Love Mom

THE
BLACK VAULT

JACK KING

For Rosie, without whose many sacrifices this book would not have been written.
With thanks to Caroline Cooke, Bryan Cooke for taking a closer look.
Above all thanks go to Elizabeth.

PART ONE

1

A single shot thundered over the cheering crowd, its echo multiplied a hundredfold by triumphant fireworks exploding high above the stadium. With the rifle butt at his cheek, the sniper savored the bullet's impact raising hair on the target's temple, the telescope magnifying the death in its glorious violence. He watched as the smile vanished from the lips of his victim, wide open eyes augmenting the somber and surprised expression on the suddenly lifeless face.

"They always seem surprised," the killer thought without remorse, and watched as the body slowly slumped onto the podium floor.

The clean-slate entry of the bullet and the rapid recoil of the head were registered by cameras and projected on jumbotrons above the stage. The cheering subsided gradually as the understanding of the incident dawned on the stupefied crowd, and at last silence fell upon the arena. It lasted mere seconds before a single cry resounded in the still air. The cameras pan, and focused on a woman in the middle of the crowd, her outstretched arm and index finger pointing high above.

"There he is!"

The speakers amplified her voice, the monitors magnified her face.

He recognized her. It was his love… His soul… She has betrayed him.

Suddenly the doors flew open with the impact of strong shoulders.

Four plain-clothed men filed into the projection room above the arena, surrounding him and shouting orders, their voices fusing into one incomprehensible clamor yet remaining strangely familiar. Barrels pointing at his heart, they advance on him and press him right against the cold wall. Someone switched on the lights. He gasped out, recognizing every face. They were men he worked with, his oldest friends, who now turned into hunters. They advanced on him further, their faces contorted in dogged hatred.

"He's one of us!" The men cried out in unison.

"He's one of us!" The audience doubled from the speakers, in thousand voices the final judgment.

One of the men stepped forward, the others followed. One of them raised his arm, the cold barrel of the gun pressing into the assassin's ribs. The leader's voice penetrated deep, it shattered the dream, had the power to wake him, "You son-of-a-bitch! You killed the President—"

Martin woke up with a gasp, his heart in cold grips. It took him a long time to realize that it was only a dream — the same dreaded dream that haunted him since the day he parted with the Company. The dream became more physical with each occurrence, and today was the culmination of hallucination and reality. He could still hear the echo of the shot reverberating in the woods across the bay.

Too real. He shook his head, and instantly regretted it. His temples throbbed with pain. It was unbearable, excruciating to the point that his eyes covered with fog. He blinked and struggled to raise his eyelids, only to find that milky mist was in the air, rising off the still lake in thick clouds resembling cotton candy. He labored to sit up, but the weight of his soaked clothes was constricting his movement. It took extraordinary effort to raise himself on his elbows. The movement startled a bird. A blue heron that was perched several feet away spread its wings and flew away, into the mist. Only now did it occur to Martin that he was lying on the floating dock, next to an upturned canoe, the cabin barely visible in the fog.

The cabin was located in the middle of a steep, wooded hill, overlooking the lake. It stood not more than a hundred feet from shore, but it might as well have been a thousand — before Martin reached the house he was breathless, panting like a dog. It was cold inside, but he did not feel it, his body covered in sweat caused by the strenuous climb. A rusty smell hung in the inside air, resembling something between blood and gun powder, bringing to mind images of a butcher shop. He shook his head to rid his mind of the intrusive vision, and almost lost his balance as the room spun in his eyes. Braced against the fireplace he waited for the dizziness to subside. At last he gazed about the room, his eyes glazing the beer and liquor bottles, and landing on the holstered pistols that hung on antlers mounted on the wall. He listened. The house was quiet, in stark contrast to the clamor that reverberated in its walls all night. The image brought vague memories of joyful hours spent with his friends, together after months and years of separation. Where were they now? He made a step forward, and tripped over something, but regained his balance. He looked down. One of his friends had claimed the sheepskin by the fireplace, sleeping face down, hugging the furry patch like a primeval lover on his primeval woman. Everything was good. Martin turned abruptly to go to bed. Too abruptly. His head exploded, spinning faster, and faster. He staggered only as far as the couch, and slumped onto it, involuntarily. He did not see the shadow lurking outside of the panoramic window. He did not see the growing patch of blood seeping into the sheepskin, next to his friend's head.

He felt the commotion around him through his skin. The sounds of voices penetrated his mind as though from a deep well. It took him a moment to realize that it was not a dream, not this time. Someone tugged on his shoulder and Martin came to. He opened his eyes to the blurred figures that moved purposely around.

One voice came on top of all others, "He's alive!"

Suddenly the blurred figures came to a still, and centered around him. Someone neared, closer, and closer, until Martin could smell the onion breath, and see the windblown face of a man with a thick mustache, a sparkling metal badge on the man's chest shooting painful sparks.

"How you feelin', son?"

He did not reply. The living room was bright, the sunrays touching the floor, and creeping up the walls. He tried, and succeeded, in pulling himself up to a seated position. The headache was gone, but he felt groggy. Casting curious looks around, such as those of a newborn, he stood up, and staggered.

"Easy there, fellow!"

A pair of strong hands slipped under his arms, preventing him from slumping back onto the couch. The cabin was filled with uniformed police officers, and civilians with badges around their necks, or clipped to their belts. Everyone paused and focused their attention on Martin. He stood in the middle, bewildered. The presence of cops did not alarm him. In fact nothing could upset his mind at this moment, for he was observing the events as though through an out-of-body experience. He was here, and not here, all at the same time. His eyes wondered from face to face, from person to person, and from an object to object, resting at last on the fireplace, and the furry patch beside it.

Something clicked in Martin's head, rising him from numbness. He took a step forward, toward the white sheepskin that was no longer white. He towered over it, struggling to focus his eyes. At last succeeded, he could scarcely believe what he was looking at. He knelt down and stared in numb disbelief. What was once his friend's face was now a bloodied and unrecognizable mass of lifeless shreds of skin, bone, and brain matter, and, as though in some gruesome exhibit, one eyeball was dislodged from its socket, hanging on the optic nerve.

He sprung to his feet, and the room reeled in front of him.

2

With twice as many passports and various other identification bearing photographs of only five men, and scrambled mobile phones equipped with military-grade encryption preventing identification of their owners, the case stank, and the sheriff was taking no chances. He had arrested the suspect, and, acting on request from the worried mayor, he had instructed his officers to refrain from discussing the particulars of the cabin murders to the press. The summer season might be winding down, but the tiny township of Apsley depended on tourism to such extent that, unless under strict damage control mode, the event could have a devastating effect on the approaching winter snowmobiling season, perhaps even spilling onto next year. Tourists were the principal source of income for residents, a money crop for the community located in this pristine lakes district. With any luck the whole affair will have died down, as the sheriff was convinced it would — after all he had arrested the only suspect, the culprit, a sick bastard. He felt no particular sympathy for the victims. Those rich city boys vacationing in their fancy log cabins, driving fancy vehicles, and drinking fancy liquors, had it coming anyway. Damn fools. Not a season went by without some damn rich kid crashing his ATV, or a water scooter, alcohol playing major role in each and every event. The sheriff knew that where drinking was involved there were no accidents. Alcohol — the devil's weapon — was always an invitation to trouble. It was responsible for all that was wrong with the world today, and sheriff Bob Foreman knew it better than anyone: His own son fell victim to alcohol when he slept with a male prostitute while on honeymoon in Thailand. Was the subsequent contracting of HIV not the result of being drunk, perhaps even drugged? Now this city boy killing all his buddies in drunken stupor. Terrible? Sure. Surprising? Hardly. Not where alcohol and drugs were at play. The latter must have been at the center of everything that happened, it was the only explanation for the multiple documents, and the firearms. The sheriff knew instinctively what had transpired even if the forensic results were not in yet, and would not arrive before Monday. Sheriff Bob Foreman did not need forensics to tell a killer. He had seen them aplenty during a career spanning three decades. After his only son's untimely death, in the days before AIDS became a treatable disease, the sheriff went on a crusade, becoming a self-professed guard of morality, and his efforts turned Apsley into a dry community.

A loud laughter broke the sheriff's reverie. He put down his the morning coffee and looked up from his desk. His deputy was chatting up the weekend temp, a daughter of a woman his son once dated.

The recollection stirred unpleasant memories, and the sheriff called out, angrily, "You got them replies, yet, Harv?"

Deputy Harvey Connaught glanced at his boss, then winked at the girl. She giggled. They both knew what happened this morning, on the way to the station. After the night of filing reports, checking the evidence, and absorbing shit from the increasingly anxious mayor, the two officers had enough time to run home in the wee hours, only to shower and shave. On their way back, riding together, they had an incident that threw the sheriff into a foul mood, and his deputy into amusement, the particulars of which he later shared with the temp.

The sheriff had pulled a woman over. She tailgated his unmarked cruiser for several miles along the curving road before passing him on the double lane. She was a young woman, under thirty, attractive. He asked for the license and registration. "Officer," the woman pleaded, her eyes aflicker, flirtatious, "I'm awfully sorry. I'm so-o late for work, today, on a holiday. Can you cut me some slack? Could I just buy a ticket to a police ball, or something?" Who knows, the sheriff would have, perhaps, let her out with a warning but for the wrecked night and the prospect of a whole day's work ahead. The nerve of her! Making misty eyes, thinking she could bribe her way out of a ticket. His mind not as sharp as it would have been, as it should have been on a restful long weekend, the sheriff replied, "Maam, the police department does not have balls." A split second later, his face red as the morning sky over the horizon, he drove off to the station, picking on everything that he could find to make the day hard for his deputy.

Twenty-five years his boss's junior, and thus better suited to miss a night's sleep, the deputy did not let the boss's mood get to him, thinking the sheriff a good officer. He approached the printer, which was located next to the coffee percolator. He scooped up several sheets of paper, separated them, and brought two sheets to the sheriff. With his eyes scanning the time stamp on the printouts, he placed the papers on the desk. Before the papers touched the wooden surface, the deputy's eyes caught several words, his face turning the color of the documents.

Twenty minutes later, and a second cup of coffee in his hand, the sheriff walked into the ten-by-twelve room painted in a mild cappuccino color, two thirds of it divided by a steel crate. A cot with a mattress and a soft throw of undetermined color, and a latched table top attached to the wall underneath a small window beneath the ceiling, completed the decoration of what was the Apsley jail. A plastic tray with untouched breakfast was on the tabletop.

Sleepless and restless fourteen hours had passed since Martin was locked up in the small cell. When he did not feel sick to his stomach, he spent most of the night pacing. The thoughts that tormented him were painting an ominous picture in his mind, and one thought dominated all others: It had finally happened.

"Ready to tell me what happened there?"

The sheriff took a loud sip from his coffee cup.

Martin did not react, too absorbed in his own thoughts. What could he say, anyway? At times he wanted to pinch his cheeks in order to bring to an end a dream that went on too long. But he knew that it was not a dream. He passed the night awake, thinking about his murdered friends. They were killed, as he knew they would be, sooner or later. Such was the fate of most operatives — expendable pawns in a game of the mighty. They all knew that the day would come. "You will die someday," their instructor would say, "but not with your loved ones by your side. You will die in some shit-drenched gutter, knifed in the back, abandoned, forgotten, deserted by your government. You will die for your country, but your country will deny the association." Indeed, from the day he graduated from the Farm, Martin had lived with the instilled conviction that it would happen some day.

"You're in serious trouble, son."

The voice had finally reached him. Martin stopped pacing, and faced the sheriff. He said nothing, his mind still elsewhere.

"You're in serious trouble," the officer repeated, cherishing every word. He had never had a case that reached so high. He had just hung up with the Feds, after having found a connection between a name on a prescription bottle found at the scene, and one of the passports, a diplomatic one at that. He contacted the State Department not expecting much, but the passport proved authentic. The Feds were sufficiently alarmed to convince the sheriff that poor old Apsley would not see the end of the affair any time soon. Those were no ordinary city boys to have the State Department officials scrambling to ensure that not a word gets out, and vowing to dispatch a team of special agents.

The sheriff sipped from his coffee cup. He wanted to take a good look at this man, who, at first impression, seemed no different from the hundreds that passed through the town every summer. But underneath the scruffy exterior the sheriff recognized intelligence in the bloodshot and glazed eyes, the same intelligence he saw in the eyes of some of the most notorious criminals he ever came across. This one was one of them — on the face of it an ordinary city boy, but a sick bastard, a killer.

"You don't want to talk, that's fine. You will. It won't be as pleasant as in here, it won't."

The prisoner raised his head.

"Got your attention, ha?" The sheriff took a swig and leaned casually against the doorframe. "Yep, they'll be 'ere soon. You know what they do to guys like you, do you? He-he. There ain't no lawyers, and judges, to keep creeps like you locked. Know what I mean? Dee-tain for good is what they do. You'll talk, you will." Goddamn junkie, the sheriff added in his thought. The drugs found at the scene had checked out. A call to the pharmacy had confirmed that a legitimate prescription had been filled by the property owner, but it meant little to the sheriff. These rich city boys had doctors wrapped around their fingers. What was more important than a prescription was staring him in the face, and the signs were obvious — the vomiting, the restless night, and the disorientation the prisoner exhibited while in custody, told the sheriff whom he was dealing with. A junkie. A rich, goddamn junkie.

"Sheriff, I'd like to make a call," Martin said at last, his voice betraying sudden anxiety, but remaining firm, reminiscent of a hesitant order. The night he spent in the cell, sick as a dog, trying to recall the events at the cabin, and remembering nothing, made him wary.

The sheriff's eyes gleamed. Those were the suspect's first words since detention. It took the threat of the feds to open his mouth. Not a good testament for a tough cop. He sunk his lips into the coffee cup to prevent himself from lashing out.

"From now on you'll be doing only what you're told, son."

Another swig.

Martin approached the grate. With his hands on the steel bars, he said through his teeth, "I want my goddamn call."

The sheriff grinned, sipped again, and swallowed hard. He observed the prisoner for a time, with curiosity, but made no attempt to accommodate the request. At last he shook his head, and smacked his tongue.

He said, not concealing his contempt, "Had you not been so pissed last night you would've had your call." Swig. "Shoot a man in rage, or drunk, I can understand. I've seen it before. But what in the hell did you blow their faces for? Couldn't stand the dead eyes staring back at ya? Or did you think they wouldn't be recognized? Hell, son, have you not heard about dee-en-ay?" The sheriff paused, smacked his tongue again, and exhaled in a hiss, "You sick son-of-a-bitch!"

Martin wanted to object, but bit his tongue instead. He saw no point in telling this man that highly placed intelligence operatives were gunned down. He could not do it, even if he wanted to. The procedure called for contacting the Company, but he could not do this either. On the back of his mind was the persistent thought that he too should have died, slaughtered together with his friends. Yet, he was alive. This, if an oversight, was highly unusual from a hit that must have been carefully planned and executed. The realization of it was as troubling as it was hopeful. Trying to explain it to this officer, who looked at him with contempt, was pointless. It was not that intelligence operatives were slaughtered, but that Martin could remember nothing about the night. Worse still — he exhibited signs of incapacitation, from vomiting, to dizziness, to blank memory. He spent a restless night trying to makes sense of what had transpired, but came up with no more than what was on the surface. He kept the deputy up all night, throwing up, but his mind remained blank. A hangover? He had had hangovers before, but never as bad as this. Bobby thought him the trick in high school: Eat plenty of fatty foods before and during drinking, and you'll outdo the heaviest drunkard. But the amount he drank that tragic night did not warrant such a reaction. A drug, then. But who could have done it? Who could have drugged five spies that met in utmost secrecy — a secret shared with no one?

"Sheriff!"

The voice came from the office. The young deputy appeared in the doorway.

"The suits arrived."

"So quick?" The sheriff glanced at his wristwatch. He could not hide the surprise on his face. It should take the feds at least two-and-a-half hours to get to Apsley, unless they flew in. Such expediency only confirmed his suspicions. This case was big, very big.

"Sheriff!" Martin called out, the urgency in his voice stopping the officer in his tracks.

Their eyes met. The officer saw no anxiety in the prisoner's. Something else was in those deep brown eyes, and it made him shiver. He shivered the more at the sound of the words that pierced his skin like icicles.

"Sheriff, make sure they are who they say they are."

The sheriff did not reply. Something about the prisoner had changed, and it shook the officer's confidence. He turned on his heels, and walked into the office area. The Apsley police station was no different from many such establishments in tiny hamlets scattered around the country. A long dais separated the official section from that for the public, which, for the most part, consisted of the officers' families delivering lunch, and the like. The large three-pane window, unthinkable in a bigger city, where crime statistics called for walled up fortresses, provided enough natural illumination to eliminate the need for artificial light during the day. The sheriff walked passed the dais and the young woman who gave him a short smile. He approached the window, and peeked through the Venetian blinds. It was not a helicopter, nor a float-plane that brought the feds, which would have explained the expediency of their arrival. A black SUV was parked in the gravel driveway, several antennae protruding from its rooftop. Two square-jawed, black-suited men were approaching the building.

"Send them to my office," the sheriff said to his deputy. State Department or not, he would make it clear whose domain this was.

"Oh, and Harv?" the sheriff said to his deputy before disappearing behind the door to his office. He nodded to the jail cell. "Get that food outta there. This junkie's gonna feast on federal cuisine from now on."

The two men identified themselves as federal agents. They gave the sheriff no time to question them, nor offered any explanations. They opened with a bang.

"This is a national security case. Borneman will be transferred to our facilities in Peterborough."

The sheriff tried to conceal his surprise. The name appeared on none of the ID that was found at the cabin. He repeated, "Borneman?"

One of the suits raised an eyebrow, exposing a small scar that resembled a crescent. He raised his voice to indicate that no details would be forthcoming, "Here's the paperwork."

His partner, a skinny man with pale face resembling a knotty pine drew out a folded manila envelope from his pocket, straightened it out, and handed in over across the desk.

The sheriff did not hurry. He sipped from his coffee mug, and studied the agents, before lazily reaching for the envelope.

Deputy Harvey Connaught walked into the office.

"Sheriff, you want me to pull out the boxes?"

His boss glanced to the newcomers.

The knotty face said to the deputy, "Give you a hand?"

The two disappeared behind the doors.

The sheriff turned to the man with a scar.

"What about the bodies? They're still at the coroner's. The forensics reports aren't ready."

"We're here to take the living one," replied the agent. Something mortifyingly cold in his voice should have alerted the sheriff.

"Who is he?" the officer asked while trying to suppress intense curiosity.

"I'm afraid I'm not authorized to share this information."

The sheriff sunk his lips in the mug. "To hell with you, city boy," he thought. "The sooner you haul away the killer the sooner it'll be off my head. Fewer questions will be asked, and life in Apsley will return to its pace again." He picked up the envelope again.

"Say, sheriff?" the agent started, his shrewd eyes scanning the office. "Have you found out anything yet? Anything that could ID the stiffs? It would make our job easier." He finished with a toothy smile.

"I'll bet it would," the sheriff murmured. "Here," he reached to a desk organizer, suddenly feeling good about himself. He pulled several sheets, and said, "The firearms were untraceable; the fingerprints came back negative; all vehicles were rentals. We're checking the names on rental agreements against the names on the passports, but I'm willing to bet they're all fake. The only positive is the prescription bottle, which matched the name of the property owner, but figuring out which one of the stiffs it belongs to won't be so quick, what with their yaps blown away." Thinking that the quandary should be appreciated by the agent, he asked, "Some sort of drug deal gone bad?"

The agent scanned the documents but did not reply. Instead he asked, "Is that all?"

The sheriff could not hold back his frustration. He repeated, "Is that all? It's a long weekend!" He has had enough of this. Is that all? You've got to be kidding me! He was reeling. He reached for the manila envelope to sign the release papers, and to rid the station of these pricks. What he saw made him grind his teeth. The envelope contained a single sheet of blank paper. This was too much. The sheriff looked up, ready to express in words what was building up at the tip of his tongue. His jaw dropped at what he saw. The image hurt his soul. It was the culmination of the worst day in his career. Staring him in the face was a barrel of a gun, swollen by a silencer.

3

The Apsley police station was understaffed this morning, with every duty officer working in the field, talking to the residents about any suspicious activity they might have witnessed. With the deputy sheriff collecting the boxes of evidence from the basement, the floor was held by the young woman, a temporary help who appreciated the extra check for her weekend and holiday duties — it would come in handy in several months, after she gave birth. Jobs were not easily attainable in this small and remote community, and she was grateful for these few hours, hoping to stay on, since as a new mother she would not have the time for a full time employment even if she could find one. She was sitting at the dais, in front of an unfinished Sudoku puzzle, her mind wandering to the dark SUV in the parking lot, thinking what it would be like to live in a larger city.

She was engrossed in the thoughts, stroking her hair, when the scarred man entered the office area. At the rustle behind her she turned around, and smiled. Her body slumped onto the floor with the smile remaining on her lips, a small black spot on her forehead quickly filling with blood.

Voices from behind the doors at the farthest wall drew the killer's attention. The door swung open and deputy Harvey Connaught appeared with a large semitransparent plastic box in his arms.

He addressed the man with the scar, "I was asking your partner how much more action you guys must be getting in Peterborough, if this small hole in the woods sees five murders in one night?"

Hid did not receive an answer, but was not surprised having previously encountered a similar reluctance to conversation from the knotty face who was following him from the basement. He shrugged his shoulders, and asked, "Where you want this?"

The man with the crescent scar said nothing.

Miffed, deputy Connaught started, "Look it—" The gun with a silencer in the agent's hand made him bite his tongue. Thinking it was some kind of a joke, or the agent was showing off to impress the temp, he looked to the dais. The woman was not there. "Gina?" His eyes wandered to the coffee percolator and the fax machine stand. Only then did his eyes catch a glimpse of a pair of legs stretched on the floor, the rest of the body obscured by the desk. He looked back to the agent. "What the—" He did not finish. His body jerked back with the impact of the bullet in the throat, then bounced off the wall, and fell forward, landing on the storage box he still gripped in his arms.

"Have you found it?" the killer asked his companion who appeared from the basement with a similar box in his arms.

The man shook his head. "Don't know. It's all sealed. They haven't even gone through this stuff yet, the hicks!"

They proceeded to open the boxes and fingered through them methodically, their frustration rising with each passing minute. At last they realized that their search was useless.

"Damn," said one of them, "it must be at the cabin."

17

"We searched it already."

It was no point arguing. They searched the cabin, but did not find what they were after. The police did not find it either. There was only one thing left to do.

While his companion carried the boxes into the SUV, the man with the scar pulled the bodies deeper into the corner between the fax machine and the filing cabinets where they would not be seen by anyone entering the station. He cleaned up small items that fell out of the evidence boxes, and, satisfied, he went back to the sheriff's office. He collected the passports and other ID that belonged to the murdered men, and added to it the results of the paperwork already completed by the officers. At last he bent down over the sheriff's body to detach the key chain from the officer's belt.

Martin was pacing within the confines of the small cell. He heard unidentifiable noises, and although he could not quite make out their source, he did not like what he was hearing. It did not sound right. The last thump, like that of something large falling on the floor, breaking, was not a sound that should accompany the arrival of federal agents. He expected the worst, and was not surprised when, at last, it appeared in front of him, dressed in a black suit, holding a pistol in its hand.

The two men observed one another without a word.

At last the newcomer said, "Step back and face the wall, arms behind your back."

Martin complied. He heard the sound of keys being inserted into the lock. He turned his head. Something oddly familiar in the stranger's countenance made him focus on the face. The scar. It was barely discernible, but it was there, and it was very unique, in the shape of a perfect crescent, not more than a centimeter long.

"Put these on," the scar face said, and placed a pair of handcuffs in Martin's hand, all along keeping watchful distance.

Martin strapped on the cuffs. The man approached and frisked him. He was a pro. The pat down told Martin that the stranger was looking for something.

"Have they left any belongings on you? No?" The man checked anyway. He pulled the blanket off the cot, and upturned the mattress. Disappointed he withdrew from the cage, and said, "Okay, walk out, slowly."

The killer's companion had already moved the evidence boxes to the SUV. He waited in the office, watching the main entrance.

Martin walked by the dais, seeing nothing that should alarm him — nothing, except for the eerily emptiness and silence. Where were the officers? Where was the woman whose glimpse he caught in the morning when she handed the food tray to the deputy sheriff? It told him that something was terribly wrong. He knew that these two men were no ordinary federal agents, and vague glimpses of memories were beginning to take shape in his head. The crescent scar. He could not quite place it, but he was certain of what the man bearing the scar signified. Danger. This, in turn, triggered an instinctive reaction. It told Martin to offer no resistance, and to look for the first opportunity to change the equation. It told him, that despite the sheriff's conviction, Martin was not the one responsible for his friends' deaths. The killers, he was certain of it, were the two men who were ushering him toward the black SUV.

4

Two Days Earlier
Martin had hitched a ride with Arthur. Old college friends, they have grown closer since parting with the Company, the bond made the stronger for both men being labeled renegades, and ostracized by the intelligence community. The three-hour drive to the cabin passed quickly — the result of an animated conversation centered around rumors concerning a mutual friend. They speculated whether they would ever see Derek again, alive, or otherwise. The rumor had spread as rumors do — that is to say it was on everybody's lips and sparked the wildest ideas.

"Get a hold of this," Arthur started, his voice signifying the urge to start the topic. His excitement was such that the steering wheel swerved momentarily, the car crossing the divider lane. He regained control of the vehicle, and continued, "I ran into Chris in Geneva. He's been busy with the State."

"The State Department?" Martin's curiosity showed on his face and in his voice.

"A special *envoy* for Eastern Europe."

"They're never short for euphemisms, that's for sure."

Arthur switched on the radio, located a music station, turned up the volume, and carried on, his voice barely audible above the musical tunes, "There's more. Chris had some insight on Bobby and Derek. Said he ran into the two of them. In Riyadh, of all places! The money-laundering capital of the world."

Martin felt a hot flush on his face. He looked out the window to cover his reaction. He asked, trying to conceal the anxiety in his voice, "Bobby too? I thought he retired to some sunny destination?"

Arthur did not seem to notice his friend's sudden anxiety. He continued, "There's only one way to retire in this profession, and you'll never know when it hits you. I tell you, I'm wondering if our time has come. If the rumors are true— If Derek really did it, perhaps with Bobby's help— You know what that means, don't you?"

Martin was stunned. The connection and its implications did not escape him.

He said, "It means he's as good as dead."

The driver did not reply, his concentration on the wet pavement, and the approaching curve. In the attention with which his friend's eyes pierced the windshield Martin read what words did not express: All five of them were as good as dead, if only by association. He wanted to curse, but what good would it do?

Arthur read his mind. "I suppose one can't even blame him. Who wouldn't be tempted when operating millions in cash, no receipts, and no official acknowledgement of the service rendered?"

Could it really be true? Could Derek have done it? Martin leaned back and recalled a conversation he had with Derek some years ago. Their paths had crossed, as they sometimes do between operatives, least of all by coincidence. Martin had just arrived in Mexico City from Morelia where he was scouting the area for a planned hit on one of the most notorious drug barons. Derek was en route from the Cayman Islands. They sat on the rooftop patio of a hotel with views over the main square, drinking Modelos. After several bottles Derek opened up. He bragged about going through the Cayman customs with suitcases full of banknotes that were fingered by the officials and waved through. It was not until this moment that Martin grasped the meaning of temptation that his friend dealt with every day.

He said, "He should've known that it would implicate the rest of us!"

"I hear it's a truly substantial amount," Arthur added fuel to fire. "And the funds were meant for a major black op, perhaps the biggest since 1962."

Martin looked into his friend's face. "We're all dead, then, whether we had anything to do with it, or not."

"I suppose whoever said it was right — You mustn't make friends in this line of work."

Arguing was pointless. From the Company's point of view they made the perfect team to hatch and execute such an action. The only thing left to do was to minimize the damage, to ensure that the suspicions would not spill beyond the five of them and onto their families. Then they would have to convince their employer that they were not guilty, while protecting their friend, because friendship was first, duty second. The coming weekend would have to accomplish just that.

"You think he's going to be there?"

"We made a deal, didn't we?"

"That we did," Martin said.

They drove in silence, each pondering the events of the past that led to the present. Martin watched the trees on the side of the highway. They were like the people one meets on the highway of life, now close, then becoming distant, dissipating behind, in the rearview mirror. Would his friends

be the friends he knew from the past, or would they have
drifted into a distant world? He recalled the September long
weekend, twelve years ago. They were the best of friends,
having graduated from the same college earlier in the Spring.
After four close years, and a summer spent together —
fishing, drinking, and pissing away the last days of freedom
— their ways were about to part. They were young, still
idealistic. Years of shared experiences could not be simply
thrown away. And thus, that memorable long weekend,
twelve years ago, they made a pact: Every year, later
amended to two years, they would meet at Chris's cabin,
regardless of the circumstances in their private and
professional lives. They kept the promise. Every other year,
come Labor Day weekend, the cabin came alive with joyful
glass-clinking and laughter. How would the meeting go this
year when troubling thoughts abounded? It was an open
secret within intelligence circles, that the Company's most
prize possession, the black vault — the dirty money that
every intelligence agency cherishes and defends with zealous
fervor for it offers freedom from oversight and
accountability — had gone missing. In no uncertain terms
the rumors pointed to the man who was tasked with
laundering the ill-gained funds. Martin never took the
rumors seriously. He knew Derek intimately, and would not
accept that his friend had anything to do with it. Derek must
have known better than any that the Company would not
stop from pursuing the thief, that sooner or later the
perpetrator and his associates would be caught. Martin
thought it was all a misunderstanding, but the rumors had
never gone away, becoming firmer, pointing to possible
scenarios that were required to pull off such a stint. A rumor
circulating within an intelligence agency is nearer to truth
than an equivalent in a civilian sector. Still, Martin could not
accept it at face value, not without first having confronted
his friend. True or not, his friend deserved the benefit of
doubt based on long friendship. They were friends with
plenty of shared memories, and whether guilty, or not, the

friendship would survive. Of that Martin was certain, and it was not the matter of the black vault that had him blushing and raising his voice. It was not the mention of Derek that had him look out the window, avoiding Arthur's eyes. It was the mention of another name that made his heart run faster, his breath rate increase, and his palms moisten with sweat. Sometime during the weekend two friends would have to come to terms with a much more troubling issue, one that actually threatened the friendship, as affairs of the heart usually do. Such was the way of the world that two men courting the same woman did not have good prospects for a lasting friendship. What fate awaited two childhood friends who had the misfortune of falling for the same woman, and both had their affections returned? Martin was about to find out, for this weekend he would face Bobby — the man with whom he grew up on the same street, the man with whom he went to the same elementary school, and later reconnected in college. The man who now stood between him and the woman he loved.

The rain was subsiding when they neared the cabin. Chris was unloading provisions from the pick up when Arthur and Martin pulled in behind him at the wooded parking lot. The roar of the engine, as Arthur spun the wheels in the mud, had brought out two more men. They came from the cabin, extra beer bottles in their hands.

"I can't believe he's here," Arthur said, and turned off the ignition, his eyes on Derek — the man at the center of the rumors.

"Neither can I," Martin replied, his eyes on Bobby — the man who took away the woman he loved.

Still, seeing Bobby and Derek laugh gregariously, without any pretenses that would be present where devious and insincere thoughts might abound, he smiled, knowing that tonight all troubles would be forgotten. The weekend was long, the beer was plenty, and the time to talk seriously would come after the needs of the friendship were satisfied

— sometime the next day, the day he woke up on the dock, shooting pain at his temples, and mutilated bodies of his slaughtered friends lying only steps away.

5

The log cabin overlooked a rocky point across a small bay. Several acres of spruce forest surrounded the five-bedroom bungalow, sheltering it from cold winds, and noisy speedboats. Here and there a trolling boat carried fishing aficionados who were devoted to their hobby, rain or shine. Despite the bad weather, the long weekend attracted plenty of visitors who longed to catch the last breath of fresh air before returning to the daily grind. The cabin's location was an oasis of serenity, with birds chirping in the dense foliage, and chipmunks harvesting the abundance of insects and acorns. Wet ground and moisture in the air added to the stillness, creating an aura of tranquility.

Two men were lurking on the deck of the pine log house, careful not to raise attention of the fishers who were soaking in the light rain in the quiet bay — after all one such boater had called the police after he heard the shots the previous day.

"Careful with the footage! It's your balls on the line if anything happens to it."

The technician shrugged, then tore the police tape, and jimmied the lock. His companion's comment was uncalled for. He knew the equipment by heart; it was his baby, and, if possible, perhaps even more precious. He was surrounded with it from the day he joined the Federal Bureau of Investigations. Setting up bugs, and debugging, were his passion. He loved everything about it, from ensuring that field stations around the country, as well as legat offices around the world, were clean, to setting up surveillance, and eavesdropping equipment. This was one such operation. He was ordered to bug the cabin, and to remove the equipment when the job was done. He did not have all the details about the targets, nor did he care to know; he was told only to take special precautions as he was dealing with pros. He was not a man without curiosity, though, and seeing the police tape, and the obvious signs of bloodshed inside the cabin, made him wonder what had transpired here during the weekend. He promised himself to take a peak into the footage before submitting it further.

Dense conifers whizzed by the side of the road as the black SUV sped along the wet highway. Martin's mind was working fast, trying to isolate the moment in the past when he came across the man seated next to him. He knew that their paths had crossed already, and the circumstances, though yet unclear, did not bode well for him.

"Where is it?" The man with the crescent scar turned to Martin as soon as the car left the Apsley city limits. The two of them occupied the back seat, while the knotty-face sat behind the wheel.

Martin gazed back, focusing on the scar. He did not reply, his mind desperately probing his memory.

"Don't make it difficult, *Mother*. Where is it?"

So they knew his handle! It confirmed his suspicions. These were men from his past, a past that came back to haunt him. He looked outside. The road followed a meandering creek, passed an old abandoned barn, and a beaver dam that someone had disassembled and then piled the sticks on the side. This was the road to Chris's cabin.

Martin turned abruptly to face the man sitting next to him.

"Who are you? I've seen you before."

The answer was not forthcoming, and was no longer necessary. It was the last sentence that brought an image to his mind. The scar. The crescent. Personnel files. He remembered. The man sitting next to him was one of the most notorious contract killers in the employ of the Company. He was used extensively in some of the most demanding cases, until an accident left a deep, if small, scar on his forehead, rendering him useless for clandestine operations.

"You are Croissant," Martin said calmly, his eyes scanning the road ahead, in search of the right moment.

A riveting pain shot through his right leg. He exhaled a muted shriek, and leaned forward to embrace his knee, tears of pain flooding his eyes.

"Let this be a warning," said the man called Croissant, a pistol in his hand, its butt having just inflicted the pain. "By the time you reach the door handle you will loose a kneecap, and if you still try to open the door—"

The butt of the gun struck the fingers embracing the knee, and Martin clenched his teeth in pain.

"You bastard!" he hissed.

"You have about twenty clicks to recall what happened to it. If I have to waste time searching through the shack again, you will remember this as nothing more than a tickle."

The man raised the pistol as though to strike again.

"All right!" Martin cried only to stop the deranged man. It was no point trying to explain that he knew not of what the man was referring to. His mere presence here meant that the rumor was not a rumor, after all, and that Derek had brought tragedy to himself and to his friends. That was all that mattered.

"The cops didn't find it, so were is it?" Croissant pressed on.

"At the cabin," Martin replied with conviction, his objective to buy time.

The answer seemed to have satisfied the assassin. It gave Martin the space to gather his thoughts. He knew that, unless he came up with a plan, he would be dead in twenty minutes. His mind worked frantically, but he could not think of a way to escape the inevitable. His heart accelerated and he felt sweat drops on his forehead and around his collar. The changing scenery, and above all the narrowing road, indicating the approaching cabin, were stifling his ability to think. Talk! If he made the killer talk maybe he could clear his head, and learn something that he could use.

He said, "The scar — it rendered you useless even before my term."

The man presented something of a smile. "You turned down my services, remember?"

Yes, Martin remembered. The personnel file in his hands. The distinctive scar precluded Croissant from taking on the assignment. But why was he still at work? And for whom?

"Who do you work for now?"

"Forget it, Mother," the man with a scar replied with a toothy grin. "You know how it works, so save your breath."

The inevitable outcome was almost paralyzing. It made Martin understand why he never made a good field operative: He could not conceal the overwhelming anxiety. What he was good at was the technical aspect of survival, having planned them for agents under his command, agents in the field. He realized thus, that if only he could control his growing anxiety then he would stand a chance. One of the ways to achieve it was to think less and do more, trying to draw strength from the opponent's weakness. He had to find Croissant's weak spot. The best way to achieve it was to unsettle him.

"Was it you?" he asked.

"What?" The killer did not understand at first. Something in Martin's eyes made him click. "You mean that gruesome mash-up at the cabin? Did you like it?"

"You son-of-a-bitch!"

The outburst amused Croissant. He grinned with an expression of a high school bully amused by the resistance offered by a meeker student.

"Whatcha gonna do? Spit on me?"

"I'm going to watch you die." Martin pronounced the words with conviction, finding no trouble in getting into the necessary role.

This time Croissant burst out laughing. The driver glanced in the rear-view mirror and joined in.

Martin went on. "You made it personal. I'll see to it that you pay for it."

Croissant stopped laughing. He shot Martin a quick glance, and said, soberly, "Fuck you, Mother. It's just a job."

It was working. He had to step up the pressure.

"You've lost your touch."

"Did I?" The assassin showed curiosity.

"I'm still alive."

"Not according to the body count."

"A body count?"

Croissant shrugged, and extended his hand, showing five fingers.

"Probably a neighbor. You must've passed out somewhere outside. Neighbor came in. The body count added up. Sure, it's a fuckup, but not that bad that it couldn't be fixed."

Martin still felt the effects of the night spent on the dock, shrouded in cold mist. His body ached, and the remnants of nausea lingered in his throat. How did this happen? How did he end up sleeping while his friends were being slaughtered? This was no time to ponder the questions. He would find the time to ask them when the balance of power shifted in his favor.

He provoked, to keep Croissant talking. "You killed an innocent man, a civvy. His family will want answers. That's a mistake. I heard you were better than that."

The killer shrugged, and patted the barrel of the handgun. "Small mistake, easily remedied."

Martin ignored the threat — he had to, and it came surprising easily to him with the realization that a man has a threshold of threats he can absorb. The situation he found himself in was threatening enough, and that threat had already overwhelmed him, keeping him numb to any more such stimuli, as though he had received a local anesthetic. But, as any anesthetic, this one would eventually wear off, and before it did, Martin had to find a way to remove the source of the pain.

"How did you do it? How did you manage to kill them all?"

"Magic." Grin.

Something about the way the killer said it led Martin on to the answer.

"You used drugs. You had to. I can still feel the effects."

Croissant's grin was the only answer.

"Me and the others — we don't exist, technically. But you killed a civilian. You can't cover it up. That's a big mistake, Croissant."

It worked. The killer took the bait. He snarled, "That neighbor son-of-a-bitch! Once his face was blown off who could tell who's who? A screw up, for sure. Gotta tell you, though, what a surprise it was later to hear the cops chatter on the radio about a survivor. Petrifying. When I heard it I was petrified." He savored the word for a moment. "Jimmie here will vouch for me, won't you?"

"That I will. Sure will." The driver replied over his shoulder. "It was like stepping on dogshit. A nasty surprise."

"Yeah. Shit, I says to Jimmie, you don't screw up in this business and get to live to see the light of day. So we come back to fix it, and before you know it the headquarters calls. Not so fast, they say, something's come up: You gotta retrieve the merchandise. So, you see, it's a good thing that happened—"

"Merchandise?" Martin cut him off.

"You're gonna give it to me, or it won't be pretty."

The SUV turned onto a narrow dirt road that wound its way through the woods and led to summer homes, the only indication being hand-made signs nailed to tree trunks. The resolution was nearing, and Martin had to step up his efforts.

"Suppose the cops took it away?" he suggested.

"It wasn't scooped up with the rest of the evidence. Besides, they're too dumb to know what to look for."

"Do you?"

Croissant gave him the look of injured pride.

"Don't be insulting."

"You drugged me. I might not remember where—"

Croissant cut him off. "Trust me, I know modes of persuasion that open all memory glands." He looked out, and added quickly, "And, Mother, save us the unpleasantness. There are less painful ways to go."

The road narrowed, becoming not more than a path in the woods, barely wide enough for a single vehicle. Two minutes later they drove over a small bridge spanning a seasonal brook. A passenger car was parked on the side where trees were cut down to make room for passing. Cabin owners were responsible for the roadway, and they made several such cut outs to allow the passing of vehicles. Occasionally someone would park in one of the areas, especially during shoulder seasons, when the ground was too soft for cars to go further, as it appeared today, after several days of heavy rainfall. Croissant and Jimmie became suspicious of the vehicle, chiefly due to long antennas protruding from its rooftop, and decided not to drive directly to Chris's cabin. Instead they drove past, until they found another clearing, where they parked the SUV, and retraced their way on foot. Chris's private drive descended a steep hill and turned sharply onto a small parking area. Here the killers drew their Glocks and proceeded cautiously until the end of the tree line. The driver approached the house alone, while Croissant and Martin stayed behind. They watched Jimmie reach the door.

He stood flush with the wall, listening, the gun at the ready. With his free hand he tried the door knob. The police tape was torn, lying on the ground, but the door would not open. Jimmie holstered his weapon, and drew something else out of his pocket. He spent the next several seconds fiddling with the lock. It gave way, and Jimmie slowly opened the door.

A powerful blast filled the quiet air.

6

The knotty-faced Jimmie flew back, and landed on the grass with a wet thump. Before his body hit the ground another shot followed, the bullet splitting the bark of a tree not far from Martin's head. He ducked to the ground. Croissant followed suit and returned fire. In response several bullets thumped into soft moss nearby.

With the trees not providing adequate barrier to the bullets, Martin began to retreat. He crept away as quickly as his tied hands permitted. It was not fast enough, and he decided to roll. It helped, and soon he found safety behind a large granite boulder.

Croissant was not as lucky. He was hit when attempting to cover the distance to the boulder in a stooped position. He landed next to Martin, reaching the rock by the centrifugal force. He lay on the ground, one hand holding onto his abdomen, the other clutching the pistol.

"You must've pissed off a lot of people," he hissed through his teeth.

"Who are they?" Martin asked.

Croissant clenched his teeth, and pulled himself closer. The move proved fatal. A bullet reached him, hitting him on the neck, ripping through the artery, the pistol falling out of his hand. His legs began kicking spasmodically; blood from the wound was gushing, browning the fresh green moss.

Martin watched the agony in stupefaction.

"Who sent you? Do you hear me? Croissant! Who ordered the hit?"

It was no use. Croissant was dying with a grin on his lips, his legs kicking, slower, and slower, until, suddenly, he was gone.

With the break in the shooting, the first thing on Martin's mind was to free himself from the shackles. Not certain whether the bullets came from friend or foe, he acted with extraordinary caution. He pulled on Croissant's foot, the only body part not exposed to gun fire, inch by inch, until he could reach the jacket pocket. The keys were there, but it took him a while to unlock the cuffs, his hands trembling from anxiety. Having succeeded at last, he looked for the Glock. The pistol rolled too far to attempt to retrieve it safely. Perhaps, in the end, he did not need it?

"Hold the fire!" Martin shouted at the top of his lungs. Slowly, he raised himself to his knees, and peeked over the sharp edge of the boulder.

The move was not missed, and a series of bullets chipped the granite rock.

It was no time to question the intentions of the mysterious assailants. He crept away, making sure the boulder remained behind his back, shielding him from bullets. Two dozen feet later he rose to his knees, then to his feet, and ran stooped. A cacophony of shots erupted, bullets shaving branches of surrounding trees. Martin did not stop, and ran until the cabin was out of sight. He stopped for breath and to calm his nerves. He recognized the area — a small pond that he remembered from previous years. He would often come and sit by the pond, allowing his mind to be carried off into the starry night on soundwaves of croaking frogs. Those were good times, spent with good friends. He owed it to his friends to find out what happened.

Martin made a large circle and doubled back. His advantage was in the times he had spent in the woods during all those visits to Chris's cabin, climbing rocks, jogging, or just wandering. He knew his way around. He had spent the next quarter of an hour lurking in the thicket of small but dense conifers, some twenty steps from the cabin, before the door opened and someone emerged, a rifle in his hands. The man cautiously approached Jimmie's body, his eyes scanning the tree line. He kneeled down, touched the artery, and stood up. He gave a silent signal to someone else who remained in the house, and proceeded toward the boulder.

The scene told Martin that at least two men were present. He stood no chance against two armed, and determined, enemies, but his chances, though still not equal without a weapon, grew exponentially one on one. He proceeded to approach the cabin from the side least likely to be hiding the remaining assailant, when all attention would be focused on the front where the first of the assailants was nearing the boulder. Martin reached the pine wall, and ripped the vinyl mosquito screen, before sliding open the wooden window. He then lifted himself up on the ledge, and slid into the bathroom. It took extreme concentration to enter the wooden house, and to proceed without making its floors squeak, alerting whoever was hiding inside. The humidity was his savior, making his cautious trek soundless. Soon he found himself in the living room, behind a man was glued to a crack in the door, observing his partner.

The same concentration and tension that was making Martin perspire with every step, had also made the stranger concentrate on the view in the front of the house, and making him oblivious to the events taking place behind his back. When the creak in the floor had finally registered in his mind, it was too late.

7

"We called for backup as soon as we heard you approach!"

The technician attempted to sound threatening, but his trembling voice suggested that he was far from feeling secure. When he came to he was met with a terrifying scene. The man, whom he recognized from images captured by the surveillance equipment, was standing over the body of his companion, tying his hands with bungee cords. If that was not enough, the face, seen now in person, seemed familiar. He recognized whom the surveillance operation was aimed against.

"Your reputation precedes you," he said, "but even you won't get away with it."

"Away with what?" Martin asked, a butcher's knife and a sharpening stone in his hands. He decided to use a bit of theatrics, expecting to achieve better results this way. The ominous image of the knife was a better guarantor of the answers he so needed, and was determined to receive from this peculiar team. It was the most ill-matched pair he had ever seen. One was a typical thug — the way he moved about the woods, the way he held the rifle, and the look in his eyes — all the traits resembling Croissant, spelling a killer. But the other, with his thick glasses, and a shaky voice, was something else. Who were these men? Martin saw only one way to find out. He approached the nerdy man, and, with cold precision, he pulled the blade against the porous surface of the sharpening stone. He watched with satisfaction as the sound made the man shiver. The old maxim that fear of pain, not pain itself, was a more affective interrogation tool, seemed to come true.

"Away with what?" Martin repeated in a grave voice.

The man clammed up. As his fearing eyes darted between the knife and the stone, Martin saw that he was right about his first impression. This was the most peculiar twosome he had ever seen.

"Who are you, and who do you work for?"

No answer.

Zzing… Zzing… The blade scratched the stone.

"You won't get away with!" the man repeated, his voice at a higher pitch.

It was time to step up pressure.

"Listen to me, you son-of-a-bitch! The men you just shot and killed were professional hitmen. If someone is not going to get away with it, its you. You, and your loved ones."

The last threat seemed to work.

The man replied, struggling to conceal his fear, "I don't know anything. I'm here only to collect the equipment."

"Equipment?" Martin repeated, disconcerted.

"Cameras, mikes—" The man's eyes shot somewhere over Martin's shoulders.

Martin followed the gaze to the dining table. It was topped with several aluminum cases that he did not notice in the heat of the events. He approached the table in several quick steps. The cases were filled with various electronic components secured neatly in static-free compartments. He knew the purpose of the equipment, some of which he used himself in preparing his operations. The cabin had been bugged, and it confirmed that someone had the foreknowledge of the friend's meeting.

Martin returned to the couch where the man was seated, the blade of the knife glistening ominously in his hand. His was thinking intensely, seeing only two possibilities, and liking neither.

He towered over the cowering man, and asked, "Who do you work for? The Company? The Feds?"

The man did not reply, his eyes focused on the blade.

Zzing… Zzing…

No answer.

"Why did you kill these two men? They were with you."

"N-no! I didn't kill anyone!"

"Who—" Martin started and followed the man's gaze to the companion who was lying by the door. "Who is he?"

"I don't know. Just someone they paired me with."

"Who did?"

No reply.

Zzing… Zzing…

"I was here to secure the equipment. They sent him along to sterilize the place. At least that's what he said."

Martin stood motionless, only his eyes darting between the two men. Something did not add up here, and in the unknown was the answer to all that happened.

He pressed, "Why the hell did you kill Croissant and his sidekick?"

"I told you, it wasn't me!"

"Who ordered the hit?"

A reluctant shrug of the man's shoulders was the only reply.

Martin took a step toward the couch.

"The surveillance, those cameras, the mikes— Who requisitioned all this?"

"He already told you! We don't know nothin'!"

The voice startled Martin. He swung around. The thug had come to. He was sitting, propped up against the door, struggling to stand up. Martin approached him quickly. He studied the face, trying to recall the image from the countless personnel files that went through his hands. It was no use. The only resemblance to any file photo was what connected all such men — a nondescript face, and something in their eyes, something indistinguishable to a civilian, but something that Martin learned to detect instinctively. This man was a killer. It was that realization that told Martin that the man would not divulge anything. He turned around, and approached the couch.

He pulled the blade against the stone, and said, "One of you better start talking—"

He did not finish. Martin's momentary distraction was seized by the thug, whose hands Martin had improperly tied. The killer had managed to untie the bungee cord, and lunged at Martin with extraordinary zeal, something not expected after a blow to the head that he took earlier. What saved Martin was a shadow reflecting in the geek's glasses — that, and quick reflexes. He spun around on his heels while simultaneously raising his left arm in guard, thus absorbing the impact of the short, decorative canoe paddle that Chris had hung above the door. The wooden stem of the paddle shattered on impact with the sharpening stone. Before any of the pieces hit the floor, the knife in Martin's right hand had reached the throat and cut through the assailant's windpipe.

Martin stood over the whimpering body, watching in awe as life departed the mortal coil. The geek's uncontrollable stammering and shattering of teeth, roused his attention. Electrified by had just happened, he rushed to the couch, pulled the geek to the ground, and kneeled on his chest.

"Talk, or you're next!"

"Jesus! I didn't even know this guy! I swear. I'm just a tech."

"The surveillance, who ordered it?"

"The Feds, counterintelligence, who else!"

Martin was taken aback. Something did not sound right.

41

"This man," he nodded to the dying thug. "He was a killer. Since when does the FBI send assassins to set up surveillance?"

"I told you! I don't know him! But I think he was with the CIA."

"The Company?"

"The surveillance. The targets— You were all CIA agents. So it's normal that Langley would want its own men on the operation."

Martin sat back. This was too much. The Company had sent an assassin to sterilize the cabin! Sterilization was a term of endearment. It mean that the CIA wanted all traces covered, professionally cleaned, so as not to link back to the agency. The realization opened a new can of worms.

"If your buddy was with the CIA, then who the hell was Croissant working for?"

"I don't know anything."

You better know something, Martin thought. He could not let go, not after the explosive bits and pieces he had learned so far. He had to learn more, and right now this trembling man he was sitting on was the only route to the truth.

Martin raised the hand that held the blade.

"Talk, or I swear—"

He did not finish. The sound of a roaring engine reached them from the parking lot.

The geek began to tremble more. He was visibly losing self-control. He began to laugh spasmodically.

"Who gave the order to bug the cabin?"

The man kept on laughing, nervously. He could not stop.

"It's over!" He cried through tears. "It's over. You son-of-a-bitch! It's all over!"

It was over. Martin could get nothing else out of him, least off all because of the man's nervous breakdown. He could hear footsteps outside of the house. He could feel the bodies coming flush with the walls. Soon he could hear the thump of something hitting the doors, breaking it. But at that time he was already halfway outside the bathroom window.

8

Martin could not tell how long he had been running. He could not tell how far he had gotten way from the cabin, and whether anyone had followed him. He ran in a trance, motivated by only one desire — to escape the terrifying realization that he had been betrayed by his former employer. He would have run as long as his legs would take him had he not tripped over a tree stump and fallen, embraced by a patch of thick, warm moss.

Raindrops tickled his face and he came to. His knee was throbbing and he stood up with difficulty. With his back against a tree, he inspected his head. He detected no wounds, nothing hurt, save for the knee, and he saw no signs of blood on the moss where his face left a pressed mark. He concluded with relief that his unconsciousness was the result of a shock rather than an injury. Now that the shock was wearing off he felt cold. His clothes were soaking wet, and his teeth began to chatter. It was time to move forward.

He could not pinpoint his exact location, but he knew that the area was a popular tourist destination, and sooner or later he would find a road. But where would it take him? Where could he go? What would he do? The questions mounted, helping his blood circulate faster, and soon he was able to form a plan, or rather a seed of a plan.

A trucker picked him up at a gas station, and drove him all the way to Dupont Circle. The warm truck cabin did not help his knee — it throbbed the more with every mile that brought him closer to Washington. The pain diminished considerably after he walked several blocks, the rising anxiety pushing the pain aside. He was stricken by doubt, not at all certain that he should involve his parents, but the desire to find the truth and to punish the killers of his friends told him to cast all doubts aside. His parents were the only people with the experience and the necessary connections to help solve the mystery.

Lydia and Oliver Borneman founded The Hill Gazer on the wave of the counterculture movements that swept through the world in the 1960s. It grew from a fringe publication into a weekly government watchdog. Its contributors ranged from politicians who were frustrated with the policies of their government, to whistleblowers, and to grassroots organizations. Some observers thought The Gazer had hit its zenith during Nixon's days of shame, while others saw its brightest star shine during the years of George *Dubya*. The publication remained at the top of the game for decades, and the Bornemans were people not without some influence. That influence, or the contacts built during decades of hobnobbing with the brightest, the most progressive thinkers in the country, was what Martin was pinning his hopes on. Someone among the many acquaintances of Lydia and Oliver would be in the position to makes sense of the madness.

The quiet street with stately mansions looked just the way he would expect it on the late afternoon of the last long weekend of the summer. If any danger was present, it would loom in the shadows of the tall elm and maple trees that formed an umbrella over the asphalt and concrete, but Martin could not discern it. The street was quiet, and nothing out of the ordinary drew his attention. Students had already arrived in town, and rental vans were parked here and there, but the overall atmosphere of Georgetown was that of the end-of-summer nostalgia, with the sporadic passersby moving about slowly, as though dazed.

Martin peered from above the white picket fence of Mrs. Pankrac's corner property, just as he used to do years ago, when, as a child, he would hide from his parents, in order not to be driven to school. His parents' home stood across the street, the fifth house askew from his current position. He had already scanned the street, including every car that was parked along the curbs, and was satisfied. He straightened his back, and stood erect over the fence, ready to move forward, when something drew his attention. At first he thought it was a flicker of sunrays, but the sun was not present on this grey, rainy day. He looked closer. The blue sedan almost in front of his parents' house. The windshield's angle reflected the moving clouds, and the swaying tree branches. It was only a reflection, then. He breathed in with relief, and then he saw it again. It was barely discernible, but it was there: A silhouette of a man inside the sedan.

"Hi, mister B!"

The voice startled him. Martin spun around to face the unknown. His arm shot up in self-defense.

"Jesus!" He recognized the neighbor's kid who was walking a dog. "Ben! You shouldn't sneak up on people like that, or one of those days you're gonna get yourself a black eye."

"I'm not afraid of your karate! I'm taking classes myself. Tay-kwan-doh. Look—" Ben took a step back and shot up his right leg, while exclaiming, "Ap chagi!"

The sudden move startled the poodle. The dog pulled on the leash, in turn drugging Ben behind. The boy fell to the sidewalk.

Martin looked up the street, alarmed, but the commotion seemed to have passed unnoticed.

"That's what I meant," he said, and helped the boy up. "You alright?"

"Oh, sure, it's nothing. You should see what we do in class. Here, let me show you. Hold Cassie, will you." He offered the leash to Martin.

"That's okay, I believe you. Listen, Ben, can you do me a favor?"

"Sure, Mister B. What kind?"

Martin explained.

9

Martin was observing the scene from behind the picket fence, his heart pounding. The anticipation was no lesser from those he felt during the operations where lives were at stake. In none of them were the lives of his parents involved, and the realization of it made him want to bite his fingernails. He watched the boy cross the street, and wanted to shout. Faster! Faster! He wanted it over with, but was only able to remain in place, and watch as a boy of about twelve approached the house, a small white poodle following him on a leash. He walked up the narrow flagstone pathway and rang the bell. So far everything went according with the plan. As Martin had predicted, the appearance of the boy at the door drew the attention of the man in the sedan. This was the moment when Martin was supposed to cross the street, while the man's focus was on the house. As the boy pressed the bell, and the man stiffened in the car, Martin started for the curb. He did not reach it when something in the boy's body language made him freeze. Ben appeared uncertain, even scared, a trait most unusual in a boy this self-assured.

And then it started.

The sound was incomprehensible at first, muffled by the distance. The boy spun on his heels, and darted for the street, pulling his dog behind, the animal slowing him down. The sound became louder, words becoming discernible.

"Run, Martin, run!"

Stunned, Martin watched the commotion that erupted at the entrance to his parents' home, where an elderly woman stormed out of the doorway, a step behind her a man her age; both were following the boy.

"Mom! Dad!" Martin took a step toward them.

At once another figure appeared. It was a burly man, stooping, and holding onto his groin with one hand, the other grasping a pistol.

Martin froze as in a spell, not able to move or utter a sound, as he watched the events reel in front of his eyes as though in slow motion. The arm holding the weapon rose up, aiming at the backs of the elderly couple. The door of the blue sedan swung open just as Lydia Borneman ran past it. The impact of the door threw her back into Oliver, both falling to the ground. The huge man who followed them from the house had caught up. He towered over the couple, and looked around, scanning the street. He did not see Martin. He aimed the pistol at the couple.

"No!" Martin cried out. "No! You bastards!" He jolted to the curb.

His voice gave away his location. The thug projected a smile. His companion, the man from the blue sedan, spun around to face Martin, a shotgun in his hands.

Shots whizzed in the air. Martin veered off to the side, and ducked behind a gray station wagon, its windshield shattering, bullets ripping the metal hood and frame. He pressed to the ground and gawked from underneath the car. The boy was still running toward him, fear and panic on his face matching only that of his dog's. Martin focused beyond.

49

Something odd was in the assailants' behavior. They were ducking behind the sedan, its windshield shattered, shards of glass landing on Martin's parents.

What had happened? Martin looked up along the curb, where, across the street from his parents' home, two men were ducking behind a van with a logo of a moving company, pistols in their hands, aiming at the thugs. Who were they? It did not matter. This was not the time to question. This was the time to seize the situation. Martin stood up, and immediately ducked as the man from the sedan aimed in his direction. This sparked a fire exchange, as Martin's unexpected allies fired back. The two groups battled as only in gangster movies, firing round after round.

It was madness. Pinned to the ground, Martin analyzed the situation. He noted with relief that his parents had enough sense to remain on the ground, embraced, drawing as little attention as possible.

The boy, on the other hand, did quite the opposite. He continued toward the wagon Martin used for cover, as though drawn to it by a magnet, the dog yelping, being dragged behind. The boy was shouting. His words could not be made out in the shootout, but they drew the attention of the thugs. The one with the shotgun appeared over the hood of his sedan, and aimed at the boy.

"Get down!" Martin cried, his lungs filled with helpless rage.

The shattering spat of the heavy weapon could be heard above the other. A split second later Martin watched in painful amazement as the boy flew several feet in the air and landed on the dark gray pavement in front of the wagon, his eyes wide open, fixed on Martin. The dog was yelping, shivering, its tiny tail pulled underneath its belly.

Martin's eyes slowly lifted off the boy's, focusing on the scene in front of the parents' home. He did not hear the shots that reached the killer, but he saw his body spin around, his arms shooting upwards, throwing the shotgun into the street. He watched as the killed slumped onto the ground. He saw as his companion returned fire, and he saw as one of the men who came to Martin's help was shot, pivoted, and fell. He saw as the remaining one aimed, and fired, hitting the last of the standing killers. He watched as everything and everyone suddenly stood still.

The silence did not last long, but it felt like an eternity. The first to break the spell was the remaining of Martin's allies, who started across the street, toward the thugs. Martin could see as his legs touched the driver of the sedan, and then his companion. He watched as the man holstered his pistol, and approached the Bornemans. He watched as they struggled to their feet, embracing each other, their heads turning as though in disbelief, their eyes scanning the area for their son.

Martin struggled to his feet.

A screech of tires startled everyone. A large SUV started abruptly from a parked position some two houses up from Martin's parents' home. It approached the blue sedan, coming to a sudden halt. The event took everyone by surprise, including the man who helped the Bornemans up. It would cost him his life. Before the SUV stopped, a shot was fired, and the man fell to the ground.

Martin watched in amazement as several men emerged from the vehicle. They approached the elderly couple. One of them drew out a pistol, lifted his outstretched arm, and fired two silent shots, one at each of Martin's parents.

Martin watched in paralyzing terror and stupefaction as his parents slumped onto the sidewalk. He watched as the newcomers moved briskly, picking the two bodies, and shoving them onto the back seat of the SUV, the vehicle reversing at high speed.

The entire scene lasted no more than sixty seconds, but the events that reeled in front of Martin's eyes would remain etched in his mind, frame by frame, forever. A nightmare that never ends.

10

The Director of the Federal Bureau of Investigation stormed into the office of the attorney general.

"James, there was a shooting in Georgetown," he said in a composed voice that concealed emotional storm.

"I know, Bill. I'm on the phone with the chief of police."

The attorney general motioned his guest to a leather chair, but the offer was declined. He continued the telephone conversation, his eyes tracking the nervous pacing of the tall figure. He hung up some two minutes later.

"Talk to me, Bill, because I don't know what to make of it. The cops are talking about a war zone."

"It is only the beginning, James."

The attorney general gasped. He studied the director's face. He saw the strained effort to remain in check, and he did not like it. It would make his job much more difficult, if not impossible.

He said in a muted voice, "Talk to me, Bill."

The director appeared to gather his thoughts before replying, "It's a long story. It goes back."

"Condense it. A lot of angry people who are waiting for answers."

The director stopped the pacing as though to collect his thoughts. He wiped his forehead several times, a clear sign of the weight of what he was about to share, and continued back and forth about the office as he narrated.

"A routine background check on a state department diplomat led our agents to his friends, all CIA agents. It wasn't long before our counterintelligence was alerted to some dubious activities involving the CIA."

The attorney general said nothing, the expression on his suddenly pale face suggesting that the importance of the disclosure did not go amiss.

The director continued. "All in all we put five men under the microscope. For a long time we ran around in circles. Not really surprising, given the background of these men. They're experts at concealing their identities, and leading investigators astray."

The man behind the large desk picked up a scrapbook and scribbled something in it, only to occupy his trembling hands, his face ash pale, the reaction partly concealed by the need to lower the head. He adjusted his shirt collar, the move exposing a thick silver chain that supported a large cross. He was known as a devout Christian.

The director continued. "Several weeks ago we received intel about these five men planning a meeting. We found out where the meeting was to take place, and we planted surveillance on them—"

"You, what?" The attorney general dropped his fountain pen. He raised his hand to his mouth, and coughed to cover the reaction.

The director was taken aback by his superior's behavior.

"Why was I not appraised of this operation?" The attorney pressed, his voice at high pitch.

The director looked into his face, and turned his eyes. He answered factually, albeit with detectable caution in his voice, "A routine procedure."

"Since when is keeping tabs on the CIA considered a routine procedure?"

The tall, slim, slightly hunched director towered over his slouching superior. He replied in a voice that made the attorney general shiver. "A routine background check on a state department officer led us on." He paused, giving the interlocutor a chance to voice his concerns, confident now that none would be forthcoming. He then went on to describe the events at the cabin on Lake Ruther, as he knew them from the retrieved surveillance footage. He concluded, "Five men — three CIA agents, one, a diplomat with the state department, and a neighbor who wandered in at the wrong time — were slaughtered."

"Who did this?"

"We can't be certain at this stage. We know, however, that one of the men survived."

"Survived?"

"We can only guess, but it looks as though the body count added up — a neighbor walked in, while one of the CIA men, Martin Borneman, was elsewhere. He survived the hit."

The attorney general exhaled deeply, avoiding eye contact.

"And the shooting in Georgetown?"

"Whoever killed those five men had realized that a mistake had been made, and Borneman survived. They waited for him at his parents' home, and were met with a CIA team, who, presumably, was dispatched to protect Borneman."

"Then it's a CIA matter."

"Not exactly. They killed a state department diplomat."

The attorney general raised his head as though he came to a sudden decision. He glanced at his wristwatch, grinned, and asked after a moment's consideration that resembled resigned hesitation, "What do you need, Bill?"

"We must find Borneman before the killers do, or before the CIA silences him. I suggest we go national, full board, involve the police."

The doors had barely closed behind the director when the attorney general picked up his mobile phone and dialed a number. It took his shaking hands three attempts before he picked the correct entry in his smartphone's phone book. With the connection established he was unable to control his emotions.

"Bill has just left my office! He knows something's up! He had the cabin bugged!"

The man who answered the call replied in a carefully choreographed voice, as though speaking laboriously to conceal a trait of some kind. His tone was stern.

"We know that."

"For God's sakes, they've been onto you for a long time—"

The voice cut him off. "Just what do they know?"

The attorney general was stumped. "I don't know. I couldn't pry. I think he suspects me."

"Did he mention names?"

"No— I don't know!"

"Then he knows nothing."

"But he's on the right track. It's only a matter of time before he finds out about the Group, and from there he'll be onto us—"

The handset vibrated in the attorney general's hand when the recipient shouted, "Get a grip of yourself! Everything's being taken care of—"

"Is it? Your plan is in ruins, and we are going down with it!" The highest official at the justice department was at the brink of a nervous breakdown, and his voice showed it.

"These things happen. It's a rare operation that goes without a glitch. The Group has struck, but they failed to stop us. Borneman is alive. He will carry on, alone."

"Oh, Jesus God." The attorney general's lips trembled uncontrollably. His words were barely discernible through the chatter of his teeth when he said, "If this fails we'll all lay our heads—"

"Now, listen to me, you whining old fool." The voice was an ice pick piercing soft flesh. "We won't fail."

"The Group has proved resourceful! They knew about the plan, that's why they struck. Now the director is onto you, too."

"Keep an eye on him. It shouldn't be difficult since you're his boss. Stall him. It won't be for long. The operation is in motion, and cannot be stopped. By anybody."

11

Martin spent the better part of the evening wandering the Rock Creek Park, and crying until he no longer could. Pulling his hair and cursing the unknown murderers, he vowed revenge. Images of his parents slumping to the ground, the killer's grin, and the young boy running for his life, his falling body exposing the image of another killer, would remain etched in Martin's memory forever. Two elderly and a child were slaughtered with cold determination. He failed to find a reason. He searched for answers until confusion and physical exhaustion brought his mind to a state of numbness. Unable to come to any conclusions, he could no longer grieve, nor curse. He needed peace. He needed help. Lonely, and desperate, where could he turn? Whom could he trust the way he could trust his parents? The question brought an answer. He raised the collar of his jacket, and headed out of the park, careful to remain in the shadows as he covered the way on foot.

The doorman studied Martin with suspicion. In all those years as the concierge he was used to seeing all kinds of people come to professor Sabria. Some of them were well-dressed, professional people, perhaps even civil servants; some were students, and then there were the others — the writers, or artists, who didn't pay much attention to appearances. Ever since the professor picked up the pro bono cases from the community center, the concierge had seen his share of unemployed come for their free legal advice. But this one, although still young, was the worst of the bunch. His clothes were wet and soiled, and he looked as though he had just crawled from under the bridge. A bum! The concierge rang the apartment anyway, reminded once by the professor that it was not the clothes that made a man. Still, he would prefer to see more of them government people, and would even settle for the students, but not those types.

"Martin?" Dan Sabria stood in the doorway to his apartment, wide smile vanishing at the sorry state of his guest's appearance. "What in God's name happened to you?"

Martin approached unsteadily, his shoulders slouched, a tired and resigned man. He walked by the stunned lawyer and entered the living room. He gazed around the modest apartment he knew so well from childhood, as though not recognizing it, and slowly slouched onto the sofa.

"Martin?" The professor repeated worriedly.

"They're dead, Dan. … Killed. … They're all dead."

It took a great deal of compassion and quiet understanding to coax Martin to open up. Once he started he could not stop. He told Dan everything, beginning with the stolen black vault funds, the meeting at the cabin, and the mutilated bodies, and ended with a broken description of the events that took place at his parents' doorsteps. Relating the tragedy had a cleansing effect in so far that he no longer wept. A new sensation came over him entirely. With no traces of doubt, grief, or guilt, a dogged and burning desire to punish was gaining ground.

Dan Sabria listened with growing anger. When the story came to the second shooting at the cabin he could no longer remain in his seat. He began pacing within the confines of the small living room, his large and heavy figure making the glasses on the dining table clink. When the story reached the shooting of Lydia and Oliver, he froze in place, motionless, his eyes immersed in Martin's. He could not believe his ears, and he had seen a lot.

Dan Sabria's firm represented numerous members of the subversive groups of the 1960s and 1970s in their suits against the Federal Bureau of Investigation and the State. He was no stranger to abuse of power, but those were distant days he thought would not quickly come back. He was wrong. Nowadays such obstinate forages beyond security agencies' sanctioned duties were back with full might. Dan himself had witnessed how far the State was prepared to go when his firm's computers and files were seized for daring to speak out against the increasing invigilation. Still, even in the terror-obsessed age, with homeland security issues reaching unprecedented measures, often grotesque, and certainly not without mistakes, Dan could not accept Martin's evaluation of the events. The boy — oh God, he still thought of him as a boy — Martin had gone through a terrifying ordeal, and his perception must have been skewed by agitation. His friends were murdered, and the preliminary investigation had lead to Martin. The sheriff's decision was justifiable — letting Martin go would have meant letting a potential killer on the loose. The murder was shocking to Martin, but the sheriff's conviction that he had found the killer was not unreasonable. Sabria did not see a conspiracy, as Martin suggested. There might have been overzealous judgment on the part of the law enforcement agencies involved, but to suspect the CIA, or someone else connected to the government, of killing the young boy who was walking a dog, and then assassinating the elderly and harmless Bornemans could only be the effect of a strong emotional shock. It had to have been.

"All right, let's go through it once more," Sabria started in calm, reasoning voice of a lawyer. "Why do you think those two men who picked you up in Apsley were with the CIA? Had they identified themselves?"

"Yes— No— The sheriff said they were on the way and would be taking me to Peterborough on a case of homeland security. The cops released me and let them take me so they must've had some proof. In doesn't matter anyway because then, in the car—"

"They roughed you up in the car, Martin, but it doesn't make them killers."

"There is more! I recognized one of them, Dan! He's known as Croissant, for the mark on his forehead. He's been with special operations. His file went through my desk. Besides, he knew me, too! He knew my CIA codename. I'm telling you, Dan, this hit was ordered by the CIA. It had to be."

"Sanctioned?" Sabria raised his brow in a studied expression of doubt that was projected in an effort to make his young friend elaborate.

"I thought it over, and over. It was a professional hit disguised as a maniacal murder-suicide. Their faces were blown off, for crying out loud! It was made to look as if Derek did it. You see, we had a few drinks that evening. In effect, it looked as if Derek went nuts, killed everyone, and then turned the gun on himself. It was a convincing set up. Only something went wrong. I survived, Dan!"

"How?"

"Bobby and I— We had an argument brewing, so I went outside to cool, and— I don't know what happened after. I woke up on the dock."

"What argument, Martin?" Sabria asked with concern. During his law practice he had learned that arguments lead to consequences.

12

Martin said, "It was about a woman."

Professor Sabria pried after a moment's silence, "Is it the same woman for whom you left the CIA? … Don't be surprised, Martin. I know about it because your parents and I are good friends. You're almost my nearest relations, you know."

Of course, he should have known that his parents, mother especially, would have shared whatever there was about their only son's most serious relationship. They liked, perhaps even loved Jeannie, and the parting hurt them nearly as much as it did Martin. He realized that recapping the incident and dwelling into its implications was helping clear his mind from the terrible shock caused by the killing of his parents. He was starting to regain his strength and the desire to find and punish those who caused the tragedy. And thus his words were purposeful, his voice clear, his thoughts defined.

"Mum's, as always, melodramatic. There wasn't one single reason for my leaving the CIA. A whole string of factors led to the decision. Jeannie— She came between me and Bobby, and at such a time when leaving the CIA was no longer a question of if, but how soon. Bobby and I, we never really talked about it, but it couldn't be left in limbo. I thought this weekend we should finally clear things out. I didn't want to lose my cool, so I drank, hoping it would calm me down. I had too much, walked out drunk, and fell asleep on the dock. They died."

"The argument." Sabria reminded.

"Dead end, Dan. I did not kill Bobby and the others because of the woman," Martin replied with irritation.

"Why are they dead, then, Martin?"

Martin shrugged. "I can't think of anything else but the money. Word on the street is that Derek took off with the black vault. He denied it, of course, and said it was a set up, but what in the hell for?"

"Did the killers retrieve the money?"

"How could they? There was no money."

"But they must've been darn sure it was there if they killed your friends. You just said that this Croissant was convinced that it was hidden somewhere in the cabin."

"I don't think they were looking for money. They mentioned that the cops wouldn't know what to look for."

"And you have no clue what it might have been?"

A helpless shrug was the only reply.

The professor spread his arms in a gesture of sheer curiosity. "About the money, then. How much are we talking about? A pocketful of change, or a briefcase full of diamonds?"

"I don't know, but it would have to be substantial. Derek dealt with millions in cash, literally. I can imagine how it would be tempting to pocket some of it, to nibble now and then, but to grab the whole lot and run? He has been at it for close to ten years, and he wasn't stupid. He must have known about the consequences."

"If he has been nibbling, as you put it, all those years, and was never caught, he might have become careless and complacent."

"He worked for the CIA long enough to know that he could never get away with it."

Sabria stood up, and went to the kitchen, remaining visible through the wide-open doors. He put the kettle on. He tapped his fingertips on the countertop, crease between his eyes. Some gut feeling fueled by years of experience, of dealing with real thieves and framed scapegoats, was telling him that the answer was close but for whatever reason they could not find it. The conversation resembled a trap door with no handles, a door that needed to be tapped in just the right spot to open.

He changed the approach. "What have you been doing since you left the CIA?"

"I've been taking over The Hill Gazer. You know it."

"No connection with the CIA?" The professor observed his young friend carefully. "No? And, what's his name, the friend who left the CIA with you?"

"Arthur? You've met, I think. Arthur Latki. He used to come to our house a great deal. Bushy red hair, skinny as a broom, and a very good friend—"

"I remember. That's why I asked. A promising law student. What has he been up to?"

"He took up a position with the International Criminal Court," Martin replied slowly. "Why?"

"You seem fixated on the money, which you doubt your friend had taken, and which, in my opinion, seems rather improbable, and for the same reasons you pointed out. Then, of course, the whole thing sounds quite improbable, starting with the killing of the only persons who could have returned the stolen funds, and ending with the most dubious part — that of carrying the cash around and bringing it to the cabin. You said it yourself — the loot went into millions. Who in their right mind would carry this much on them for so long, especially if they were being pursued by one of the most notorious agencies in the world?"

"What are you suggesting?" Martin asked, suddenly stricken with the significance of Sabria's idea.

"This Croissant was looking for something that would not have raised the attention of the police. You don't know what it might have been, but your friends, or one of them, might have. Start by looking into your friends' background. How well do you really know them? What have they been up to? Take for example your friend Arthur. Dissect his life."

"Arthur?" Martin repeated hesitantly, dumbfounded.

"Well, I admit, the United States does not recognize the jurisdiction of the International Criminal Court, and it seems hardly a reason to murder someone who advocates the ICC's principles, but what about the others? What do you really know about your friends? For instance, what do you really know about Arthur's reasons for quitting the CIA?"

"Dan, I'm through with the CIA, and so was Art," Martin said with intonation that meant for Sabria to press on in this direction. He felt instinctively that they were getting somewhere.

"I hear one is never through with the CIA."

"Urban legends." Borneman shrugged, unconvincingly.

"Perhaps." Sabria studied Martin's face. "But then, why are you convinced that the CIA killed off your friends? To think that they would be so quick to get rid of their former, and current, operatives is rather improbable. I remember you say once, in this very room, four or five years ago, that nothing happens on a whim, that everything the CIA does is carefully planned. By that reasoning would they not confirm that you took part in the theft? Would they not have irrefutable proof of your guilt before writing you off?"

"Dan, I assure you, I had nothing to do with it. And no — they would not hesitate to get rid of anyone who crossed them, as they would kill anyone who knew what Derek did for a living. Do you have any idea where the black vault funds come from? From the most notorious black operations! And they finance more black operations, drug trafficking, arms dealing, sex trade, assassinations, robbery—"

"Robbery? Really, Martin—" Sabria interjected doubtfully.

"Yes, Dan, robbery!" Martin said without hesitation. Seeing the skeptical look in Sabria's eyes he explained, "Alright. Do you recall the pharmaceutical truck that went missing several weeks ago outside Seattle? It was all over the news. A truck like that can transport drugs worth twenty or thirty million dollars. These drugs likely ended up in some of those Internet pharmacies, or on the streets, and it would not surprise me in the least if the CIA had a hand in it. A good percentage of organized groups in this country, as elsewhere around the world, are stealing for intelligence agencies, for the most part unwittingly. The money that comes from these activities has to be laundered, and in cases where the loot is merchandise, it has to be cashed. That's where Derek and people like him fit in."

Silence followed his words.

"Martin, what have you gotten yourself in to?" Sabria said after the initial astonishment wore off.

"Every intelligence service in the world works this way. They all need funds free of governmental scrutiny," Martin said unapologetically, as though stating a fact.

"I'm sure, but that's not what upsets me. I'm worried about you being mixed up with those—" Professor Sabria began pacing about the room, breathing heavily. He stopped, wiped his forehead with a handkerchief, and continued, "You know how critical I am of our secret services, but I still find it hard to believe that the CIA could be behind it."

Martin shrugged, weary of the stalled progress. "If the hit was not ordered because of money alone, then perhaps it was tied to the purpose it was to serve. The black vault exists to sponsor covert ops that ought not to be tied to the official budget. In other words black funds are not only unaccountable — they provide the CIA with freedom to engage in operations that go beyond its sanctioned duties."

"So what you're saying is that covering the truth about the operation the money was to finance might've been more important than getting the money back."

Martin stared at the old family friend, wide eyed, shocked by the thought he has unleashed.

13

"My God, Martin. What have you gotten yourself in?" Professor Sabria's voice came from the kitchen where he collected a large pot of tea, and another of coffee. Bustling about the kitchen he continued, "I don't know the details of your parting with the CIA, I don't even know what you did for them, and I'm not sure I want to know, though I understand there was, perhaps still is, some bad blood between you and the agency."

"Of course there is some bitterness left, and I'm not the only one! Plenty of good officers resigned, or were forced to quit."

Sabria came back to the living room, two steaming pots and two cups on a tray.

"Dare I ask why?"

Martin replied wearily, it was clear that he was not ready to venture into specifics, however close the friendship,

"Most were expected to fix intelligence around the policy, and quit in protest."

Professor Sabria could not guess whether his young friend was mum on the subject because his job involved vile duties, as he suspected it did, or purely out of concern for the safety of those within his inner circle, as the common knowledge had it. He was thinking aloud as he paced between the table and the door to the balcony, a cup of tea in his hand.

"That could not have made your employer happy, but what company kills disenchanted employees? The events take on a whole different meaning when we consider that your parting with the CIA parallels, time-wise, the disappearance of the black vault. Can the two be a mere coincidence?"

Borneman was taken aback. It was true that he left the CIA just as the rumors about the black vault began to spread. But this could only be a coincidence. It had to be.

"If you had worked for the CIA and seen the way it operates, you'd sooner believe your friends than your employer. Derek said he did not touch the vault, and, despite everything that happened, I would sooner believe him."

"But you agree that it's a possibility. Otherwise you must ask yourself: What is it that you and your friends did that precipitated such an extreme measure?" Sabria watched Martin who appeared to struggle with his conscience. "I understand you are bound by secrecy, but do not forget that the CIA has broken that agreement by killing your parents and friends, if you truly believe that's what happened. I intend to do what's in my powers to help you bring those responsible to justice, but I must know what I'm dealing with."

Martin hesitated.

"You realize that once I tell you, there will be no going back. You will be subject to the same repercussions that I would be if I ever decided to break the gag order."

"Martin, the sort of things I heard from my clients would have me locked up in any number of those secret detention centers if I didn't know what I was doing."

Martin took a minute to reply. He had decided to come forward the moment the thought had crossed his mind to seek Sabria's help, but he was still holding back. Everything he knew, or suspected, about what had occurred on the lake, were suppositions. And suppositions were not a good way to solve a mystery. He hated to admit this to himself that he was more of a cold analyst relying on facts rather than instinct that his job so often required. Gut feeling and hunch were not part of his professional vocabulary. Careful, painstaking planning were what was needed when lives were at stake. Lives were at stake, he reminded himself. Lives were lost. The dearest lives of all. He owed it to them to come clean, and to solve the mystery.

"My friends and I, all five of us, were tied to the CIA. Even Chris, who worked for the Department of State, was reporting to the CIA."

"What are you saying?" Sabria asked quietly, the tea cup frozen in the air.

"If you can't work together then you must keep an eye on one another. I'm sure the State Department has sympathetic people inside the CIA, just as the CIA snoops on the State. Derek laundered money for the black vault. Bobby was discharged from the military only to be pulled in to the CIA; I suspected it was my own department, on the field side, but he never admitted to it."

"And, you?"

Martin did not bicker. He stated simply, as anyone might when asked about their occupation, "I headed a cell that facilitated the disappearance of some very bad people."

Professor Sabria studied his face as though looking for confirmation that he understood correctly. Martin thought that the professor's face turned green, but it could have been the effect of the fluorescent street lights that entered the room on the gust of winds that spread the window curtains open.

Sabria composed himself, and said, "Jesus. It's no surprise at all. If you combine the missing money with your employment records, and your secret meetings on the lake, it all adds up to a pretty scary scenario. You see what I mean? You fit the profile."

"The profile?"

"Whatever the hell they believe you were planning to do with the money," Sabria clarified.

For a moment they pondered the answer in silence, both stunned by the connection.

"We'll get to the bottom of it, Martin, I promise," Dan added quietly but firmly, without looking into the young man's eyes, still visibly uncomfortable about the revealed employment details. In any case, no words could comfort a man whose parents were killed in front of his eyes, and whose friends were slain in his presence. Martin was a man convinced that his former employer was responsible, and Dan's words were not intended to comfort. The professor was angry. Damn angry. Lydia and Oliver were killed, their deaths somehow tied to the preposterous conspiracy that almost claimed the life of their son. Whatever the case might be Dan would not rest till those responsible answered for it. God help him, he would not rest.

"First off," Sabria continued in a changed voice, "Tell me what you intend to do."

"I want to kill every son of a bitch who was even remotely tied to this affair. And I want you to help me." Martin's eyes glistened from the newly found passion to inflict his own justice.

"Kill? Martin, I—"

"I meant — help me in your capacities."

"How?"

"Perhaps you are right. Perhaps there is more than meets the eye, but if what you suggest is true — that it is not only about the money — then what? I must find out what my friends were up to these last couple of years. I must, because whatever precipitated their deaths must be linked. I've got to start somewhere. I need help, and you're the only person I can trust."

"Where do you want to begin?"

Martin pondered the thought, "You're a lawyer, and so was Arthur. It's a starting point."

"I hardly knew your friend."

"But you know about the world he was a part of. After quitting with the CIA, Arthur embraced the same sort of ideals that make you who you are. He became committed to change, and to helping those who are underrepresented."

"The International Criminal Court?" Sabria shook his head. He continued thoughtfully, "No, not really my cup of tea, but we may try here in D.C. There is a man here who's been advocating the U.S. joining the ICC. He's a former Supreme Court justice and a professor emeritus here, at Georgetown."

"That's a start. Where is he?"

Sabria explained, and added, "But Martin, do not rush into anything. Let me try other ways first. We must act justly."

"Other ways? There are no other ways. Not after what they've done."

14

Further discussion was pointless without proper understanding of what exactly had transpired at the cabin and outside the Bornemans' residence. Both men needed to rid their minds of anger. Martin was agitated and desperate — traits not helpful where finesse and a cool approach were necessary. A bath and a drink, the professor hoped, should allow his young friend to grab hold of his carnal emotions. He filled two glasses of strong whisky and led the way to the wardrobe. Martin was roughly the same height, definitely less wide around the waist line, as Sabria had observed without envy — after all age has its prerogatives — and the clothes might not fit snuggly, but at least they were fresh. He drew a bath, and returned to the living room. He had several telephone calls to make.

It was almost thirty minutes later that Martin had emerged from the hallway, bathed, shaven, wearing clothes that looked more casual than loose. He appeared weary. The bath brought out the physical stress, the alcohol somewhat taking care of the emotional. He froze at the entrance to the living room, sensing more trouble.

The professor was pacing in front of his liquor cabinet, a pair of reading glasses on his nose. He kept adjusting them up and down, nervously. His face was pale, almost paper-white. His hands trembled. He did not try to cover his agitation. He could not.

"The sheriff—" Sabria started, his voice breaking. He cleared his throat and continued, "Apsley police station. They're all dead, including a woman named Gina, the pregnant temp. The federal agents who followed you to the cabin were killed too. And then— And then— Oh Jesus, Martin! An innocent boy in Georgetown! They have it all pegged on you!"

Martin was stunned. He stood in the doorway gaping at the old family friend.

"Of course, I don't believe any of it, not for a minute!" Dan added with conviction. "Please forgive my initial reaction, but hearing all those absurd things was so terribly shocking! How could they be so blind? How could they be so set on pursuing the wrong person for the wrong reasons? How can they be convinced of your guilt?" He shook his head violently. "There must be more to it than we are given to understand. We're missing an important piece of the puzzle. Either that, or something seriously wrong is happening to you and to this country. The sheer fact that it could come to such charges against you makes me very afraid, and very mad. Very!" Sabria approached the bar and poured himself a tall drink. He swallowed it in one swig with a theatrical gesture of pushing his head back and slamming the glass on the tray. He licked his lips and resumed his pace.

The old man did not expect a reply. He merely expressed his thoughts aloud. Even if some answer was due, Martin was unable to utter a word, stunned beyond speech at the confirmation of his fears. He was being framed. He stood frozen, his eyes following the professor.

"I spoke with a good friend at the Justice Department. A nation-wide warrant has been issued. The FBI has been watching you for months. They claim you and your friends were plotting for a long time. Jesus, Martin! What have you gotten yourself into?" Sabria continued in an emotionally charged voice, cracking his finger joints as he crossed the room back and forth several times. "You can't stay here—" He paused abruptly and approached Borneman. "We have to get you to a lawyer. I know one who can help. But first we need to talk to someone else. The judge we spoke of. He is retired, but very influential. He knows plenty of people in just the right places. Some of them very high, the highest. Come, let us go to him."

Martin did not move. He watched the old friend in numb bewilderment.

Sabria walked over to a built-in closet in the hallway. He fingered through hats and scarves on the top shelve, and handed something to Martin who accepted it mechanically — a baseball cap.

"Put it on. And pull the visor down to cover your eyes." The professor took out a knee-length trench coat and fumbled with a hanger. Finally he threw the hanger angrily away, and offered the coat to Borneman. "Raise the collar up." Satisfied, he quickly draped a similar coat over his shoulders, and headed toward the doors.

Martin did not move. He spoke at last, forcing his voice to remain calm.

"What about my parents, Dan? They were your friends! Say I turn myself in, what then? How will they ever pay for the killing of my parents, and is there punishment enough? No, Dan! I can't do this. I won't."

"I grieve with you, my son. I do! I understand what you feel, just as I know all these charges against you are preposterous! I know it is all a mistake. But they— They think you're a bloodthirsty monster. Somewhere a mistake was made that cost your parents' and your friends' lives. I promise you — I will not rest until they pay for it. But it must be done in a lawful way." He pulled on Martin's elbow. "Come now, we'll find you the best lawyer this country's schools ever produced."

Borneman jerked his arm back. The numbness and bewilderment were giving way to anger. He spoke with determination and conviction, "Don't you see? I'm being set up. I was supposed to die, but I survived, and I got away from them. Now they're making sure that no one talks to me, that no one asks questions, just as they did not ask any before shooting my friends and my folks. Whatever is going on it must be of the highest priority, and not something they're going to discuss, nor would they want to see it go to trial. Conspiracy. Killing all those people. Me? What a crock of lies! It's all made up from start to finish. They won't permit me to talk to lawyers. If they get their hands on me they'll finish what they've started. I'm dead, Dan, anyway you look at it, because they want me dead. Only, before it comes to that, I will settle scores my own way."

"Revenge? No, Martin, you mustn't!"

"What else have I got? I lost the people I love!"

"No, Martin, you mustn't contemplate revenge! It may seem like the only thing to repay them with, but you must not give in to your most primitive desires. You are better than that."

"You're right. I am devoid of any and all human feelings right now. And they are responsible for it. They killed my parents and my friends. I shall respond to them in the only way they deserve."

"Let us work together. Let justice prevail. It is all the distinction there is between us and the killers. Besides, look at it from another perspective — what if they want you to act in a certain way, what if they want you to use violence?"

The thought got the better out of Martin. He stopped, thinking about the implications.

Sabria pressed on, "If your suspicions are true, if you are being, as you put it — set up — then it is not inconceivable to assume that it may be aimed at eliciting a certain reaction."

"A reaction?" Martin repeated.

"Just one of many possibilities. Unfortunately, we can't get into the mind of those who are doing it to you, without knowing who they are. Come. Let us find out."

15

The house stood in a quiet residential area a short stroll West of Potomac View. It was one of those quickly disappearing neo-colonial residences, with clear signs of neglected grandeur. Tall grass grew along the meandering flagstone pathway, several rose bushes sprouted out of the confines of trellises, their branches hanging to the ground under the weight of flowers, and the small artificial pond had dried out together with the funds, or a will to maintain the property. Despite the neglect the property conveyed a sense of established ownership, passed down through generations.

Ezra Ferguson was nearing eighty, but with his vigorous bearing and piercing eyes he could easily pass for seventy. Having retired close to a decade earlier he devoted much of his time to what he missed the most in his thirty years behind the judge's bench in the Supreme Court: after his wife passed away, and following a short but unsuccessful attempt at up keeping of Morna's rose garden, he voraciously devoured books. He felt no guilt about it — the roses flowered year after year, somehow tending to themselves without his contribution, while books that he and Morna purchased over the years with the intention of sharing them together in their retirement, drew him like a magnet. He read many of them aloud, as though reading to his wife, the way they were supposed to enjoy them.

Though a retiree, Ezra Ferguson kept himself busy. Apart from reading books, he consulted for a variety of organizations, and chaired an even greater number of committees. As though these activities were not enough, he liked to exercise. That evening, as every evening and early morning, he dressed quickly, put on his wrist pulse monitor and opened the door to start his routine: an hour-long walk around the neighborhood. He opened the door, and was met face-to-face with an old friend.

Almost an hour later Martin was convinced that the visit to Ezra Ferguson was a dead end. The retired judge listened to Martin's narrative with indifference of any lawyer, or a judge, who had heard and seen it all. Crime, abuse, misery — these were all terrible for the victims, but hearing, and often seeing the evidence, day after day, for decades, could desensitize anyone. While he nodded during the narrative, as a judge would from the bench, Ezra Ferguson remained unmoved. It was not until he heard the name that his attitude had changed entirely.

"Arthur Latki is dead," Martin repeated.

Suddenly, Ezra Ferguson aged beyond his years. Gone was his stamina, and as before he seemed ten years younger, he was now far older than his actual age would have it. He seemed to have shrunk in his deep, and plush, lounge chair. He leaned forward, embraced his face, and remained in this position for several minutes.

His guests dared not move. Breathless, they awaited for the judge to come to. When he did, his words had stunned them.

Ezra Ferguson said, his voice barely above a whisper, "Your friend, Arthur, was right. It has begun."

Sabria and Borneman exchanged glances.

Having found himself this close to the truth Martin was unable to play riddles. The pent up anticipation was explosive.

"What has begun?" he asked.

"I advised him against it, you know," the judge continued in a quiet voice.

Martin did not press, though his head was throbbing for answers. He wanted to know, everything, now. He dared not press, though, knowing that the elderly can be as outpouring as they are stubborn, and a single word uttered at the wrong moment could shut the judge forever. His tactfulness was rewarded.

"I was against it all along," Ezra Ferguson continued. "I believed it could only lead to deeper division, and throw the country on a downward spiral. But Arthur would not have it. Every new generation in a changing world believes in different approaches to old rules. Don't get me wrong, young man, fresh wind can bring the vital forces that are required to bring about change, but a wind too strong can cause damage. It seems that the wind has been gathering inside a huge balloon that is about to burst. God help us all when it does."

Bewildered, Martin stood up. With his hands at his temples he crossed the room several times. At last he paused. He said in a voice filled with desperation, "I don't understand any of this. It's as though I don't know my friends. What was Arthur up to? What change are you referring to?"

Now the judge seemed perplexed.

"Have you not said that you and Arthur, and three other men, formed the Group?"

"The group? We were friends. Five of us, going back a ways. Yes, we were a group. A group of good friends."

The elderly man looked him up and down. He stood up, suddenly alert, and began to pace. He murmured something to himself. Then he said aloud, "But that means that you were all dupes."

"What are you saying?" Martin pulled the man's elbow, stopping him in his steps.

The judge shook his head a notch, gazed into the young man's eyes and said, "You must tell me again what happened. How it happened. And tell me all you know about your friends. Be attentive to the smallest detail, however insignificant it may seem."

And so it was that Martin related the events of that fateful night at the cabin yet again. It did not escape him that it came much easier this time. He began by speaking quickly, but gradually the narrative facilitated reflection, and with it came pacification of mind. Martin became deeply entrenched in his words; reliving the events helped him form rational thought. He began to see more clearly.

"What you have stumbled upon is the most challenging threat our country has faced in decades," Ezra Ferguson said when the narrative ended. He turned to his friend, Dan Sabria. "You were right to connect Arthur Latki with everything that's happened."

"You're the only one I know who could have a connection to that boy, as remote as it may be."

"I met Arthur Latki on a committee advocating our joining the International Criminal Court. At that time he was already deeply involved, working in Europe. He sought me out. He was concerned about something peculiar that he had discovered. He called it — and I remember his words as thought he said them just now — a sinister conspiracy."

"A conspiracy?" Martin repeated.

"Involving you and your friends."

"Nonsense."

"Yet Arthur was convinced that you and your friends were a part of this conspiracy. He couldn't quite make the connection, though, and became quite paranoid. He became convinced that the rest of you conspired behind his back."

"Conspired?"

"Arthur made some assumptions based the evidence he found. He made some predictions. There is but one difference in what Arthur predicted, and what has actually transpired. It makes me hopeful that not all is lost."

"Judge, what you say is… a riddle. I understand none of it. It's as though you're talking about someone else, not my friends!"

"Arthur said the same thing about the rest of you. Now I see that he was wrong. You were all involved in something that you were not aware of. You weren't aware of your destiny, of what you were chosen for." The judge took several turns around the room, the visitors following his very move. At last he stopped, faced his young guest, and said, "Where to begin? How is one to explain it now, in a few words, a game that's been in the making for years?" He ran the palm of his hand against his cheek and chin, as though wiping away constricting thoughts. He said at last, "What happened in the beginning is not for me to tell. I could not quite understand it when Arthur tried to explain the workings of the intelligence world to me, so I shan't try to relate it to you. You will have to make sense of it yourself. What I can tell you falls under my sphere." He fell silent, as though searching for the right words. A while passed before he spoke again. "It all starts with the International Criminal Court. Not many Americans are even aware of its existence, little else about its mandate. Not a surprising turn, what with the attitude our country holds toward international accountability. You see, our country lost a lot of its credibility on the world stage. All those unilateral aggressions gave America very bad reputation. Many relations were severed. Some were patched by the new administration, but many remained broken. The world was afraid of us, could not trust the assurances that our policy has changed since the last regime. The wars, the economy, and other factors, crippled our stance. Demands were placed on our new president. To show his goodwill he was expected to make an example, to prove that he meant what he promised in his platform of change. That's when Arthur came in on the stage. He and other like-minded people formed a unit that was supposed to make amends with the world. Under the umbrella of the International Criminal Court Arthur worked on a very delicate case."

Martin dropped his head, and closed his eyes. Out of the very many unknowns a picture was forming in his head, and he did not like what he was seeing.

"A case?"

"Yes. Arthur was building a criminal case against those officials of our former administrations who were deemed responsible for many alleged crimes. Bringing them to justice was what the world considered crucial in rebuilding mutual trust. Do you see where this is leading?"

Martin did, though it created more questions in his head than it provided answers.

The judge seemed to be reading in his mind. "During his assignment Arthur came across something very peculiar. His, and the names of his four close friends, had surfaced. He burrowed deeper, until he was able to form a better picture out of shattered fragments. Arthur found that the former officials against whom he was building a case were prepared for just such eventuality. They made plans that would ensure that no such actions would ever be undertaken against them. That's were you and your friends come in. A plan that was hatched twelve years ago is about to be executed… or has already… I don't know. I don't know what to make of the events of which you are an unwitting, but crucial part. I'm afraid that only you can answer this because… you are it."

"I am it," Martin repeated, wearily. "Yet, I am unaware of the things you talk about. How am I to act? Where begin?"

"I am surprised that Arthur hadn't discussed his findings with you, and your friends; the more so for he was convinced that a resolution was near."

Could this really have been the motive behind the murders, Martin wondered, the mysterious case his friend had come across, the case twelve years in the making?

The judge continued, "What Arthur undertook was unprecedented in the history of this great nation."

"Judge, are you saying that my friends died because Arthur took up a case against certain members of this or the previous administration?"

"Arthur died because of the group that he unearthed. A group that was formed twelve years ago."

Martin took time digesting the judge's words. What was the mysterious group that he was supposedly, and unwittingly, a part of? What did the equally mysterious plan that was set in motion years ago entail? What was the event the judge had in mind, the resolution that was near? And how did it all tie with the black vault? Once the questions formed in his head, Martin was ready to present them to the Judge. He opened his mouth, and remained in this rather undignified position, for he suddenly understood. Everything that he learned in the last several hours formed a cohesive and clear answer. Martin was stunned by the realization, and the thought was so overwhelming that he had to sit down.

He barely touched the couch when he jumped to his feet. The judge appeared equally alarmed. Professor Sabria's face turned pale.

The telephone was ringing.

16

Judge Ferguson glanced at the grandfather clock. He hesitated before picking up the receiver. A call at this wee hour could not possibly mean good news.

"What? Who is this? Now, hang on a minute!" The judge listened intently, his face becoming paler with each second, eyes ever wider. At last he passed the handset to Martin. "It's for you."

Martin approached, and placed the receiver to his ear.

"Borneman?" The voice on the line was stern and short. "You will do exactly as I tell you, or I shall make sure that you get to watch your parents die all over again. This time it will be final."

Before words could form in Martin's mind, his mother's voice came on the line.

"Martin, we're all right, a little woozy, but all right. Your father is here… Martin… For Godsakes, don't do anything you will be ashamed of! …"

A rustle followed the words. The telephone switched hands. The stern voice came back.

"Borneman?"

The shock was complete. Martin stood motionless and speechless, his face pale. He could not believe his ears. His mother! Alive!

The voice in the telephone rambled mercilessly. "Borneman? Listen to me. Both your parents are alive. What you saw outside your home was a tranquilizer pistol. With all that happened since that night on the lake we could not afford any more mishaps. You heard your mother — your parents are alright, and they will remain that way, so long as you do exactly as told. Borneman?"

"Yes," Martin answered mechanically.

"Listen carefully. A car is waiting outside. A silver sedan. Get in. The driver knows nothing so don't bother asking questions. On the back seat you will find a mobile phone. Pick it up. Sixty seconds. Go."

The line went dead.

He dropped the phone and numbly crossed the room, the hallway, and approached the doors. He peered outside through the stained glass window. A silver sedan was parked in front of the house, its engine running.

"Martin?" The two elderly gentlemen followed him.

"They are alive!" He replied over his shoulder. "They've got them, but my parents are alive. Nothing else matters. I have no choice."

"How is this possible? Who's got them?" Sabria was baffled.

Borneman did not answer. He reached for the door handle. He struggled with it, in his state of mind not seeing the simple bolt that kept the door locked.

"Martin!" Sabria cried.

He replied over his shoulder, while continuing to fumble with the handle, "They were only tranquilized!"

"Wait!" The judge approached the doors with swiftness unexpected of his age. "Wait, I have something." He ran back to the living room and returned momentarily, pushing something into Martin's hand. Borneman was unresponsive, his entire attention on the sedan parked along the curb. The judge slipped the item, an envelope, into Martin's coat pocked. "Take it. This is the answer you are looking for. You have a better chance of surviving and making use of it."

Ezra Ferguson slid the bolt, and opened the door.

Martin started for the sedan. He approached it and let out a gasp. The back door was open. In his confused state of mind he expected to find his parents inside the car, but the only occupant was the driver. Martin hesitated, but it lasted only a moment. Changes ran through his face, but were obscured by the darkness of the night. Those who could see his eyes would tremble before their expression. The disappointment of not finding his parents inside the car had triggered something in Martin's head. Gone was the numbness created by shock. Born was a desire to inflict pain on those who wronged him.

A mobile phone began to ring inside the vehicle. Martin noticed an illuminated keypad on the back seat. He slid in, and the car started immediately, centrifugal force closing the doors behind him. He answered up the phone.

"Very smooth, Borneman!" The stern voice opened.

"Where are they? Where are my parents?" Martin cried out.

"You'll join them soon enough. Now, listen to me—"

"No! This time you listen to me. I want to talk to my parents. Now!"

"This game will be played by our rules, Mother."

Martin froze, his eyes gazing out the window. The traffic lights ahead turned yellow, the driver applied pressure on the brakes, his eyes in the rearview mirror, locked with Martin's. Borneman forced a smile to his lips, placed the receiver on the seat and with one swift move smashed the edge of his hand into the driver's neck. The man's head drooped to his chest. The car swerved and rear-ended a pick up truck that was parked along the curb. The car was moving slowly and the damage was insignificant but the impact was strong enough to activate the pickup's alarm. It whizzed and honked, drawing the attention of early pedestrians and drivers. Martin was not hurt. The driver, however, slid onto the steering wheel, unconscious.

Martin reached over to the floor where the mobile had slid off. He felt for it and opened the door. He started back on the sidewalk, the receiver at his ear. The connection was alive.

"Borneman?! … What was that? … Borneman?! …" The voice lost its stern intonation. Apparently the caller had his trigger points.

"You've already killed them once in my heart. You can't do it twice!" Martin said coldly. "You need me, so you listen to me, you son-of-a-bitch! This game will be played by my rules! I want to talk to my mother! You have sixty seconds to put her on. Go." He switched off the phone.

Martin was playing a risky game, but the gamble was necessary. He stood to lose as much as he stood to gain from the kidnappers' next move. He considered that the caller may be bluffing, and that Oliver and Lydia were dead, the message he heard on the phone prerecorded. But if they were alive, it would suggested that the kidnappers had plans for the son. Martin believed this to be the case, and a belief was a stronger propeller for one's desires than mere hope, though hope was not absent from his thoughts.

He quickly dialed a number.

"Dispatch." The phone was answered before he could hear it ring.

He used his old handle and a password. It worked.

"Patching through."

A familiar series of high-pitched sounds indicated a sterile line. A woman's voice answered.

"Glad you kept the old codes," Borneman opened.

It took her a split second to recognize his voice.

"Martin?" she gasped, confusion in her voice. "God, it's a surprise—"

"Jeannie!" he cut her short. "I need your help. Please. I don't have time to explain. Can you put a trace on this phone?"

The urgency in his voice left no doubt as to the gravity of his plea.

"Hold on. I'm on it." Whatever confusion might have been in her voice was now gone. Jeannie was a professional. "I have to patch it through, conference with the office. You've actually caught me in bed, you know." The process took under thirty seconds. "Okay, you're locked in. Now what?"

"A call will come through. Find out who it is and where the call is coming from. Anything you can. I'll call you as soon as possible. I'll owe you."

"You do owe me. You owe me a conversation, in the least."

In retrospect he really did owe her, though not in the way she understood it. Her affair with Bobby had helped him make up his mind about leaving the CIA. If he and Jeannie had stayed together he would, perhaps, still work there, doing what was increasingly becoming repulsive. She was all that kept him there those last months. The truth about her affair with Bobby did not make it a whole lot easier to part. While he missed her, he found solace in renewed bond with his parents. Reconciliation was long overdue. Martin's relationship with Lydia and Oliver hit a snag when they found out about his working for the CIA. He never offered details about his job, and they never asked, purposely giving him the cold shoulder. The details did not matter, anyway. The CIA was what they and The Hill Gazer stood against. As the years went by, and the family drifted further apart, it weighed heavily on both sides. His parting with the CIA put the long and unpleasant spell behind them. His involvement with The Hill Gazer rekindled the family bond. The periodical benefited too under Martin's editorial guidance. From general criticism of the government it steered toward outright condemnation of its policy, and the readership increased significantly. Indeed, the breakup with Jeannie was a blessing — Martin found fulfillment and satisfaction in his rejuvenated passion for work, and reclaimed rapport with his parents. The parents he though he lost forever.

The phone rang. He waited two rings and picked it up.

"Martin?"

"Mum! Are you all right? How's dad?"

"Oh, Martin! We're all right! What do they want from you?"

"I don't know yet, but don't worry, mum! It's nothing I can't handle."

"They say you've done such terrible things—"

"No, mum, don't believe anything they say. How's dad?"

"Shaken, but is taking it rather well, considering—" Without a warning, evidently to surprise her captors, she changed the subject, "We're in the air, over water. I think it's—"

Her voice was cut off and rustle could be heard on the line.

"Borneman?" The stern voice came on.

"Goddamn you, put her back on!"

"Listen to me, Borneman. You've shown that you're a perceptive guy, but don't try me anymore. My patience has its limits."

"You've just proven that you need me. I swear to God, if anything happens to them—"

"What happens depends on you. You survived that night on the lake, but you should not bank on living forever."

"Goddamn you! I meant it!"

"So do I!"

They wrestled in complete silence for a few brief moments.

The caller broke the silence. "How's the driver?"

Borneman did not reply, the sudden change of questions took him off guard, though the anger that permeated his mind and body did not lose its veracity.

"Ah, never mind!" the man continued. "He's just made contact. I say, that was a nice move. You are more than just a pencil pusher, after all. That's good. That's very good. It is time to put your bravado into use, and if you want your parents to live you will do what I say. You are mine, now. Is that clear?"

Any other person would cower in the face of such hopeless circumstances, but Martin was not any person. Having already suffered the loss of his parents, and having reconciled with the need to punish the guilty, he was propelled by determination. Martin could crunch the mobile phone if doing so would punish the man on the other end.

"Who are you?"

"Insignificant contractor. It is whom I represent that matters."

"Whom?"

"Let's just say that when they need something done, it is done. And believe me, it will be done. And you will do it. Your parents' lives depend on it. Do what you're told and they walk away unharmed. Do you understand?"

"Do they guarantee this?"

"They? They don't care, so long as the job is done. I guarantee this to you, as one professional to another."

"That's not enough!"

"I'll prove it to you in a minute, but first things first. Aren't you interested in what the job entails?"

Martin did not reply. His heavy breathing from a strenuous walk was the only indication that he was still on the line.

"You know the charges against you?" the voice continued.

"You're kidding, right? It's a bunch of lies that can be easily disproved."

"Wrong. Your friend, the professor—"

Martin froze. They listened in on the professor's phone line. They were a step ahead.

"He pulled the information from the right source. Everything that happened at the cabin, in Apsley, and in Georgetown, is attributed to you. The charges stand. Cops nationwide will get the files, and a warrant for your head will be out in under an hour."

Baffled, Martin did not reply immediately. At last he said with sarcasm to cover the worry in his voice, "You sound pretty cheeky for someone who hired a burnt out contractor."

"I admit, using Croissant was not very smart. A man with a mark like that is useless, too recognizable, alas we had no choice and had to act fast—"

Perhaps it was only a hunch, not a tool at a disposal of an analytical officer, nonetheless something in the caller's voice, and in the way his words hung so suddenly, made Martin stop in his tracks. Did the kidnapper reveal more than he intended?

"The CIA needs better contract killers," Martin fished for a clue.

"Is that who you think I work for — the CIA?"

"Don't deny it."

"I don't. And I don't confirm it, either. I wish, though, that I had you on my team when we planned this operation. Perhaps it's not too late. Perhaps you'll warm up to our ideas, after all. Do what you're told and we can talk about it."

"You killed my friends."

Martin glanced at the time on the phone's screen and eased — Jeannie would have the call traced by now.

"Did they not warn you at the Farm against forming attachments?"

"You son-of-a-bitch—"

"Focus, Mother! You've been trained to acquire a very particular set of skills. You will use them now, and the job must be done exactly as I say if you want me to follow through with my promise."

"If you as much as touch them—"

"Empty threats! Besides, I gave you my word, didn't I?"

"You know where you can shove that word of yours?"

The man burst out laughing. "Yeah, I have an idea. Still, you don't really have a choice, do you?"

Martin did not reply immediately. His mind was searching for alternatives, anything to reverse the course of action. He found none.

"What is it?" he asked.

"The president must be dead before the election day."

17

Martin stared at the heavy sky, stunned. The assassination of the president. His worst dream, an irrational nightmare, has come to haunt him. It was the recurring dream that has been a cause for many a sleepless night since his parting with the CIA. A vivid event that he was forced to watch through the eyes of the guest star of his dreams.

"The sooner he's dead, the sooner your folks will go back to their comfortable lives." The stern voice did not allow Martin to daydream about his nightmares,

"You can't be serious!" Martin roared, as anyone would upon realization that his worst nightmare has materialized. "It takes time to prepare such an operation!"

"There's more, Borneman. In an hour every news station in this country will broadcast your mugshot, and the details of the conspiracy you and four other intelligence operatives were plotting. The FBI will be looking for you. You are already found guilty of the crime you have yet to commit.

You may as well do it, just don't be caught." The voice paused for a moment, only to add in a sarcastic tone, "See? I'm giving you headstart."

Martin did not know what transpired at the attorney general's office. Had he known about the conversation and the request made by the FBI director he would have perhaps found a keen ear, and reverse the course of action. It would not be inconceivable to expect that many lives would be saved and the country would avoid the catastrophe that a handful of madmen had orchestrated. Alas, Martin could only play by instinct —the instinct that he used to downplay in his work was now telling him that no security force in the country would believe his innocence. The most important, indeed — the only objective — was to save his parents, whatever the devilish plans. Once his parents were safe, the kidnappers would have no leverage to hold against him. In order to save them he had to find out as much as possible about the kidnappers, their objectives, and thus about their identities and whereabouts.

"Are you out of your mind? It can't be done! Not anymore! Not after you've plastered the country with my picture and details of the op." He was stalling, his mind racing. The caller possessed the skills and resources to get as far as he did, this much was evident. From killing of the friends, to locating Martin, the man held the upper hand, and yet he did not seem to realize what incredible resources were required to pull off what he had just suggested.

The voice seemed to read his mind. "It should be no obstacle for you. You can do it. In fact, you will do it."

"If you so much as lay a hand on them—"

"Your parents' lives are in your hands, Mother."

There it was again, the use of Martin's handle signified that the caller knew what he did while in the CIA's employ. It was a reminder that Martin was thrust into a game played by a mighty adversary. He felt trapped, loosing whatever self assurance he was able to muster up to that point. He had enough presence of mind, and just enough strength left, to mask his weakness. The lives of his parents depended upon it.

"Very few people have access to this privileged information," Martin said slowly and deliberately.

"You're wasting your time if you think this will provide clues for you. Trust me. Oh, and Borneman? I said I'd prove my word to you. I know this line is being monitored. Don't object! It doesn't matter, anyway. The ciphers we're using are non-governmental. They can't be broken, and the call can't be traced. Here's the thing, though. I want you to know I'm serious and my word actually means something. The girl, Jeannie… She'll live, but you should not have called her. We'll be in touch."

The line went dead.

Martin was stunned, unable to utter a word. And then, the magnitude of the last words came to him with full force. He tried to re-activate the mobile phone, but it would not. He ditched it and started up the street, toward the lights of a busy intersection. Two blocks further he spotted a phone booth and dialed Jeannie's house directly. There was no answer. He tried several times before giving up. Something was wrong and it did not take much to realize that the mysterious kidnapper played a part in it. It reiterated the connection to the CIA. Who else would have live access to the CIA's tapping system?

Jeannie Domagala lived in a bright town home in a quiet neighborhood not half an hour away. She was thirty-two and free spirited, as she often thought of herself. Tramp, was what male colleagues called her, behind her back of course, because being openly sexist was no longer politically correct even in Langley. Regardless of the nickname Jeannie had a hungry appetite for men and no desire for steady or serious relationships. She changed men as some women change shoes, that is to say she needed a new pair for every season. She was not a glamorous beauty, as could be expected from someone of her professional specialty, but she sported the magnetic looks that steered everyone's attention toward her. Jeannie had an incredible personality, an aura that won the hearts of everyone she met. She had a girlish naiveté about her, combined with a permanently etched smile, and a spark in her eyes, that opened hearts and doors. Jeanie headed the CIA department responsible for recruitment of, predominantly Western European, diplomats, who were posted in the United States. Having started as a recruiter herself, she mingled in Washington's diplomatic circles and exhibited skills that caught the attention of the deputy director for operations. When her cover burned as she attempted to recruit an attaché of a European embassy, Jeannie was assigned a desk job, eventually rising to head of the department. With the promotion came higher clearance and a new circle of friends. It was then that her paths crossed with Martin's. They became lovers. They parted less than a year later, when Jeanie's interest in the relationship lapsed, seemingly, behind her attention to work. Some men would argue that Jeanie's devotion to work always took precedence over her lovers. No one knew the true underlying reasons that separated Martin and Jeannie's paths, and destroyed friendship, not only that of the two friends who enjoyed her affection, but of the entire group of five.

Martin stood on the corner of a quiet cul-de-sac. The street was poorly lit due to the city lampposts hovering over tree crowns, and the rising fog that covered the neighborhood under its cold veil. He lurked under the cover of the trees for a while, his eyes glued to the townhome he knew so well. The house was dark. The street was quiet. He climbed the five concrete steps to the front door and listened. He tried the door handle. It turned. He opened a notch. He noticed a faint glow coming from the breakfast nook at the back of the house. He remembered that it overlooked a small ravine, with a narrow stream meandering through the woods, and a small artificial pond where the residents held neighborhood events. Martin instinctively followed the light and froze at the entrance to the nook.

A woman lay on the area rug, flat out, arms stretched alongside her body. He rushed in and leaned over.

18

"I dressed, and waited for your call in the living room. I thought I heard something downstairs, in the nook. I thought it was you, coming through the back door. The last thing I remember was reaching for the light switch."

Jeannie was sitting on the couch in the living room, pressing a cold wet towel to her forehead. She was wearing casual clothes, soft sole shoes, and a pony tail. She managed to shake off the trauma of the event rather quickly, over a single cup of coffee Martin made in a percolator that he found in its usual place. He knew the house well, and noticed with some nostalgia that nothing here had changed. Neither did Jeannie. Over six months had gone by since he last talked to her, touched her, but it felt as though it was only yesterday. Time did not erase all the feelings that he still held for her, but, as he realized now, the feelings left were those of compassion derived from the emotional closeness that once existed, closeness that ended abruptly at the height of his affection when Jeanie betrayed him with his best friend.

"I'm so sorry, Jeannie. I brought it on you, but I didn't expect it to come to that. I had no one to turn to."

He really was sorry. He often fantasized, particularly in those first weeks since their parting, about punishing her for the breakup she had caused — a helpless folly of every broken heart — but these thoughts were long gone, replaced by nostalgic longing for good times they shared together.

"The call?" she said simply.

Martin nodded. "They traced it to you." He added with anticipation, "Did you?"

She shook her head and grinned apologetically. "Scrambled and relayed through so many networks it would take a day to pinpoint the location. The boys at the station say they hadn't seen one of those yet. The network was setup with the knowledge of our intercept routines and cipher codes. It was developed to slip through these measures. You know what that means—"

He nodded. No words were necessary. The mysterious kidnapper had the knowledge about the inner workings of the CIA.

"What have you gotten mixed up with, Martin?"

The question brought back the image of professor Sabria. Same words, but a startling contrast in intonation; a reminder that the break up ended a relationship that was purely physical, at least for one party. Where the professor's words were filled with intense concern, Jeannie's did not venture beyond curiosity, heightened somewhat by personal involvement. The realization pained more than Martin wanted to admit.

"I wish I could tell."

She replied with reproach and pointed to a reddish mark on her forehead where the assailant struck, "I think you owe me for this."

"I meant — I wish I knew the answer."
"That bad? What can I do?"

"I should not have involved you in the first place—"

"Forget about it, what are friends for? Besides — it's personal now. Someone whacked me over the head, and I'd like to know why. I want to help. Let me."

"Jeannie—" Martin hesitated. He could not involve her. The warning was clear. He did owe her the news, though. "Bobby—"

"Is now the time to talk about it?" she cut him off, her back suddenly straight and she leaned against the back of the couch, as though pulling away.

"It's not that," he replied, trace of anger in his voice. It still pained to think about what happened between Jeannie and his best friend, but the source of anger was elsewhere now — in deep regret that he and Bobby did not make amends. "Bobby—" He took a deep breath. "Bobby was killed. He, Arthur, Derek, and Chris, they were all slaughtered. I walked away with nothing more than a headache."

She gaped at him without a word. Her face expressed what words could not. He could almost taste the tears that formed in the corners of her eyes. She refused the hug. He did not persist, knowing that tears were a reaction she wanted suppressed. They made her angry. Jeannie was a tough build, or at least believed herself to be. What exposed her vulnerability made her weaker. She was most vulnerable where affairs of the heart were involved. It was one of the reasons why Jeannie could not hold relationships. They made her weak.

Martin described to her the events at the cabin.

Jeannie appeared composed when the account came to an end. Something of a cold resolution formed in her eyes. She dropped the wet towel, stood up, approached the table, and began fussing with the small stove-top percolator. She thought best when her hands were occupied.

"I thought your meetings were pretty hush-hush?" she said over her shoulder as she began to clean the machine.

"I can't think of a single person who'd know about them—" He bit his lip as he said the words.

"I knew," Jeannie picked up, and froze, as though stricken with a sudden realization. She added, without facing him, while continuing to clean the percolator, "Perhaps that's where the answer is. You ought to look close. Who else, close to you, might have known?"

He did not expect to be surprised after everything that happened, but the thought made him sit back. Someone close! So simple, yet so painful. Only someone close could know about the meetings at the cabin, and about the relationship between Jeannie and Martin.

"Someone who knew about us! The man on the phone, he knew that mentioning your name and uttering threats against you would have an effect on me."

He caught her eye, and blushed. He had inadvertently dressed in words what he tried to suppress all those months. He still had feelings for her.

Martin could not hold anything from Jeannie. It was as if he were back to those days when he would lean on her when things did not go well at work. Being in his business was hard on the mental balance, one had to let open from time to time, and since he had no one else to turn to — the world of spying was a lonely one — he found the relationship with Jeannie so rejuvenating. They could always talk about the CIA without pretenses. He told her now about the events in Georgetown and the kidnapping of Oliver and Lydia. Having lost her parents in her early teens, Jeannie often inquired about the Bornemans during their relationship, reminding Martin to call and visit regularly. Having met them several times, she had nothing but the kindest regards for them.

"That does it!" she cried. "Like it or not — I'm with you on this."

"These guys are serious, Jeannie. What happened to you was a warning. Next time they won't be so lenient."

He offered her a chance. He hoped she would not change her mind. He needed her.

"I'm with you on this, Martin." She reiterated.

He gazed deep into her eyes. "Good. I could use another set of brains because right now I am low on ideas."

"Where do you stand so far?"

"You know it all now."

"Is that everything?" she gasped out.

Did he detect a trace of relief in her voice? Good Jeannie! Perhaps her fresh outlook would help find a solution; perhaps not all was lost yet. He was glad he came to her for help.

"No clue about the kidnapper?" She did not let him ponder pointless thoughts. He shook his head and Jeannie continued, "Have you got the license plates, anything particular, identifiable, about the vehicles used?" She watched him closely. "The weapons? Clothing? Shoes?"

He cut her short, "I was too upset to think about that. In any case, it's unlikely they would flop on something so silly."

"You'd be surprised," she said with a sigh. "Too many ops flop on the silliest of details. What about the assignment? Do you have any idea who in the world would want you to kill the president?"

"I can guess, but I don't like what I come up with."

"Say it," she encouraged with a curious look in her eyes.

"We're weeks away from the elections. There has been enough rhetoric thrown around during the campaign that any simpleton could come to the obvious conclusion."

He did not answer the question directly, but it was not necessary, Jeannie understood.

"Why do I detect doubt?"

"You've been with the CIA long enough to see that it is just too obvious. It's good for conspiracy theory aficionados, and other blabber mouths, but between you and me, I think we have to agree that suspecting the opposition is just too simple. Verbal blows during presidential campaigns are nothing unusual, it's the established American way. It does not mean that contenders plot each other's assassination."

She shrugged. "The nation is polarized. The president was elected four years ago on a wave of euphoria, following two terms of a deeply unpopular predecessor. That euphoria waned somewhat, many people turned away from the president. If anything, he managed to turn his friends away. His progressive policies do not go well even with his own administration. There are many who want him out, regardless what the outcome of the elections."

"What are you saying?"

Jeannie put down the percolator.

"Look, I'm just throwing ideas. Perhaps it is not the opposition camp, per se. Maybe the extreme discontent comes from the opposition's support base? There are enough powerful and determined extremists in this country."

Martin thought about it.

"I still don't like it. It's too obvious."

He wanted to add something else but glanced at the clock on the wall and flicked his fingers.

"The news!"

She watched him, bewildered.

"It's two minutes to the hour. Let's see if they really mean it."

She remained puzzled.

Martin explained. "About going public, splashing my face on the screen."

He found the converter on the coffee table and switched on the television set.

"That is perhaps the most peculiar aspect of the plan. How do they expect you to carry it out after they've told the world about you?"

He was fumbling with the remote, searching for the news channel, and said absentmindedly, "If they really intend to kill the president, then it means that I'm only a patsy intended to tie the resources, while the real killers are waiting for the right moment to pull the trigger."

Jeannie froze, and watched him intently.

He noticed, and explained, "That's exactly what I'd do in the circumstances."

He did not finish. The anchor came on the screen, but they were not meant to hear the news.

"What was that?" Jeannie whispered in alarm.

"Someone at the door," Borneman replied in like manner, and turned off the television.

19

They stood quietly, side by side, listening intently, until they heard it again — the unmistakable sound of someone tampering with the lock, like a key being inserted, only instead of the key turning, a knocking sound followed and continued on. Someone was attempting to bump the lock.

"Boyfriend?" Martin suggested doubtfully.

"Come!" Jeannie sprung up to her feet and walked briskly to the hallway, no trace of fatigue in her bearing, the unknown and danger adding determination and strength. She approached the telephone table and quietly and slowly slid open the top drawer. She took out a holstered pistol. She then picked up a small fashionable knapsack-purse that was hanging on a hook, and hurried toward the back of the house. She deactivated the sensor floodlights and slid-opened the doors. The backyard was dark, on either side a privacy fence provided shelter from the neighbors' prying eyes, and straight ahead was the tree line of the ravine.

Distant lights from surrounding backyards provided enough illumination to find one's way without a flashlight.

Jeannie's townhouse stood roughly in the middle of the cul-de-sac. To approach it through the backyard one had to walk back around the block and find his way through the dark ravine. If the unknown assailant had companions they would have corroborated their efforts and someone would have been out back. Caution, thus, was the name of the game. Jeannie led the way through the lawn and toward the gentle slope that would eventually turn steep and end at the narrow creek.

Rising fog was obscuring visibility. They had barely reached the end of the lawn when a dark shadow appeared from around the corner of the fence.

"Shit!" a male voice cursed.

The man was startled momentarily but regained his composure and leaped toward the woman. His arms grasped the air when Jeannie swayed her torso to the side. The man did not expect to miss the target at such close range, and by putting his body weight forward, he had now lost his balance. It lasted only a split second but it provided Jeannie with enough time to grab onto the man's wrist and pull. The momentum caused him to trip over his own heels and fall to the ground. He did not have the time to stand up. Martin landed on the man's back, his arm strangling his throat. It was not long before the body wilted.

Everything happened in silence, save for the rustle of the clothes and the gasping for air.

"Dead?" Jeanie whispered.

"No, just out. Let's see what he's got in his pockets."

"No time. Come, we'll take my car."

Following the ravine to the street entrance was too dangerous, with who knows how many more assailants lurking in the shadows, and Jeannie led the way through the neighbor's backyard instead. The sliding glass door to the house was secured with a broom stick meant to deter forcible entrance. No force was necessary. Martin lifted one panel out of the slide, pulled it out, and proceeded to do the same with the second panel. They were inside. The layout was identical to Jeannie's home. She led the way, tiptoed through the dining room, then the living room, and to the front door. She opened the lock and peered outside.

They descended the flight of stairs to the sidewalk and peeked from behind the decorative cedars that grew on the neighbor's front lawn.

Martin started toward Jeannie's house.

She grasped onto his arm. "What are you doing?"

"I can't run for ever!"

He jerked his arm and started for the house.

She held onto his sleeve.

"Don't! We don't know how many there are. You give yourself up, and they'll have no use for your parents. They'll kill them!"

She had a point, but pondering it was out of the question. The commotion was not missed by a man who waited beside the car parked several parking spaces up the street. They notice him too late.

"Borneman?" the man exclaimed in surprise. "Miss Domagala! We have a warrant—"

"Warrant this!" Jeannie replied in a hiss.

Bullets whizzed by Martin's ear, but they did not come from the stranger.

Jeannie fired over Martin's shoulder. She missed.

The stranger ducked behind the car.

They had no way out. The street was a dead end. On the one side was Jeannie's house with an unseen assailant lurking inside, and on the other side was a killer blocking the way to the vehicle and the main street.

They were thinking alike. They spun around in place and leaped into the darkness of the neighbor's lot where the cedars blocked the light from lampposts. Martin was first to reach the door, but it was no use — they had inadvertently locked themselves out! Jeannie braced her back against the door, her pistol pointed to the street. In order to free her hands she threw the holster to the ground, and scanned the area.

The stranger was inexperienced, and not used to clandestine work, which explained why he was left behind, in the car. He assumed that the targets returned to the neighboring house. His inexperience would cost him his life. He approached the staircase not prepared for what awaited there. Jeannie and Martin were standing on the porch, as exposed as targets at an amusement park, but they had the advantage of a split second. Jeannie's outstretched arm was ready to fire.

"Borneman!" the man called out with astonishment, and paused at the sight of the barrel aimed at his head.

He raised his pistol, and said something that Martin thought sounded like *FBI*, but it could have been anything, since his words were drowned by a deafening sound.

Jeannie had fired.

The first bullet hit the man in the head, and another in the chest. By the time he fell flat to the ground, Jeanie and Martin managed to negotiate the five steps to the sidewalk, then leaped over the body, and headed up the street.

"Stay where you are!" a voice followed them from the direction of Jeannie's house.

A shot thundered through the thickening fog. Then another.

They ran stooped along the black pavement, covered from the bullets by a row of vehicles. Jeannie's car was parked further up the street, and she worried that they may not make it in time. She was grateful for the car the assailants arrived in — the driver's door was wide open and the flickering light reflected off the dangling keys that were left in the ignition. Their minds continued to work alike. Jeanie started for the driver's seat, while Martin circled the vehicle, and jerked on the passenger side handle.

Another shot sounded in the cold, still air, as Martin swung the doors open. He was hit. The bullet threw him into tailspin, but he remained on his feet.

Jeannie turned around in the driver's seat, stuck her arm out, and fired a round.

"Get in!" she cried, and turned the ignition key.

The engine started. Martin fell into the passenger seat, his legs still outside as the car made a u-turn with a screech of tires. Martin struggled to a seated position. The car approached the intersection, where it made a right turn, and the passenger door had shut itself. All the while Jeannie's face was tense, her eyes frantically scanning the rear-view mirror as she drove along the empty street.

"Are you hit?" she cried out.

He did not reply immediately, pressing tightly onto his left bicep, a grin on his face.

"You've killed them, Jeannie!"

She misunderstood him. "It's kill, or be killed! It was self-defense!"

"No, Jeannie! You killed my parents!"

It took her a second to grasp his meaning, several more to answer. "I don't think so. From everything you said they gave you an ultimatum that is time-framed. Your parents are safe, until you carry out the assassination."

He clenched his teeth, and Jeannie was not certain whether it was a reaction to physical pain, or the emotional.

Jeannie drove for a quarter of an hour, changing lanes and making frequent turns in an effort to spot pursuers. None were obvious. They abandoned the vehicle at the curb of a downtown street and proceeded on foot. Jeannie calmed down eventually, the walk making her mind work efficiently and to the point. She considered her options and settled for a safe house she knew in the vicinity. Her department operated several such locales in the DC area. She could shelter Martin in one such apartment without having to go through the requisition process, she was after all the one who issued such permits.

20

The wound proved painful, but not life threatening — the bullet had only grazed the flesh. Jeannie cleaned and treated the arm with a medical kit she found at the safe house. Fortified with a painkiller, Martin was able to think clearly, though clarity was far from what the two were able to achieve after hours of deliberation. Questions mounted, and frustration grew with each new one.

Jeannie brought up what both understood to be the only logical step left at their disposal. She announced, after yet another rehash of the events, and a failed attempt to find reason behind them, "We've turned every angle, and so far haven't come up with any answers. There's only one thing left to do. I've got to dig in Langley."

"Like hell you do." Martin's voice lacked the vehemence his words suggested.

"You know that it's the only logical step."

"Jeannie, I am worried about you."

"Relax. I won't post questions on the bulletin board. Have a little faith in me. I've worked in the field. I know how to cover my tracks."

He gave her one more opportunity to turn back.

"I should not have involved you in the first place."

"I'm in."

Jeannie's top clearance was their best chance. They both understood it, and all that was left to do was to work out the details. They agreed that Jeannie would make quiet inquiries on the inside, while Martin would concentrate on the field work, his tasks determined by the woman's findings. The plan, while lacking precision, was the first important step to taking charge of the situation. It brought certain relief, as only decided action does in circumstances of overwhelming unknown.

Once the next step was agreed on, they had breakfast — a tin of beans in tomato sauce, and toasts from bread found in the freezer — provisions supplied by adepts of the spy trade, usually students whose task it was to stock safe houses with non-perishable foods, medical kits, and the like.

Their parting was an awkward one, without goodbyes, or goodlucks. Too many things were left unsaid to precipitate the closeness that such a parting would require. They both breathed in with relief, welcoming the circumstances that postponed the inevitable and painful conversation that awaited, though their reasons for delaying it differed.

Outside, on the street, Jeannie dialed a number.

"How is the bruise on your head?" The call was answered by a stern voice.

"Believable enough," she replied.

"He suspects you?"

"I doubt it."

"And the document?"

"He had it on him."

"So, he knows?"

"That's the strangest thing. He appears clueless."

"Or is playing you."

"I'd know."

"Alright, then. It's time to pick up Borneman before they catch up and kill him."

"I'd say. There was an incident outside my house. The feds. They've gotten awfully close."

"Unfortunately we were unable to reach a consensus with the director."

"Am I burned, then?"

"It won't be for long. The resolution is near, and once it's over it won't matter anymore."

"Meanwhile?"

"Remain at Langley. You will receive cover there."

"It's going to happen, then, isn't it?" She could not conceal her excitement. "It is actually going to work!"

"We still have work to do. But it cannot be stopped."

Meanwhile, knowing that Jeannie's job required time to produce results, Martin attempted to nap, but his mind, despite two sleepless nights, was restless. Jeannie's closeness, after painful circumstances that led to their abrupt separation, had brought confusion. Mourning the loss of his friend, and having reconnected with the woman who caused the rift in the friendship, he was torn between the feelings that he thought were gone — but proved to be only suppressed — and the pain that she caused — and which he could not put behind him. He yearned to clear things between them, but it had to be postponed. More important things were at stake. The waiting, combined with the personal affair, was unnerving. He was pacing about the apartment trying to find something to occupy himself with, but in the sterile environment of a place furnished with nothing but the bare necessities, he found no solace. He went to the kitchen to boil water for yet another coffee, and his eyes rested on the digital clock on the microwave oven. It was five minutes to the hour, and thus to the news. He returned to the living room, and turned on the television. The weather report was coming up. He sunk into the couch, waiting for the newscast. He blinked once, twice, and closed his eyes.

The door chime woke him up. Dazed by inadequate sleep he stumbled to his feet, the persisting chimes drawing him to the door.

"Who is it?" he asked in a sleepy voice.

"Martin—" a woman's voice started, and paused abruptly at the sound of the lock being open.

"Jeannie—" Martin swung the doors open, and froze. It was not Jeannie. Martin did not know the woman, nor the man who stood beside her.

It was a reflex reaction that made him slam the doors in their faces. He had no belongings to speak of, and was out on the fire escape in seconds. The apartment was on a second floor, but the ladder was pulled up. He did not waste precious time unfolding it. Instead he hung himself off the platform and landed softly on the ground. He lost his balance and fell backwards, onto some aluminum garbage canisters. The noise was shattering, enhanced by the walls of the buildings on either side of the narrow alley. He glanced from side to side. The street to his left was closer and he could reach it quickly, but so could the couple. He took off in the opposite direction instead. He did not slow down until he reached the end of the alley, and looked back. He saw them at the far end, two silhouettes against the harsh light of the midday sun.

It was lunchtime. Office workers were emerging from the confines of their prisons. A coffee shop with a payphone logo drew Martin's attention. He had to warn Jeannie. He started for the doors and froze in place. Dan Sabria's photograph filled the screen of the television set inside the shop. The image was followed by shots of police cruisers outside of a mansion that he recognized as that of judge Ferguson's. Martin's mugshot flashed next, followed by a written description of his physical particulars. Drawn to the screen like a moth to the light, Martin pressed his face to the window. He no longer paid attention to the street, his entire concentration on the screen, but the images changed, replaced with some celebrity gossip, the usual fillers of newscast — the gory and the mindless.

He pulled away from the glass, his head spinning. Did they kill Dan and the judge? Why? They knew nothing! Unnecessary, ruthless killing! He was walking, unaware of the direction, or the purpose. He walked several blocks, all along struggling to come to grips with the television images that still flashed in front of his eyes. He found himself in a small parkette where a woman was throwing a tennis ball for her dog, the animal's happy barking at last rousing him, bringing awareness to the surroundings.

It was too late.

What happened next was so unexpected and quick that it gave him no time to react. He heard a rustle, and his peripheral vision registered movement in the direction of what he thought was a trunk of a tree. The trunk came alive and moved toward him. He turned to face it, and froze. In front of him stood the woman in whose face he slammed the door not more than half an hour earlier. Her blue eyes were smiling.

It was the last thing he saw before a dark veil covered the world around him.

21

"Tell me we are not engaged in indiscriminate killing of America's children!" The director of Central Intelligence Agency was beside himself. His fury threatened to burst the walls of his seventh floor office.

"Of course not." The deputy's defiance contrasted with his squinty eyes casting ironic glances. He was speaking condescendingly, and made no effort to conceal it. The director was only an appointed civilian, a temporary hindrance in the workings of the agency, while the deputy had spent years in the field, being the de facto chief spy.

"Then how do you explain to me what role our men played in Georgetown?"

The deputy director considered his reply carefully. He despised himself for having to lie and play a dual role at a time when unity of thought and action was required to successfully carry out the plan.

The director pressed on. "Known agency contractors were engaged in an open war in the capital city. What can you tell me about it?"

"They were freelances, we've used them in the past, through subsidiaries, and no firm connection to the CIA can be established. Complete deniability."

"What am I supposed to tell the press?"

"Damn the press."

"Damn it? Borneman's on the news. The Bureau made sure of that."

"We cannot deny Borneman's past. We can, however, conceal most of his service record behind operational secrecy. Tell only that, which is expandable."

"What is the truth?"

The deputy swallowed hard. He had to take charge before the situation got out of hand. He was lying to his superior, but he was quite confident that his lies would not be caught, not before it was all over, anyway. And at the point it would not matter anymore. Still, he was too experienced to burn bridges, and settled on the established spy trick — that of mixing facts with disinformation.

"About a year ago we uncovered irregularities in our black vault fund. We put our chief courier under surveillance, and it led us to a conspiracy."

"A conspiracy?"

"Five of our agents, meeting secretly, at a remote cabin, plotting to assassinate the president."

Stunned silence met the deputy's words.

"What's worse — our black vault was to finance the assassination."

"Have you stopped it?"

The deputy appeared uncomfortable.

"What is it?"

"We tried, but someone beat us to it."

"Come again?"

"We dispatched a team to the cabin, but they were late. The conspirators were already dead, save for one."

"Who did it?"

"Borneman, of course. He killed his friends. Then he killed our team, and the local cops."

"Jesus."

"We traced him to Georgetown, to his parents' residence. And, yet again, he killed the team that was sent after him."

The director shook his head in disbelief.

"Jesus. This man leaves a trail of death. Who is he?"

"Borneman was one of our best men."

"Was?"

"Left the Company about six months ago." The deputy director shoved a manila envelope across his boss's desk.

The director shook out the contents of the envelope — the service records of Martin Borneman, a senior analyst — and studied them.

"How serious a threat does this man pose? How does an analyst become an assassin?"

"That's his official title. Borneman worked with the special ops. He was taking care of the logistics of the ops carried out by field operatives."

"What kind of ops?"

"Assassinations."

The director looked up.

"And now he's turned against his own? How did it come about?"

"He's not alone. He's been planted on the inside by a powerful force. The Group."

The director needed several moments to understand.

"The Group?"

"They are hell-bent on placing their candidate in the Oval Office."

Long silence followed the revelation.

"What's the plan of action?"

"Everything we can do to stop them."

The director dismissed his deputy, and fingered through the documents. He picked up a photograph, and studied the face of the man who was at the root of the trouble. His service records, the unique set of skills acquired over the years of employ with the CIA's operations department, combined with Borneman's parents' influence would support the accusation. The director would buy his deputy's claim had it not been for a conversation he had earlier that day with his old friend, the head of the Federal Bureau of Investigation. It seems that his friend was right: Something very wrong was happening inside the Central Intelligence Agency. The director picked up his scrambled phone and dialed a number.

"Bill, we must talk."

22

His head was throbbing. A humming sound was irritating, with every second becoming louder, penetrating under his skull, piercing every nerve. How could he stop it? He tried to focus his eyes to find the source of the noise, but to no avail — he could see nothing. Darkness. Why was it dark? The painful realization came as his eye lids slid open a notch. Slowly, with a painful grimace on his face, he focused on a cloth surface. So close, he wanted to touch it. He could not. His arm would not move. He tried again. He jerked his arm, and cried in pain.

"He's come to."

The voice reached him as through fog.

He attempted to locate the source, but moving his head caused even more pain. He shifted his eyes instead. He was in a car, probably a van, lying on the back seat, face up. The voice belonged to a woman of bright blue eyes, and a disarming smile. She was sitting in a passenger seat, someone else behind the wheel.

"Mr. Borneman," the woman addressed him with a wide smile. "You're a very lucky man."

His time has come. He felt it through his skin. He was thrown into the back of a vehicle, his hands tied behind his back, on his way to meet the Creator. Yet, despite the odds, he was not ready to give up.

"You're lucky to be alive, despite the odds."

Indeed, with a bit of luck he might keep it that way. The fact that they were talking to him signified that he would be questioned. Questioning would buy him time. Plenty could happen during that time. He would seek the first opportunity to free himself. He had to try. Succeed he would. He had to, for his parents. Was it courageous to think this way, given the circumstances? Was it the irrational hope of a cornered prey? All hope was irrational, but given his having dodged certain death at least twice in as many days, it was not inconceivable to hope for a reprieve one more time.

"Pardon me?" the woman asked.

"Why did you do it?" he repeated through his dry lips.

She exchanged glances with the driver before replying.

"You stood no chance. You're a marked man, Mr. Borneman."

"Why did you have to involve my parents?"

She appeared to be taken aback by his question. The expression on her face was that of utter bewilderment, her vivid blue eyes, were full of concern.

"Mr. Borneman, I don't think you understand—"

"Goddamn you!" he exploded, and sat up abruptly, disregarding the pain it caused. He was surprised to find that his arms were not tied, and the reason he could not move them earlier was that they were constricted by his own body weight. This confidence of his captors made him even angrier. His right fist shot up, punching the ceiling, and he cried, "You're bloody right I don't understand! And neither would my friends if they were in my place, instead of lying stone cold in a mortuary!"

Martin's outburst startled the driver, causing him to lose control of the steering wheel, the van swerving on the wet pavement.

With the driver struggling to regain control, Martin recognized his chance. He frantically scanned the view outside, and tried the door handle.

Having not yet regained control of the vehicle, the driver turned his head, alerted by the open door, and pulled the wheel with him. The van spun out of control, and headed for a ditch, where it turned on its passenger side.

With the driver's side wheel spinning in the air, the back door slid open. Martin pulled himself over the edge, and fell head down into the ditch. The cold water caused more shock than the spinning van. He rose to his feet. His head spinning fast, he staggered, and fell to his knees. He tried to prop himself up again, but his legs trembled at his knees. He fell down, on his back, breathing heavily.

Something heavy pressed him to the ground, and he saw the woman's eyes, he felt her breath on his face.

"That really wasn't necessary," she said with reproach.

She was on top of him, pinning him down. Her hair was wet, clinging closely to her face and forehead. Her forget-me-nots eyes glistened with animation. She was beautiful in distress, he observed.

"You don't have to run anymore," she said. "You're safe now."

He heard a voice from the side. He turned his head. The driver was standing on the side of the road, speaking to a mobile phone. Martin concentrated his attention. The man was neatly dressed, his clothes out of the ordinary cut that would be expected on a government agent. He was speaking with a foreign accent.

The woman followed his gaze.

"His name is André, from the DST — the French counterintelligence. My name is Olga. I'm with CSIS — the

Canadian Intelligence Service. We were both pulled from our respective agencies to form a task group with an objective to investigate the peculiar activities of the American intelligence services. Welcome to Canada."

23

"You'll feel groggy for some time, but it'll pass." The woman said.

"You drugged me?"

"You came to twice on the way up, and we had to— Well, it was safer that way."

"For whom?"

"We had to make sure you would not make trouble at the border. But don't worry — it's a only a mild sleeping agent. Nothing you can't sleep off, so to speak." She projected a wide and sincere smile.

He noticed the holstered .38 attached to her belt.

"Why should I worry? You drugged me, kidnapped, and smuggled out of the country. That sort of thing happens to me all the time. Hell, I should thank you for not shooting me on sight."

She noticed his gaze. Her right palm brushed the butt of the pistol.

"This was never an option."

They were sitting on the edge of the ditch, on the side of a remote stretch of a highway somewhere in a wooded part of the country. The road stretched in a straight line as far as the eye could see, nothing but dark hemlock and pink granite on either side of the black wet asphalt. It was quiet, save for the subdued hum of water flowing at their feet.

The driver finished removing from the van whatever personal objects might have fallen during the crash. It was not much. Apparently the pair traveled lightly. He emerged from the vehicle with a plastic grocery bag, jumped softly to the ground, and approached the woman. He handed something to her.

"Your 'at and gloves."

"What next?" Martin asked the Frenchman.

"We wait for transport."

The woman added, "I think, André, what Mr. Borneman wants to know, is what happens to him next?" She turned to Martin. "The answer is, whatever it may look like, that it is entirely up to you."

Martin did not respond, returning a blank stare. He was at a loss. What was the meaning of the charade?

"Mr. Borneman?" The woman pried.

"Will you stop— calling me that?"

He only said it to release the bottled up anger. He watched her helplessly, aware of the futility of his resentment.

"Martin, a man of your background should know where he stands. You're wanted for the murder of your friends, all secret agents. According the warrant for your arrest, you've escaped custody by killing the sheriff and his deputy, even a pregnant woman, a temp. You then shot and killed CIA agents who tracked you down to your parent's home. You've committed all these egregious acts to protect an apparent conspiracy to assassinate the president. Those are the official charges signed by the attorney general. The first might get you on the front page on local newsstands, even get you some sympathy, you know. Don't you just see the headlines — A public servant fired from his job six months ago comes back with vengeance. But the pregnant woman, and then the boy? Those make you a bloodthirsty monster. Martin, it's a remarkable list of charges for a humble publisher. They become more dramatic, and infinitely more plausible when coupled with your previous job, that of a senior analyst with the special operations, CIA."

"It's privileged information," he said simply; not a lot could surprise him anymore.

"We like to stay informed. Our countries may share the same continent, but our visions of what's good for it, does not always go hand in hand."

"Our countries don't share any land mass," the Frenchman joined in. "We know it outright that what is good for America, is bad for France."

The woman shot him a reproaching look. She said to Martin, her voice gentle, sincere, "We're neighbors, and allies. As neighbors we like to see what is happening on the other side of the fence."

"And you kidnapped me to find out."

"Wrong choice of words. We saved you. How many times do you think you could dodge bullets?"

"I did just fine, didn't I?"

"Not for long. Your hours were numbered."

He laughed a fake laughter.

The woman nodded to the Frenchman. André reached into his knapsack, and took out a small carry case. He opened the lid. Inside were several objects — a smartphone, and two other items whose purpose Martin could not determine.

André filled him in, his English passable, the strong accent making it difficult to understand at times. "This is a GPS receiver. This is a spectrum analyzer, and this one a disruptor." He paused, and watched the effect his statement made.

Martin shrugged. "That supposed to mean something to me?"

"The GPS helped us locate you. The spectrum analyzer confirmed that you were you. And the disruptor— Well, it's a simple EM pulse generator. It did what it was designed to do. It disrupted the chip."

"Aha." Martin nodded.

Olga said, "There is a reason those people were onto you every step of the way."

"I'm not micro-chipped."

"I'm afraid you are."

"Wrong. It was removed when I quit the CIA."

Olga and André said nothing, the expression on their faces telling what words would not.

"Ridiculous." Martin said in a weak voice.

André shook his head. "It's standard procedure, albeit not made known to former employees. No one can be allowed to disappear from the radar, especially someone with inside knowledge as sensitive as yours."

Olga added, "It really brings meaning to the old saying: Once a spy, always a spy."

André continued, "When the old chip was removed, a new one was implanted. It is much different."

They had his attention. "Different?"

"What you 'ad before was an RFID chip, standard issue, so to speak. This baby is something else. It's a Tox-Chip, also known as termination chip."

Martin looked at them with puzzled eyes.

"It is commonly used in combat situations, especially on enemy territory, to prevent information being extracted from captured soldiers, or covert agents. Some of its proponents call it mercy-killing chip when an agent falls into the 'ands of torturers. It contains a toxic substance, which can be remotely activated, via satellites, or ground stations."

"And I've got this… Tox-Chip?"

"Not only you. Since its introduction it's become the chip of choice. Your combat troops, spies, and members of the diplomatic service, are implanted."

He stared at them with bewilderment.

"My friends? Were they killed remotely?"

Olga replied without mincing words. "We're pretty sure of that. How else could anyone hope to eliminate, so easily, men with your combined field experience?"

"What about me?"

"It's been known to happen. A chip may fail, or, for whatever reason, the termination signal gets disrupted. Sometimes only a portion of the toxin is released, causing some nasty sensations, but not killing."

"Nausea? Disorientation? I thought it was a hangover."

"You were lucky."

"If any of what you say is true, then what about the blown faces? The blood? The brains splattered on the walls?"

"Cover up."

"For what reason?"

The woman exchanged glances with the Frenchman.

She said, "We can talk about it at the base."

"Talk now."

They exchanged looks again.

A sound could be heard in the distance. Three heads turned in its direction. Two headlights signaled an approaching vehicle. It was nearing. This is your chance, Martin thought, his gaze fixed on the vehicle. No one moved. No one made a sound. It was peculiar, as though they left the next move up to him. He turned his eyes away from the vehicle, and looked into theirs. They were peaceful, and tired. Not the eyes of killers. They were the eyes of two sympathetic individuals who were just as concerned about his ordeal as he was.

The car neared, slowed down, but did not stop, the driver rubber-necking, and motoring on. The chance came, and went.

Martin looked at his two companions, and asked, "What would have happened if I flagged that vehicle? What if the driver pulled over, picked me up, and drove away?"

Olga replied, her voice quiet, tired, "You would have lost your only opportunity to find out what happened to you and your friends."

Martin addressed the Frenchman, "What did happen?"

He replied, "That is something most intelligence agencies in the world would like an answer to."

The woman added, "And the answer originates with you, it is you." She paused for several moments to gather her thoughts. "About a year ago the French domestic intelligence agency received credible intelligence about a planned assassination of the president of the United States. The information was beyond question, confirmed, and reconfirmed through reliable sources. To cut the story short — the usual channels were opened and put to work, yet the plot was shrugged off on this side. André, who uncovered the plot, was chastised, and the French were accused of attempting to destabilize the relations between the two countries. That's when André opted for a non-official approach. An independent task force was formed, comprising officers from numerous organizations from around the world."

"A real coalition of the— What do you call yourselves?"

They exchanged glances. "The concerned."

"The concerned?"

"You have to realize that whatever happens in the United States, has dire implication on the rest of the world. It's the nature of being the only superpower."

Their faces were sincere and he had no reason to suspect that they were anything but.

"Go on."

"The task force was able to acquire leads that pointed to rogue, and very capable assassins. All five were American intelligence officers."

"Five?"

"Four are dead, killed. One, the mastermind, has survived."

He pulled back so as to cast an all-encompassing look, a once over that was to signify his disbelief.

"I don't know what is more disturbing — the fact that you had foreknowledge about me and my friends, that you even knew of our existence, or that you believe that we could have plotted anything of the kind."

"Oh, no, we know that you did not plot to assassinate the president."

"No? Who, then?"

"The BASEL Group."

24

The facility located in the North Kawarthas was a three-story modern building surrounded by several thousand acres of crown land of dense forest, ponds, and granite hills. Established as a mineral mine on land leased from the Crown, it went bankrupt and was eventually taken over by the Ministry of the Environment and Natural Resources, and repurposed as a research center for geological studies of the Canadian Shield. In reality it was a top-secret state-of-the-art research center slash training camp for intelligence operatives. What was shrouded in even deeper secrecy was the use of the facility for housing foreign turncoat operatives until the Canadian government, the NATO, or allied intelligence agencies, decided what to do with them. Hundreds of meters of old mining shafts were transformed and adapted for the needs of the new occupant. Outside, the rugged terrain served well for training operatives whose skills could be mastered outdoors, and the high tech classrooms located underground played host to the highest talents in the world of international espionage who taught their spycraft to rookies. The unmarked trucks that entered and left the compound daily could not be singled out on the highways as those carrying some of the most advanced equipment ever developed for the use of the spy trade. It was here that ordinary consumer devices with dual-use potential were doctored to aid field operatives of the spy world. Inside, a layer of nickel zinc ferrite lined the walls of every room and corridor effectively blocking electromagnetic waves and prohibiting the use of private mobile telephones, thus eliminating the necessity for jamming technology, which could be detected on the outside by anyone with appropriate sensors. All communications were routed through and logged with the central communications command. Given the advances in technology, visitors and employees alike were greeted at the entrance with a sign: *No cameras, cell phones, smartphones, wireless tablets, netbooks, or two-way radios beyond this point.*

The two men and the woman did not speak during the car ride to the facility, in part due to the presence of the driver, and in part because Martin required time to ponder the newly acquired knowledge, one pervasive question dominating his mind: was there a connection between the assassination plan the French had uncovered, the killing of Martin's friends, and the demand put forth by the captor of his parents?

"Martin Borneman!"

The sixty-something man stood up from behind his desk. He massaged his earflaps, as he casually referred to the remnants of his once lush hair, now clustered only around his ears. He covered the distance to the door in a few brisk steps, and extended his firm hand to Martin.

Something oddly familiar in the Englishman's countenance prompted Martin to take a closer look. He was a tall, slender man who took care of his body, as evidenced with the energetic way in which he moved around. Martin studied the face but could not place it in his memory. Yet he was convinced that he knew this man. He glanced at the desk in search of a nameplate. None was present.

The man noticed his gaze.

"Douglas Burke. Call me Douglas."

During the elevator descent to the underground compound Olga described Douglas as a man with the sort of character that made him instantly endearing to his enemies — curious but not prying, sympathetic but not overly — which ensured him a long and successful field career. Having faced the man, Martin discovered something oddly uncomfortable. Whether it was his posh British accent, strong to the point of bordering on being forced, or something in his eyes and his entire being, Martin could not decide, but it stirred decidedly troubling emotions. What added to the reaction was the strangest sensation — that of having met before. Martin was certain of it.

He asked, "Have we met before?"

"Have you that same feeling?" Douglas replied. "Our countries and services work closely together, so it is not inconceivable."

They eyed one another with curiosity, but failed to make the connection.

"Tell me about Basel." Martin changed the subject to shake off the uncomfortable impression.

"The team has clued you in?"

"Baited enough to come here willfully, if you can call it that, being kidnapped 'n all."

"Don't blame Olga and André. They are good at what they do. The best I've worked with. The cracking best officers this task calls for. They did what they had to. What happened was understandable and necessary. Understandable of you to run, not knowing your friends from enemies, and thus necessary for us to result to measures that would bring this meeting about. Have a seat." A big smile graced the stern lips, while the grey, almost steel eyes, remained ice cold and piercing.

The contrasting facial expression made Martin shiver. He felt as though Douglas forced the smile to cover an involuntary microexpression that might have betrayed his true emotions. The observation reinforced the earlier uncomfortable feeling, and Martin promised himself to watch Douglas carefully. He chose the chair directly in front of the desk, Olga and André at his flanks.

"How much of it is true?" he asked.

"What do you make of what you'd learned so far?"

"Paranoid delusions."

"Oh, they're not delusions, Martin. The Basel Group exists, and quite openly. That is to say there has never been an official denial of its existence."

"Or a confirmation." Olga added.

"Confirmation is only a technicality when clear evidence exists, but we'll come back to that in a minute. For now we shall tackle the issue at hand." The smile vanished, Douglas was all business now. "Your friends are dead. You are wanted on multiple homicide charges and the conspiracy to assassinate the president. These are official charges from your country's security services. What needs to be established is the connection between Basel and the events that occurred in the past several days."

"Connection? I've never heard of the Basel Group until an hour ago."

"You might not have heard about it, but the Basel Group has found out about you, or more specifically — about Arthur Latki's research."

Douglas waived the sheet of paper that Martin had received from Judge Ezra Ferguson. He had never realized its presence in his pocket, and looked puzzled. Douglas did not dwell into the details of André frisking Martin's pockets before crossing the border. It was unimportant.

"Before we dive into it, there is something else you should know. It has to do with Jeannie Domagala."

Martin turned uncomfortably in his seat.

Douglas continued, "Our people have lost track of her. We think that she might have gone under after realizing the extent of the conspiracy. Rest assured that we are looking for her, and should be receiving a report in about two hours. Understandably we must limit ourselves to a low visibility approach, it is the CIA headquarters after all."

25

Meanwhile...

"We've lost Borneman." William Mittler, the director of the Federal Bureau of Investigation addressed his old colleague.

"Dead?" Paul Bosworth, the director of the Central Intelligence Agency asked with alarm.

"No. He's been helped to disappear. There's some evidence pointing to his being in Canada."

"Canada? Are they involved?"

"I was hoping you'd tell me."

The two men were sitting on the soft leather chesterfield in the conference room of the public relations firm located on King Street West, Alexandria. The firm was established as a front company to provide plausible background for CIA operatives who traveled to various hotspots, officially to provide image improvements for companies who wanted to do business with the United States, and who really carried out assignments that could not be tied to the American government. Mittler was invited on account of Bosworth suspecting serious irregularity inside the CIA.

The meeting commenced with the review of the surveillance footage taken by the FBI at the cabin on Lake Ruther. The two men watched the footage, edited by FBI techs for time, in silence. Bosworth made notes as the events unfolded.

"I think we were both lead up the garden path and we must re-examine this whole conspiracy to assassinate the president." Mittler concluded when the footage came to an end.

Bosworth replied slowly and deliberately, his eyes expressing disillusionment, "I'm afraid you're right, Bill. I think my DDO is running an op that is not exactly kosher with the CIA charter."

"You'll have to clue me in, Paul." Mittler said, sounding not at all surprised.

"Of course. I'll tell you what I found out about the activities of five men, four of whom were killed, and one who got away."

The two men were old acquaintances and friends, with Bosworth being nominated to head the CIA while serving as the director for counterintelligence, FBI. They had had a good relationship since, one without the conformability that might have come from their previous association.

"I think it's best if this be kept just between us, for now," Bosworth started. He adjusted his reading glasses and leaned over the elongated coffee table. He fingered through his leather bound notebook, scanning handwritten notes, found what he was looking for, and leaned back. He spoke in a composed voice, glancing into his notebook as he went on.

"Here's what I was able to assemble in haste. It makes your hair stand up, when you realize how far back it goes, and what precision was involved in creating this… this… I don't know what else to call it but — deception. It all started about twelve years ago when the Company recruiters spotted Chris Earle, a young fellow who'd just published a paper on the intelligence community and its involvement in media and news dissemination. The paper caused quite a stir in the USINTEL. The author's reasoning was accurate and insightful, and quite an accomplishment on the part of someone with no prior connection to the intelligence apparatus. It proved that he possessed the mind and visionary outlook that was so needed to revitalize our stagnated community. If I may remind you that was not long after the fall of the Iron Curtain, and before Nine Eleven, when so many criticized the need for the services rendered by the CIA. Earle's paper angered the CIA decision makers and so they decided to keep a close eye on him."

"But he settled for the State Department. And it did not go too well with the CIA," Mittler concluded. He did some research of his own prior to the meeting.

Bosworth nodded. "The same paper that angered and embarrassed the CIA, got him a position with the Intelligence and Research of the Department of State. Officially Earle performed the duties of an attaché in various embassies in Eastern Europe, and in due course was handed the delicate task of a covert emissary lobbying for the support for our foreign policy in the region."

"How did he get mixed up in this affair?"

"It was decided *then*," Bosworth emphasized the word as though to distance himself from what he was about to reveal, "that Earle must remain within the CIA's circle of interest. It was concluded that it was necessary to recruit someone close to Earle, a good friend perhaps. Thus, the CIA acquired one of its greatest assets." Bosworth pushed a photograph across the table. "Derek Autry's recruitment filled the holes created by the cuts imposed by Congress. Following his college graduation, Autry found employment with an international banking firm, with an office in Saudi Arabia. The bank he was working for wasn't exactly a model taxpayer, so when the CIA approached him with the recruitment offer, it wasn't something he could refuse."

"What did he do for the CIA?"

"He invested the CIA's black funds."

"You mean — laundered." Mittler stated to clarify the image of the man in question.

"Let's just say that his skills were put to better use than just keeping an eye on a childhood buddy," Bosworth replied as he glanced at his handwritten notes. "It did not solve the question of Chris Earle, and thus another man enters the scene." He pushed another photograph forward. "Robert Sadosky had dropped out of college after having impregnated his cousin. Scared and not ready to face his catholic family he joined the military. And thus, interest in Chris and Derek led the CIA to discover a man who possessed a very special skill —"

"Are you saying the CIA made its decision to recruit him based on his friendship with the other two?" Mittler adjusted his glasses as though to better see the words that came out of Bosworth's mouth.

"I'm saying that through Chris Earle and Derek Autry, the CIA found someone with a skill that could be put into better use than filing reports on the two men. When Sadosky was considered for recruitment as an informant and was under observation, he was instantly snatched by the Special Operations Command for his ability to shoot a bull's eye, every-single-time. Understand this, Bill: every-single-time, in every situation. Such skill could not go to waste. Subsequently Sadosky was discharged from the military, and quietly transferred to a unit not officially registered as a government entity."

"What are you referring to?" Mittler asked.

"Assassinations."

26

Douglas focused on small talk and did not pick up where the conversation paused until the coffee was delivered, and his assistant — a tall redheaded man with a gap between his incisors — had left the office. He poured out the drink, starting with Olga, and leaned back in his executive chair.

"It all began fifty years ago under the auspices of Prince Gerhard of Belgium. The beginnings were rather modest when compared to what's become of it today. The first conference was attended by thirty-nine men of immense power in the fields of economy and industry and representing the wealthiest nations on this planet, although not acting as their official representatives. These men became the founders, and effectively the core of what we now know as the Basel Group."

"The name is derived from the city in which the first meeting took place," Olga filled in.

"Indeed," Douglas continued. "As time went by, and as the original founders aged and dropped out of this world, the Group has maintained its core thirty-nine member steering panel by choosing successors from among some sixty to eighty annually invited guest participants."

"Annually?" Martin asked.

"The Group meets for two days every year on the anniversary of its founding: the second weekend of September." Douglas paused for impact, his steel grey eyes frozen on Martin's.

"I get it, it's coming up. And?"

"It is not the fact that the meeting will be taking place, but for the first time in Basel's history we know where the meeting is going to take place."

"Was it a secret before?"

"Was it a secret?" Douglas said mockingly. "The world did not suspect the existence of the Group until the late eighties, and even then it was in the form of rumors only: some British journalists caught the scent of Basel and attempted to expose it, only to end up on unemployment benefits. It wasn't really until the explosion of the Internet, when information could flow more or less freely, that the Group's conferences could no longer be disputed. That's when the world began to learn about the most secretive group of the twentieth century. Of course the proliferation of conspiracy theories surrounding the Basel Group is not a surprising turn of events considering the secrecy in which some of the richest and most powerful people meet regularly, year after year. Add to it the complete blackout of the event in the media and you have people speculating left and right."

"But you managed to step beyond speculation. Just like that." Martin flicked his thumb.

"I have been tracking the Basel Group for close to thirty years. I've built my contacts, learned a thing or two, and in time found keen supporters where they were lacking before: in the governments of the very nations whose illustrious citizens form the core of the Group. Did it happen just like that? Did my wife really just slip in the shower and broke her neck? Was my daughter's car crash really just an accident?" Douglas nervously pushed his coffee cup with the palm of his hand. He stroked the hair around his ear and continued composedly, "What I am trying to say, Martin, is that we have never been this close. We are finally in the position to make some progress. Indeed — we've already taken a giant leap forward by deducing the location of the coming Basel conference."

"How did you get this break, then?" Martin asked, still not satisfied.

"Analytical deduction. Think about it — this year marks a very round anniversary of the first meeting. Fifty years ago, Basel, Switzerland. Have you been to this part of the world in the last weeks? It doesn't take much effort to realize that something major is afoot. No hotels in town accept reservations for the period immediately preceding the second weekend of September. Tourists are being scrutinized at all points of entry. The streets are filled with small groups of men of considerable physical aptitudes, equipped with the latest technology available to military intelligence. Yet, it is not another G8 Summit. The annual Basel Group conference is about to commence."

"It sounds like a huge undertaking. How can this be kept secret?"

"Those are questions we all strive to explain. Media concentration comes to mind."

"What are these conferences about?" Martin asked simply.

"Officially, the conferences are said to be devoid of all political and ideological differences that divide the world, and the men who attend them are supposedly there in their private capacities. Whether it is true or not, remains within the realm of speculation, as there has never been any media coverage and no press releases. What a keen observer can deduce comes from the choice of invited guests. The core members are joined by up to eighty invited royals, media moguls, bankers, industrialists, and politicians—"

"What's strange about that? The elites keep like company?"

"Strange is what happens following their meetings. Governments announce huge economic moves that have profound global impact. Some of the guest-participants receive nominations to offices of power. The British prime minister, the European president, the secretary general of NATO, and indeed a number of your own presidents came to power within months of attending the conference. See what I'm getting at?"

"The world government of some... Illuminati." Martin's facial expression betrayed utter sarcasm.

Douglas replied, unmoved, "Look around you. Does this place remind you of a theatre stage? The Illuminati are a subject of fables, mediocre writers' attempt at mystery tales. The Basel Group is very real. The conferences are private in nature, sort of... gentlemen's clubs, or frat parties. Only invited guests are allowed. No intelligence or state security agency has ever been commissioned to provide the logistics. All security and organization is handled by private security firms with military contracts and these blokes don't talk to civilians. There is no governmental oversight, which is very troubling indeed, when you consider who the attendees are, and what happens after their meetings. That is the reason the EIA, the European Intelligence Agency, backed by several world leaders, who expressed their concerns and decided to form this task group, to find out what the hell is happening. We are living in very tense times, and no such conference should be organized in the way this one is. Not when royalty, presidents, prime ministers, top generals, and bankers, attend and important decision are made outside of the official channels."

"What's it got to do with me?" Martin asked.

Douglas picked up the single sheet of paper that was pulled out of Martin's coat pocket. He straightened out the creases, and raised it in his hand.

"This is where your friend's research lends a hand. What Arthur Latki managed to discern was an apparent connection between the coming US presidential elections and the Basel conference. According to his research, the current president will not get his second term."

Martin stiffened in his seat, and laughed a nervous laugh, Jeannie's suppositions coming to mind.

"It is the people of the United States who will, or will not, re-elect the president."

The corners of Douglas's stern lips arched downward. "The people of the United States did not elect the president in the first place, Martin. It won't be the people who will elect the next one, either."

Silence followed his words. It was broken by André's putting down his coffee cup on the tray.

"Pardon," the Frenchman said, and blushed for no apparent reason.

"What is the significance of this connection that Arthur supposedly uncovered?" Martin pried.

"There are some who do not want to see the president re-elected, and they are determined to prevent this eventuality at all cost. At all cost, Martin."

27

Meanwhile…

"Assassinations?" William Mittler repeated with his eyebrows arched.

"A highly valued profession, I assure you," Paul Bosworth replied.

The two friends were sitting on a comfortable sofa, drinking herbal teas, and snacking on biscuits that were stacked on a tray in the center of the coffee table.

"Bobby Sadosky's friendship with the other men was a major factor in recruiting him, and as Derek Autry before him, Sadosky was simply too valuable to waste on watching Earle."

The FBI Director slurped from his cup, rinsing his mouth of the biscuit crumbs. He almost choked at hearing the last words.

"Oh my God, Paul, I hope you're not suggesting—"

"My predecessors determined it to be only natural to turn to the remaining two of the five friends. No matter how you look at it, Bill, it was a pretty sweet deal. You have five very close friends, three of whom are already of paramount importance to our intelligence services. Two remain. Both could be used as drones to watch the others. The former CIA leadership determined this to be the best option."

"Let me ask you something," Mittler started, and wiped his lips with a soft napkin. "Would you have done it? Would you have hired five men for covert ops based solely on their friendship?"

Bosworth shook his head. "It goes against common sense, to say nothing of basic operational principles. The loyalty of men whose friendship dates to childhood years must be questioned every step of the way."

"Yet it was not taken into account?"

"Or was deliberately omitted."

Mittler raised his eyebrows, but said nothing.

"My preliminary research suggests that their recruitment was streamlined and their earlier friendship covered up."

"Their individual skills took precedence?" The FBI director suggested doubtfully.

Bosworth shook his head again, in this gesture disapproval of the decisions his predecessors made. "However valuable Derek Autry, Chris Earle, and Robert Sadosky, might have been to the Company, the new recruits turned out to be quite the opposite. As you are well aware — an intelligence operative shares certain qualities with a military officer, in that he must be prepared to follow orders unconditionally. But he must also possess individuality and the ability to break those orders based on his own assessment of a given assignment or a situation, it being understood that the assignment must succeed. To put it another way — an intelligence operative is alone in the field and relies entirely on his own qualities for survival. Arthur Latki and Martin Borneman had both of those qualities, alas the latter in such abundance that it became liability. Don't misunderstand me — they performed their duties exemplarily, and they were never traitors, though some suggested otherwise. It was the CIA's actions that forced their personal beliefs to take precedence over their duties. Borneman resorted to joining the hundreds who quit their association with the CIA in protest. He joined his family publishing house, a small independent press specializing in none other than government criticism."

"Wait, wait, wait. *The* Martin Borneman? Oliver's son?"

"None other."

Mittler blew out a whistle, and reached for the photograph of the man in question.

"With such pedigree it is truly astonishing that he should have been considered for the CIA job in the first place. No at all surprising that he quit, though."

"Arthur Latki went even further. He not only quit the CIA, but he sought employment with the International Criminal Court. To many of our policy makers this was treason enough. It was not enough for Latki, though. He became a strong and very vocal critic of the USG, and actively participated in preparing criminal cases against our government officials."

"But to be critical of the administration and to plot to assassinate the president are two very different things," the FBI Director said earnestly.

"Yet these men died. Someone must've thought that they were capable and ready to do it."

"That question is who, and why?"

"Why do I get the feeling that you know?"

"I wouldn't go as far. But I have an idea."

"I'm listening."

"As we just saw on the film these four men were dead before the hitmen entered the cabin and shot them. It's unmistakable, it's in the way the bodies react, or rather not react to the shots. So how and why did they die before the hitmen arrived?" Bosworth asked with a curious look in his eyes, as though he was leading onto something. He continued, "The hitmen weren't really there to kill these men, they shot them only to cover up the way the men had died, so that the inevitable autopsy would have the cause of death laid out on the platter, while the true cause would remain undetected." He reached in to his breast pocket and withdrew a small object. It was a slim transparent capsule. He opened it, shook the contents out onto a white sheet of paper, and pushed it across the coffee table.

28

"At *all cost*?" Martin repeated.

"The man who is to become the next president of the United States has been chosen. The final confirmation came last Friday. Go ahead," Douglas pushed the latest editions of several major newspapers across his desk.

The papers included notes about the opposition candidate's planned visit to Europe in his pre-election move to ease international tension between the U.S. and her allies, to gain the support from the world for his candidacy, and to show his view of America's place in the world as a partner, not a rogue warrior.

"The time of the European trip coincides with the Basel conference." Douglas summarized with a theatrical cliffhanger, allowing the information to sink in.

The coffee was almost finished. Olga and Martin drank the hot liquid with greediness that found its source in the cold two hours spent on the side of the highway. André's cup remained untouched, though no one seemed to have noticed.

"Naturally, we expected either one of the candidates to be summoned to the Basel conference," Douglas continued. "The president's circle lobbied for him, but it was the opposition candidate who was chosen instead. With the president not being the sort of man who would go down without a fight we can expect a show of strength, though perhaps not an electoral battle, but rather a confrontation with those who shuffle the offices in the governments across the world. Trouble is brewing ahead. The two powers are about to come head to head: the reigning president and his camp, versus the Basel Group."

Martin glanced over the papers, pushed them away across the desk, and leaned back in his chair. He looked at Olga and André. Both were listening to Douglas with intensity. Olga returned his look. Her eyes expressed what Martin had feared. They confirmed what Jeannie only supposed. The president was a marked man.

"How did you first become interested in me and my friends?" Borneman switched the subject. Damn the politics! His problems were personal. He wanted to find the killer of his friends and the kidnapper of his parents.

"It's complicated and it goes back," Douglas replied. "André?"

The Frenchman cleared his throat and picked up the subject.

"It started in the low 1990s—"

"Early," Olga corrected.

André nodded, "In the early 1990s Western intelligence agencies found themselves in need of a new and viable enemy now that the old Soviet Empire no longer menaced, not that the adversaries ever lost sight of each other, but priorities 'ad changed. In the 'avoc of those years—"

"Havoc," Olga interrupted to correct the Frenchman's pronunciation.

"Mais oui, avoc!" André shrugged, unperturbed. He tried a sip of coffee, but did not swallow it. He grimaced, and continued, "Every western intelligence agency scrambled to keep their portion of the budget. The former allies in the struggle against the Soviets were now able to devote more of their resources to areas previously overlooked. They studied each other. The realized and acknowledged that the objective of the race was no longer arms proliferation, or ideological supremacy, but first and foremost —economic and political domination. In sight of the approaching formation of the European Superstate the Americans re-deployed their efforts to keep an eye on Europe, which was soon to become a unified continent."

"Are you sure it wasn't China, and terrorist states, that we were concerned about?"

"Your country is concerned with everyone," André replied firmly, but without raising his voice. He continued, "The first animosities soon arose and grew exponentially with each passing year. The breaking point came with the second Bosnian crisis, where America meddled far more than Europe could tolerate, and peaked as the threat of the invasion of Iraq became reality. At some point the relations became so strained they resembled street bickering rather than diplomacy. Still, even then it was nothing unusual. At least not until our security services caught the scent of a special unit within the CIA, a unit tasked with planning for the eventuality to remove foreign 'eds of state." André paused, his eyes on Borneman.

"Heads." Olga clarified after the silence grew longer.

"I understood what he said. There's no need for the theatrics," Martin said without reproach. "I realize that you know a great deal about me, though how you came to know what you know is beyond me."

André shrugged. "We 'ad to assume that on your list of possible targets were all 'eds of state, including the president of France. So, we took special interest in the CIA, and in particular in your special unit. We probed further and that's when we came upon something truly astonishing. We found that not only were you planning possible scenarios of removing foreign ones, but also your own president."

"Bulshit," Martin said simply, and without raising his voice.

"You don't 'ave to soap our eyes," André took offence.

"I think I'd know about such plans, being the head of one of the most important sections."

"*One* of!" André cut him off, and coughed. He tried clearing his throat but it only made things worse. He could not stop. His face turned red and he coughed uncontrollably. Martin stood up to tap on his back, but suddenly the Frenchman regained composure, his face still red.

"Have some coffee, old chap." Douglas pointed to the cup that André had put back on the tray. "You haven't even touched it. It must be cold by now."

"I'd— I'd rather 'ave some water. Excuse me." He stood up and left the office, coughing.

Douglas shook his head. "I don't know what's wrong with that bloke. I thought the French loved coffee. We here have nothing but the best. Gourmet!" He accentuated the last word.

"Is there such a thing as instant gourmet?" Olga said doubtfully, and added quickly before Douglas had a chance to catch her sarcasm, "To cut to the chase, as you can imagine, the French could not let it go where their president's safety was at stake. The fact that someone could even conceive a plan to remove their own president made it that much more pressing. Thus our task force was established."

"In other words you spied on us." Martin said matter-of-factly.

"Tit for tat, old boy." Douglas blinked.

Olga continued calmly. "We merely re-examined the data gathered thus far. Remember that your country's intelligence is very active in Canada, and more so in France, in part due to its large Muslim population, so much so that the

American department within André's agency is one of the most active. We probed and we found Arthur Latki. By then he already parted with the CIA and was working for the International Criminal Court — an institution your government considers an enemy of the United States. We watched Arthur, and got a glimpse into some of his research. It was startling. What we only suspected was now confirmed. There exists a force within your business establishment, and backed by many members of the government, that wants to depose, or otherwise forcibly remove your president."

Silence fell upon the office.

"I'm listening," Martin said when the silence dragged on.

"You and your friends were chosen to remove the president." André said as he entered the office, bottled water in his hand.

Martin did not attempt to argue. The idea was preposterous, yet the words of the kidnapper of his parents still rung in his ears: 'The President must be dead before the election day.'

"Don't look so morbid, old chap," said Douglas. "We now know that you weren't even aware of the plan, little else that you were going to carry it out."

"Though it was quite believable," Olga added. "Your unusual relationship played into the scenario. Five highly skilled spies, who, despite their strictly prescribed mode of conduct, went to great lengths to elude their employers in order to meet in secret."

"We were friends."

"Precisely. And your friendship brought about the tragedy. Together with your employment and the secret meetings it played perfectly into the plans made by those who wanted to convince your government that the five of you had an agenda. Add to it yours and Latki's sudden termination of employment and you'll understand why the FBI is convinced of your plotting."

"Complete and utter nonsense!"

Douglas said, "Not so, my dear chap, when you consider that your rise through the ranks of the CIA had been carefully cultivated from the start. Your employment was no mere coincidence. The five of you had been led to play your roles when circumstances called for it. Unfortunately for whoever made those plans, a combination of events and your friend's conscientiousness, had spoiled them. You nearly crushed the devious plans of the Basel Group."

Douglas finished with a blink, an expression that resurrected Martin's earlier reservations about the man. It helped him realize what was so eerie about the Englishman — he seldom blinked, and when he did it was as though he was forcing himself, as he did just now, while his eyes seemed focused on Martin even through the momentarily closed eyelid.

Olga continued, preventing Martin from pondering, "Of course, before we could take the findings seriously, we had to verify the source. What bothered us the most was the ease with which we found it — after all a planned assassination, particularly one targeting the head of state, should be the most closely guarded secret."

Martin tapped his finger on the armrest of his chair, his irritation unrestrained. What he heard was beginning to form a believable shape. In the least it offered plausible scenario to what had happened to him.

He said, "Where are you going with this? Spies are but mere pawns in the politicians' hands, everyone knows it. And the politics is the one occupation dirtier than spying. Someone wants the president out, and is framing a handful of spies, is that it?"

"The plot exists, the events on the lake are a confirmation. You are marked as the assassin, though, quite frankly, it's unlikely that those who hatched the plan expect you to succeed. Why? For the same reason you already noted: What are the chances of succeeding, now that the entire might of the security apparatus is on your tail? The mere hint of a conspiracy to kill the president occupies your

security and intelligence services. And here lies the answer:
You're just a pawn who happens to be useful for a time."
Douglas finished with one of his forced blinks.

"Let's have it then. Who?"

"We think it originated from within the Basel Group.
Whoever planted this information wanted to be found. Why?
We can only speculate. Perhaps it's a matter of conscience,
much as it was for you and Arthur when you decided to
sever your association with the government and the CIA.
The bottom line is that we are close, and we can do this. We
can deliver a blow to the most secretive group since the
fabled Illuminati."

29

Meanwhile…

The director of the Federal Bureau of Investigation leaned over the coffee table. He adjusted his glasses, and asked in bewilderment, "Just what exactly am I looking at?"

The director of the Central Intelligence Agency explained. "A Tox-Chip. Undetectable without the know-how and the use of proprietary equipment. The chip differs from those RFID devices that are typically used by our diplomatic corps in that it not only works as a beacon but is able to accept commands, too. At first it was tested and used exclusively in the military community, where it helped us locate missing soldiers and field operatives; in cases where capture had occurred and torture was imminent, and passing of secrets could not be permitted, the toxin was released, causing instant and painless death."

"How does it work?" Mittler asked in amazement.

"In addition to the GPS locator, the chip contains a toxic substance, fully absorbed by the body when released, untraceable. To minimize the size, the toxin also works as a power source. Should our agent become jeopardized — turned, or kidnapped — the Tox-Chip will be activated via satellites. The capsule will explode, rupturing the surrounding tissue, the toxin will then be released into the bloodstream, and the host terminated. The operatives at the cabin were implanted with Tox-Chips… right here." Bosworth patted his stomach.

The FBI director raised his brows in a silent request for clear explanation.

Bosworth obliged. "The beauty of the Tox-Chip is that it can be administered without the host knowing about it."

"Just how is this achieved?"

"Orally. Usually slipped into food or even drink, it is small enough to go down undetected. When it reaches the stomach's gastric fluids, the polymers mixed in its construction expand to a size that cannot pass into the small intestine. It stays in the stomach until a special concoction is swallowed causing the device to shrink, and… leave the body the usual way."

William Mittler shook his head in astonishment.

"I don't know whether to commend, or to curse, the evil genius who came up with it."

"That's not the end of the marvels surrounding the Tox-Chip." Bosworth fought the urge to keep his old friend in suspense by holding a theatrical pause, and decided to say what he had to say without much ado, "It can only be activated via the Pentagon's satellites."

Mittler eyed his friend for a time, speechless. He understood the implication. He said, unnecessarily, only to vent out his own astonishment, "Jesus God. Do you realize what this means?"

"It means that my deputy director answers not to me, but to someone else, whose hand rests on the Tox-Chip button; someone whose office is in the Pentagon, and not in

Langley; someone who is running an operation meant to vilify the CIA."

"I shudder to think that you are right, but I do not see any other explanation to what has happened. Can you prove it, though, Paul?"

"We're dealing with an octopus whose arms reach deep into the US intelligence and the government, Bill. The question is: Can we find the main corpus? This morning our internal security detained a highly regarded officer, with top secret clearance. She had pulled Borneman's and the other men's files from our digital databases, perhaps to destroy them, to cover up the evidence, or perhaps for reasons all together different."

"Who is she?"

"She and Borneman were romantically involved."

"Jeannie Domagala?" Mittler described in quick words the shoot out and the death of an FBI agent who attempted to arrest Borneman at the woman's home.

"The very one. She was questioned, but the interrogation had to be paused for the time being. We nearly lost her due to heavy use of sodium pentothal. We did find out, though, that she knew all about the events of the last weekend, the killing of the Apsley cops and the bloodbath outside the Bornemans' residence. Unfortunately—" Paul Bosworth paused uncomfortably.

"Yes?"

"Unfortunately, she has disappeared."

"Disappeared?"

"She got away. It's clear that she had to've had an accomplice inside. Someone highly placed, someone with the highest clearance and authority."

The message was clear. Mittler said, "Your deputy director is a busy man."

"And right now he holds the keys to the secret."

"What do you suggest?"

"I suggest that the five friends did not conspire to assassinate the president, that in fact they had nothing to do with such a plot, other than being used to draw the attention away from the true conspiracy that's underway elsewhere. This leaves only one possibility — someone is manipulating our intelligence and security agencies."

The television screen went blank. The man at the center of the crescent table kept the remote control in his hand as he gazed around the surveillance observation room, the Pentagon logo on the wall behind him. His silver hair and round pale face was almost glowing in the dimmed room, giving him an aura of reverence, something the three men gathered at his flanks did not need to be reminded of — after all he was the second most powerful man in the world. He glanced around the room, bowed to the tall man who sat to his right, giving him the go ahead.

"I think I speak for all of us when I say that I don't think we can win Bosworth over to our side, Mr. Secretary," said the tall, slim man, who chaired the Joint Chiefs of Staff.

"Everyone agrees?" The man at the center of the table gazed into the faces of the remaining guests. Seeing as all three were of the same opinion, he asked, "What about the Bureau?"

"Far as can be determined from the feed that we just witnessed, I would say that Mittler is rather passive," said the attorney general. "But, he is a sly old dog who never says what he thinks. We should not forget that the two of them are good friends, and one may sway the decision of the other. Thus, I'm afraid, Mittler is lost along with Bosworth."

"I disagree," said the deputy director of the CIA. "Mittler's behavior may suggest that he is weary of Bosworth's suspicions. We should try to convince him to join our cause, or at least to make an effort to see where he stands."

"I agree, Mr. Secretary," seconded the chairman of the Joint Chiefs of Staff. "Mittler is a long-serving director of the FBI. He's amassed considerable power over the years. Not to try to win him over to our side would be a fatal mistake."

The defense secretary required a moment of consideration. He glanced to the faces of his con-conspirators, and said, "Alright then, we give Mittler a chance to come around. Meanwhile, I want Bosworth out of our way, and I want it done quickly."

30

Martin's eyes gazed from Olga to André before resting on Douglas. Everything he learned here was explosive, to be sure, but it added more questions while providing few answers.

"Why am I here?" he asked.

Olga appeared uncomfortable, and André stared at his bottle, neither volunteering to reply.

Douglas cleared his throat and took it upon himself to explain.

"We are banking that your disappearance from the conspirators' radar will make them act hastily, and haste, as you're well aware, has the propensity for making a mess out of even the most painstakingly planned operations. They will make mistakes — mistakes that we shall seize upon."

"When they realize I'm gone, they will kill my parents."

"It comes with risk, to be sure, but risk is the name of the game. You knew it when you signed up for service with the CIA, did you not?"

"It's one thing to risk your own life, but something else to risk the lives of those you love."

"Quite. I didn't want to mention this earlier, so as not to cloud your mind," Douglas replied cryptically and in a tone of voice that sounded disturbingly familiar to Martin, and he would have perhaps located it in his memory if not for the statement that followed, and stirred the deepest fears and hopes in his mind. "Within a couple of hours we shall receive confirmation about your parents' whereabouts."

"What?" Martin rose to his feet.

"Our team is verifying the intelligence right now. And when they do, our first order of business will be to ensure your parents' safety. I wouldn't expect you to agree to work with us otherwise. Will you, Martin?" Douglas asked.

Astounded by the near prospect of saving his parents he took time to reply. The news came too quickly, too unexpectedly, and above all Martin feared the consequences of broken hopes. What if the freeing of Oliver and Lydia remained but an unattainable dream? Was there anything more painful than broken hopes?

"Let me tell you where my priorities lie — my parents are first, the killer of my friends is second. After that... damn the Basel Group and all the presidents."

"But of course. Welcome aboard." Douglas extended his hand. He glanced at the set of clocks that lined the wall of his office, across from his desk. "I'm afraid the time for pleasantries is over, though. André will show you to your quarters where you can freshen up and get new clothes. We shall meet in my briefing room in precisely two hours. Make the best of this time, as you won't be able to kick back, as you Americans would say, in the next little while." With these words, and a forced grin that was supposed to resemble a smile he stood up and walked them to the door.

Outside, in the cold corridor, Olga led the way toward the canteen.

"When was there time for pleasantries?" Borneman asked.

"It must be a British expression," she replied over her shoulder.

"Speaking of expressions—" Martin started.

She understood. "A neurotoxin. The man spent most of his professional life in the field. He'd been Botoxed through and through. With the advancement of technologies, and our understanding of microexpressions, it has become popular, heck — it's a necessity these days when our opponents become more skilled at reading every minute facial expression."

"Is that all?"

"What do you mean?" She picked up speed as smells from the canteen intensified.

"It can be unsettling, I felt that way too, after first meeting Douglas," André said, trailing behind. "Is that what you meant?"

Martin did not answer. He could not explain the peculiar feeling of having met Douglas before, and suspecting him of trying to conceal the fact. He let go of it.

Smells from the canteen were overwhelming.

"I'm s-so hungry!" Olga gasped out.

"I could eat a 'orse!" André agreed.

"Eek! I know that Canadian government diets aren't exactly gourmet, certainly nothing in comparison with what you get in Farnce, but I hope it hasn't come to that, yet."

"Actually, 'orse meat is considered delicacy in France—"

"Save it, Frenchie. You're in the land of poutine!"

The cafeteria was a sterile, fluorescent-lit square room. A self-serve bar was steaming with hot dishes ranging from mashed and baked potatoes, pastas, and rice, to fish, processed meats, and vegetables. A short line of pale-faced, sad-eyed office hermits browsed through the selection of food that never changed. Few, if any, complained about the selection. Regardless of the quality and taste of the processed food offered, compliments of the Canadian taxpayer, few employees brought their own lunch, believing that food tastes better when someone else prepared it for us.

The two men and a woman picked their meals, and occupied an available table, each with a tray of generous servings in front of them. They ate without speaking. Following the meal, André had walked over to the bar, and returned with two cups of coffee, and a bottle of water for himself. They sipped their drinks, exchanging glances, and savoring the feeling of warmth and a full belly.

Olga brought them back to reality. She asked bluntly, "Did you and Arthur Latki decide to quit the CIA on similar grounds?"

"I'd prefer not to talk about it," Borneman replied, an uncomfortable tingling in his neck, visions of Jeannie on his mind.

"I thought we might get to know each other if we're going to work together."

The woman awaited a response but when none came she exchanged looks with the Frenchman and shrugged her shoulders.

"Personal, among other reasons," Martin replied at last. He added, "Arthur… he was a conscientious objector, if you can use that term for a spy."

"As were the hundreds of others, I suppose?" She was not accusing, nor judging, simply making conversation.

He appreciated it. He said calmly, "Some quit, some were let go. Differences of opinion are present in every industry."

"Not every employer asks its workforce to falsify crucial intelligence en masse."

Martin did not reply immediately. He looked into her eyes. They were tired but peaceful and sincere. Very few people knew what he did, and those who did were all tied to the CIA and his department, they had no moral quarrels about killing, and questions about right or wrong were never raised. This was the first time he felt uneasy answering the question. He sensed, rather than heard it in her voice, that she was not accusing, but sorry. His was a job that no amount of counseling could reconcile. In the name of national security or not, whether the target was a Bosnian or a Rwandan war crimes fugitive, or a political enemy of the United States, it made no difference. A killing was a killing.

"I couldn't do it anymore," he said simply.

"Conscience?" Her lips were covered by the rim of the paper cup.

"No, I don't think so. After a few hits you suppress your conscience, it gets buried so deep you don't feel a thing."

"Like shoplifting." André agreed.

Martin shot him a quizzical look. The Frenchman's eyes were smiling.

The out-of-place comment broke an invisible barrier in his mind, and Martin said, "It's just a job, made easier thanks to not having to look into your targets' eyes. It's all pictures, computer monitors, and presentation screens. It's worse for those who actually have to pull the trigger. No matter how tough you are, it eventually comes back with force that can break you, and often does. In my case it was plain disenchantment. I couldn't see how it was making any difference. You kill one bad guy, and ten others take his place."

He opened up. It was not much, but it was more than he had ever spoken about it. It felt good.

"So you turned around completely. The Hill Gazer reads like your personal vendetta against the people who create policies that make departments such as the one you headed a necessary part of daily business."

"I guess you might say that I found my calling, though perhaps I wouldn't've gotten involved with The Gazer had it not been for my work experience." Suddenly he froze. It was enough for one time. He changed the subject. "How about yourself? You're not exactly shy with a pistol."

"Bah, she's a regular Amazon, except for the man bashing!" André said, a wink in one eye.

She smiled. "All within job requirements! Besides, it isn't often I get a chance to draw the weapon. I've probably waved it around more in the last few days than in the whole past year."

"Either of you has a problem working with a killer, is that what it's all about?" Martin said, and looked into their eyes.

They did not reply immediately, surprised by the question, not noticing the light flicker in his eye.

"We were curious, now that we'll be working together, what kind of a field agent you'll make." Olga said.

"It's one thing to plan assassinations from the safety of your desk, and a 'ole other to kill in the field." André backed her up.

"Call it a pre-emptive strike." Martin corrected, giving his voice a light tone, not quite humorous, but intended to lighten up the conversation. I'm not defending the practice, nor am I condemning it. We do it. The Israelis do it. I don't know about you, Canadians, but the French sure as hell do it. And so do a lot of other services. Me? I quit because I got tired of it, not because of some moral reservations. Those died somewhere between my third and fourth assignment."

"Well, that's not the reason I mentioned it." Olga blushed.

"Sure."

"It's true!" André protested. "We've never worked with someone like you. When we learned what you did, we thought you'd be… different."

"Different? How?"

André shrugged.

Olga said, "More spooky, or something, but you turned out to be rather… you know… nine-to-five kinda guy."

"I was."

"Never actually did any of the… field work?"

"Just recon. It is essential to see the scene with your own eyes, to feel it. Satellite imagery, maps, they'll only take you so far."

They drank in silence for a time.

Olga's badge blinked and beeped unobtrusively but persistently.

Martin glanced at it. On first impression it was similar to a standard plastic ID badge, as worn by millions of office workers around the world. Olga explained the difference. Every employee, or a visitor, was furnished with a similar badge, which worked to identify, as well as to locate its bearer. The whereabouts of every person present on the premises was monitored by way of an embedded RFID chip. The chip was encoded with a clearance pass according to the level of employment of its holder. It opened doors one was entitled to enter, and warned the control room if any infractions were committed. An ultra thin liquid crystal display showed the blueprint of the facility locations the holder was permitted to enter; it helped locate exit routes and public spaces. It also allowed the security service to remotely scan the data of the holder, including photo, rank, and related information. Where communication was required, the screen displayed text messages.

One such message had just arrived. Olga read it briefly, and stood up.

"Excuse me, I'm wanted upstairs. André will show you to your room, and, we'll reconvene in an hour."

Both men watched her until she disappeared behind the doors. They both realized their eyes were fixed on the woman. André stood up.

"If you're ready," he said.

Martin followed through the long corridors and a short elevator ride up two levels. The room he was assigned to was as sterile as the entire compound. The metal used in the construction, combined with the austere decor gave it an industrial ambiance.

Under an hour later, showered and wearing fresh clothes, Martin was roused from the cot by a gentle knock on the door. He stood up with a sigh, and opened.

It was Olga, the look in her eyes expressing bad news.

"Jeannie was caught."

Jeannie was caught red handed and interrogated! The interrogation was a term of endearment. Martin knew it better than most. He had spent part of his career tracking down traitors. His team had used a score of techniques to extract information from reluctant sources — the fugitives who were marked unsalvageable and destined for silent death. In the times when waterboarding was the preferred method, the use of sodium pentothal seemed the most humane approach. Contrary to common belief, popularized by Hollywood and fiction writers, the use of chemicals, also referred to as truth serums, was neither a simple task nor a one to yield satisfactory results. An interrogation required a skilled officer and precise dosage and timing, and improper use left a shell of a person. Martin knew that while the CIA did not lack specialists for the job, the pressures to deliver answers often put a strain on quality. As a result the ratio of injuries resulting from hastily conducted interrogations grew exponentially as the various military conflicts raged on, as the hunt for anti-American elements within the society and the traitors within the intelligence community continued. Jeannie was caught, and it meant that her fate was in the hands of butchers.

"I'm sorry," Olga said. "If it's any consolation it looks as though she got away."

Sitting on the double bed tucked against the far wall of the small room, Martin looked at her with starry eyes. Jeannie got away, but what psychological and physical state was she in?

"Is she alright?" he asked.

"Anyone who gets away from those monsters is alright," Olga replied. "But we cannot confirm her physical or mental state. We're not sure how she escaped, where to, or what condition she's in."

"Can you find her?"

"Douglas thinks it's a bad idea. A hunt is already on, and we may only endanger her if we start probing."

"We can't leave her."

"She is resourceful. Years in the field taught her unique skills."

Martin shook his head, sad eyes on the floor.

"I shouldn't have involved her," he said after a while.

"You mustn't blame yourself. You couldn't have known what you were dealing with —" She paused uncomfortably.

Martin noticed. "Is there more?"

"Just how much did Jeannie know?"

"Why?"

"How much could she've told them that could make them surmise where you are?"

"Are you kidding? I still can't believe I'm here, little else had the foreknowledge of where I'd end up. Besides, what could she tell that the CIA doesn't know already?"

Olga pried. "We must be prepared. What about your friends? Did she know them well?"

"She knew what Bobby did—" Martin bit his tongue. The mention of Jeannie's lover and his best friend made his face flush crimson.

Olga made a mental note of the fact.

31

Douglas was standing in front of the conference table, using a laser pointer to highlight important points on the presentation screen. Olga, André, and Martin, watched him from their aluminum seats, pencils in hands, paper pads in front of them.

"Here's the list Arthur Latki had compiled: names, followed by basic background from intelligence and open sources. The most important are the seemingly insignificant dates of foreign travels, which coincide with the Basel Group conferences, but before we get to them let us examine the names. Two are American citizens, one is a German, and one Italian. Neither name appears on any lists of confirmed or suspected Basel Group members."

"But that is not proof that they are not members." Olga said.

"Certainly not according what we'd learned about the group so far, where members hold significant positions in the highest echelons of industry, finance, or by virtue of blue blood. Yet—"

"They are nobodies." André cut in.

"It looks that way. They are retirees — wealthy, to be sure — but unremarkable otherwise. Or so it may seem until we dig deeper — to decades before any of you were born." Douglas fumbled with a small remote control that changed images displayed on the screen. Several old photographs appeared, each taken in a setting resembling a board meeting. "They may appear to be forgotten today, but they once represented immense wealth and power. And they share yet another common denominator — each one of them traveled to the cities in which the Basel conferences took place, and on the exact dates."

The significance of the discovery was clear.

"How is it, though, that we have not come across their names before?" Olga asked excitedly.

"There are many things we don't yet know about the Basel Group, and probably never will. It isn't even about what we know, or do not know, about the Group of today. What is infinitely more important is the Basel Group in its first days, but of which we know precious little. It seems that Arthur Latki's painstaking investigation had shed a light on that period. Take these four men."

His laser pointer circled every name, one by one, as Douglas read out loud.

"Giovanni Buonarotti. Chairman. Banco Italia. Italy. Charles Archibaldi. Chairman. Council on Foreign Relations. USA. Lawrence Sexton III. Chairman. AmeriOil. USA. Wolfgang von Lutzenstein. Chairman. Bundes Auto Werks. Germany."

He let it sink in before continuing. "Now, imagine there was another name on this list, that of the recently deceased man whom we know as one of the founders of the Basel Group."

"Prince Gerhard van Eenijde?" André suggested incredulously, his eyes on the list.

"Now place his name on the list, between Sexton and Lutzenstein. Take the first letter of each man's last name, in the order that they are."

"Merde!" André said.

"That's preposterous!" Olga seconded.

Martin said, his eyes probing Douglas' face, "Arthur was a lawyer. He didn't say a word, unless he analyzed it from all angles. He must have been certain of the accuracy of his data to put it down on paper."

Douglas glanced at his wristwatch just a split second before the door opened, and a red-hair agent walked in.

"We've got something." The man announced and handed several printouts.

Douglas glanced at them, and passed them along.

They took turns studying the documents.

"This certainly puts a new light on the affair." Olga summed up.

André shrugged.

"The American Liberty League? I don't see the significance."

"It's not something that is not widely known. The League was a fascist group that plotted to overthrow President Roosevelt, and replace him with a subservient puppet."

Martin knew about the plot to overthrow president Franklin Delano Roosevelt, it was taught as part of a required course, a lesson for officers in his specialty, where planning coups, albeit on foreign soil, required thorough understanding of not only politics, but also history, economy, and social conditions. He looked at Douglas, somewhat curiously, but not entirely convinced.

The Englishman read his mind.

"The similarities are here. FDR was elected largely on the platform of change — the New Deal — promising reforms designed to stimulate the economy, creating jobs, and giving control of the economic matters to the government, instead of allowing free market to reign. The business elite were very dissatisfied with the move. The business elite are very dissatisfied with the current president."

"The times are different. The American Liberty League was a fascist group. Fascism was in then. It swept the world. Germany. Italy. Spain—"

"Fascism always exists where conditions are ripe," Douglas riposted. "Many think that such conditions exist in America today."

"Oh-la-la!" André smacked his lips as he studied the document again. "The pieces of the puzzle are beginning to fall into place, with Archibaldi and Sexton being the sons of the most prominent members of the American Liberty League."

"But the League was disbanded." Martin reminded.

Douglas replied, "In one form or another, something akin to the League has always existed, and the Secret Service has a long list of similar organizations under their magnifying glass. The Basel Group fits the picture, too, as the sort of American Liberty League on a global scale — shuffling offices around the world."

Douglas allowed them a minute or two to absorb the significance of the finding. Then he said, "This finding lays out the course for us, and should go particularly well with Martin's personal quest." He shuffled the papers in his hand, and placed one sheet in front of Borneman. "Did your mother not say that she was on a plane, somewhere over water? Lawrence Sexton III was flying on his private jet, and according to the records from the air traffic control, he was in the air over the Atlantic at the time the kidnapper let you speak with your mother."

Martin read the air traffic report, his eyes glistening with sparks.

Douglas placed yet another sheet of paper on the table.

"Furthermore, our boys pulled this little tidbit from the society pages of Sexton's home town. He has departed for Europe to attend the tomorrow evening's birthday celebration of one Vicomte de Montrose."

"Monsieur le Vicomte is a confirmed Basel Group member!" André said.

Three pairs of eyes were set on Douglas's lips. He savored the effect of his words as he went on.

"I don't believe in coincidences. I put it to you that the Basel Conference will not be happening in Switzerland after all."

Olga protested. "But the preparations! We have reports of something about to happen in Basel, Switzerland. Do we not? No hotels accept reservations. The heightened scrutiny at all entry points—"

Douglas cut her off. "Mere theatrics measured to throw the investigation on a wild goose chase. I put it to you that the birthday is a pretext to hide the real reason for the gathering of who's who. The Basel Group will meet in Paris, tomorrow, and you are going to be there."

PART TWO

32

Borneman stood up and closed the window. The noise from the périphérique — the highway encircling Paris — was so loud it made the glass panels vibrate. He drew back the curtains and poured himself another cup of coffee. He had had several already and was edgy. The realization that his parents might be close was overwhelming. He looked up at the wall clock. It was only two minutes since he last checked the time. Five and a half hours to go. He sat down to study the documents the Kawartha Facility supplied, and stood up again. The wait was killing him.

Furnished with what Douglas was able to obtain through official requisition channels from the Direction de la Surveillance du Territoire, without raising undue interest to the Canadian intelligence operation in France, the three conferred around the wooden kitchen table of an apartment building in the bustling Parisian suburb of Aubervilliers. The area was chosen with utmost care, the large and mixed populace of legal and illegal immigrants forming a busy and colorful crowd, so desired for those requiring anonymity. The three bedrooms in this unassuming part of town were on the second floor of a gray concrete high-rise. Officially rented by a salesman who spent much of his time traveling around the country, the apartment was regularly swept for bugs and served as a short-term safe house for field operatives in need of refuge. For reasons of security and convenience the DST maintained numerous such apartments across Paris. They were all maintained by the adepts of the counterintelligence services, often university students, whose duties included the stocking of the refrigerators, paying the bills, and maintaining the image of an inhabited dwelling.

"Maybe we could make better use of the time?" André suggested, annoyed with the nervous pacing of the American.

"What do you have in mind?" Olga asked. She too was nervous, uneasy feelings about the operation burrowing under her skull. She would welcome some distraction, anything to turn her mind elsewhere, if only for the time being.

André shrugged. He put aside the newspapers, picked up the converter, and turned on the television. "Merde! Those cheap bastards. I wish they subscribed to cable!"

Borneman caught on to the idea of doing something as opposed to sitting and waiting. He suggested reconnaissance to the known French members of the Basel Group who owned estates in Paris. One of them might be housing the Bornemans.

"It isn't what I meant," André said, and waived the TV converter in his hand. He made himself comfortable on the couch, and began to flip the channels. There were not many. He settled on one and quickly became engrossed in the programming.

"The waiting is driving me crazy!" Martin confessed after a failed attempt at finding common ground with the talk show host and his guests, all engaged in an animated discussion. "I feel like I should be doing something."

Olga said, "Your parents could be kept anywhere. There are numerous Basel Group members in Paris and the Ile-de-France. Any snooping around their properties would raise a red flag. I say we stay put. Let Douglas do his job. Reserve your energy for tonight." She added, "Why don't you have a nap? You barely had slept on the plane."

They had spent most of the flight talking. They talked about their childhood, high school, and college, travels, and summers in the country with their folks, not a word touched on their work. It felt good, normal. Martin missed this kind of a conversation.

He looked into her eyes, and said softly, "I enjoyed the company, instead."

"As did I," Olga replied and blushed.

"What are you whispering about?" André called out from in front of the TV. He did not wait for the answer. "Come and see this."

They approached.

"Trivia show?" Olga shrugged. Expecting something serious, she was perplexed.

"No, no!" The Frenchman objected excitedly, and pointed at the screen. "These are celebrities, minor, but it's funny nonetheless. They make fun by insulting each other. Like this man, the other guy just said that 'e is turning into a baby again, with 'is head is as bald as when 'e was a baby—"

Olga and Martin looked at one another and burst out laughing. The triviality of the show reminded each that there was a real world out there, with common issues like paying taxes, shopping, and poking fun at other people. They could not stop laughing.

"It's very funny, actually!" André took offense and raised the volume.

An hour to departure they began trying on the clothes that were provided by the DST. It was a daunting process that none of them particularly enjoyed — Olga for not being used to dress in attire that did not permit the strapping of a pistol holster; Martin for not being able to concentrate on anything other than worrying about his parents; and André for the bad luck of the draw — he would not be attending the event that would be staffed by his colleagues from the DST. Instead he will be spending the evening in the car, though wearing a tuxedo in case the events inside should call for his backup. Should such need arise he would enter through the tight security without much ado, his genuine identification ensuring compliance of the detachment responsible for the security at the event. It would be the last resort, of course, as keeping his affiliation with the Kawartha Facility hidden as long as possible was paramount.

The two men were standing in the middle of the living room, fixing their bowties, when Olga entered from her room.

André whistled.

Martin shook his head in admiration.

She was stunning. Her sandy, shoulder-length hair, contrasted nicely with the simple but tasteful black evening gown.

"You're not so bad looking yourselves, gentlemen."

The tuxedoes were an excellent fit, and both men looked the part.

André approached and reached for her hand. He pressed it to his lips, bowed charmantly, and said, "Banaček. Miroslav Banaček. Attaché of the Czech embassy. May I claim the first two dances, milady?"

Olga smiled and spun around gracefully.

"There is only one problem," she said. "A lady needs a purse."

33

They took the small Renault that was requisitioned from the DST's pool and stopped by Galleries Lafayette on the way. Olga and Martin went in for a quick shopping visit as André drove around the block. Rush hour in Paris knew no constraints, it was an all-day affair, and André did not want to attract the attention of the traffic police by stopping illegally.

Twenty minutes later André parked the car a block away from the Palais de l'Élysée. Borneman, in the back seat, proceeded to open the aluminum briefcases that were supplied and delivered by the DST. They contained a small notebook computer, a power inverter, and three mobile telephones. The set worked as a private cellular network. With a range of about three kilometers in diameter in built-up areas, it was a top of the line secure communications center. Mobile phones connected to such a network could not be accessed remotely by service providers, as often occurred on orders from state security services; each phone connected to the network worked on a scrambled frequency. André plugged the power inverter into the cigarette lighter socket and Borneman switched on the computer. He set up the base station and tested each telephone, while André proceeded to explain the added features.

"Three identical cell phone models, with rapid use functions, meaning no special activation sequence is required. All three work as mobile phones, but only one sports a functioning video camera. The others are packed with features that pro'ibited fitting the optics in. The first one delivers an electric charge, not as powerful as you'd get from a full-power stun gun, but given the size of these units it is still impressive. To use it you simply switch on the button on the side whenever you are ready to fire. The charge comes out through the charge contacts at the bottom. It is important that you keep the side switch off, or else you risk firing accidentally. The second phone is identical, except the camera is a dummy. Instead of filming, it releases a nerve gas. Same idea, switch on the side button, point and press the key. Effective range is about two meters. Now, the third mobile is actually deadly, and given the event it poses the 'ighest risk of not passing through the security. To arm, once again you switch on the side button, but also swivel the lens like so. Then, press the button and out comes a bullet, through the lens. I suggest that the firearm unit stays with me, as it is entirely impractical given the type of event. After all, we are only to talk to Sexton, not to kill him. I'd like to see a live video feed, though I'll understand if it is not possible. Olga? A lady should not raise as much suspicion as a guy would."

"Sure, I'll take that one." She placed the phone with the working camera in her new purse.

"It may not be possible to use it without raising unwanted attention. If that's the case, I want you to send a signal, so I know you're fine. I guess every fifteen minutes shouldn't be too conspicuous? In an emergency send a text and move for the exit as fast as you can."

"Whatcha gonna do, Mister Banaček? You gonna show us some special tricks?" She asked with a smile.

"I'll improvise, I suppose. Raise 'ell if necessary."

"Elle? Who's Elle?" Martin asked and blinked to Olga.

"*'ell: Ach-ee-el-el…*"

They were laughing as they left the vehicle.

The entrance to the Palais de l'Élysée was cordoned off by uniformed gendarmerie. Limousines lined the boulevard as the Sécurité officers used mirrors to scan the chassis of the arriving cars for explosives; a queue of pedestrians extended well passed the gates. The sight was reassuring. Martin worried that arriving on foot would raise attention.

"It would've in America," André assured him earlier. "But, this was Europe, and more importantly, the center of the chic and classy, where even royalty were not above walking their royal butts to various functions."

André was right: A queue of elegant men and women were being allowed through the gate on foot. After having their invitations and IDs verified, scanned, and telephones checked, they were waived through the gate. More dignitaries were lining up behind, and they were not used to waiting long.

Inside, the magnificent Ceremonial Hall was bustling with colorful gowns and black tuxedoes, glitzy jewelry, fake smiles, aristocratic titles, old money, new money, and big hopes for all of the above. The main hall and the alcoves were filling in with a steady influx of elegant men and women speaking in the tongues of their birth. The delicate notes of a string concerto descended from the balcony where the chamber music quartet was playing. Mingling, chatting, or just plain observing others, the guests awaited the appearance of the President of the République who would officially congratulate the venerable guest of honor on his ninetieth birthday.

The handsome couple, who identified themselves as Czech diplomats, had slowly weaved their way through the crowd of faces known from front pages of society magazines and daily news. They seldom spoke, and when they did it was at a whisper, their eyes scanning every person that passed by. The likeness of Lawrence Sexton, as they knew it from the photographs studied on the plane, was nowhere to be seen.

It was not until the third round of canapés that Martin's hand froze half way through delivering the palatable nibble to his mouth. The man he had so desired to find was standing under the archway. Borneman's eyes and bodily energy descended and concentrated on Lawrence Sexton III. In the hands of this aged, inconspicuous-looking man, were the lives of all that was dearest to Martin. Preventing himself from lunging at him and demanding the release of his parents was the biggest challenge Martin ever faced. He remained in place, his eyes locked on the source of his predicament, his legs feeling heavy, as if rooted in the ground, holding him back. And then, suddenly, through the distance of some ten paces and a flowing sea of distinguished patrons between them, their eyes met. While Martin's glowed with hatred, passion, and hope, Sexton's eyes remained calm and confident, save for the momentary enlargement of pupils — the unmistakable sign of recognition. As if to add fuel to fire the old man winked and nodded to the side, his eyes swaying to his left in a silent sign. The audacity of the move was more than Martin could bear. He could no longer contain the pent up emotional strain. Damn the plan! He started forward, Olga's words of caution lost in the commotion and complaints of guests being elbowed aside.

Pushing through a crowd of people not used to stepping aside was not an easy task. With his eyes on Sexton, Martin watched with sudden dismay as the man slowly turned around and headed toward the grand marble hallway. By the time Borneman had pushed his way to the archway, Lawrence Sexton had disappeared.

34

Olga's presence of mind saved their combined efforts. She slipped her hand under his arm

"This way!"

Rather than pushing head on to get through the crowd, she joined the flow of the distinguished guests.

"He went up that way!"

She led to the stairway, where several guests stood chatting, drinks in their hands. As she and Martin climbed the stairs she snatched the phone out of her purse and speed-dialed a number.

She said to the microphone, "We may've lost him. Mind the gate."

The second floor appeared to be off limits to the guests. A plain-clothed security agent stood atop the staircase, his spread out legs firmly set on the floor.

"C'est privée —" the agent started, but did not finish.

The beautiful lady in a classy gown landed a kick in his groin. He groaned and bent forward but did not fall. With one hand holding on to his privates, the other reached in to the holster that was strapped to his belt, and withdrew a pistol. With a second kick the woman knocked the gun out of the agent's hand, the gun flying upwards, bouncing off the wall, and landing several feet away from the agent — too far to reach in time. The agent made a split decision, and lunged forward.

Martin applied the contacts of his mobile phone to the agent's abdomen and deliver a charge.

"Pull him into that alcove!" Olga commanded after the agent's body wilted and slumped onto the floor.

They grabbed the unconscious agent by the legs and dragged him to the small nook where a Sevres vase stood on an ornately encrusted table. They pulled the heavy curtain and breathed with relief — the incident had gone unnoticed. Olga passed the agent's gun to Martin and they proceeded carefully.

The wide corridor was flanked by several sets of closed doors. Only one of them was open. It led to a huge suite at the end of the hallway. A dimly lit crystal chandelier, visible in the distance, drew them inexplicably. They peeked inside. Adding a mysterious aura to the quarter's rich furnishings were old tapestries hanging on the walls of the drawing room. The two windows that overlooked the gardens were entirely covered with drapes. A flicker of a cigarette lighter appeared from the right side where a loveseat and a card table with four chairs stood next to the fireplace.

Lawrence Sexton III inhaled several times on a long cigar until it caught the light. He closed the flap of the gold lighter with his thumb and slipped it into his pocket.

"You haven't disappointed, Martin Borneman. I knew you'd come. Please." He gestured nonchalantly to the seat in front of him.

It was perhaps the most trying moment for Martin. Rather than lunging at the man with his fists he had to remain calm.

"Where are they?" he asked through his teeth, and advanced one step.

"I assume that you are referring to your parents?"

The audacity exhibited by the hated man was infuriating.

"Don't play with me, old man!"

Borneman advanced another step. He was fuming, his face made the redder by the bordeaux draperies and cherry wainscoting. He stood in the middle of the room with his teeth clenched.

Olga approached and slipped her hand under his arm. Something strange was afoot. The ease with which they overpowered the agent — a single agent guarding a staircase in a presidential palace — was the first clue. The calm demeanor of the pursued man, who expected them, was another.

"Martin," she started gently, her eyes set firmly on Sexton. "I don't think this is a coincidence. Remember, we talked at the Facility about all the bits and pieces that just seemed to fall into our hands, how we thought that they came from within Basel? I think we were meant to be here."

"That's very perceptive, Miss Duchesne. Please." With a sway of his arm Sexton invited them to take seats.

Martin was not having it.

"I know you brought them with you. My mother said she was in the air, over water. Your plane was on the way to Europe when you let me talk to her. We traced the call."

"I promise to tell you everything I know, as long as you put away that weapon and take a seat, Martin. You're making me nervous."

Borneman realized he was aiming the gun at Sexton. He was angry to the point that he could find no words. He remained in place, motionless, dogged hatred in his eyes. He wanted to shoot this man.

"Martin," Sexton continued in a calm voice. "You're at the residence of the President of France. It's not the sort of place you come to uninvited, regardless of how well the forged documents and the invitations. You are here because we needed to talk."

Martin was struggling to remain in control — weakness he did not want to show. Sexton's words threw him off guard, confused, and angered. This old man had actually insisted that leads which brought Martin to Paris were planted. Desperate lies of a cornered villain! Old fool whose arrogance knows no boundaries! Yet, Sexton's words kept Martin in check, they could not be discarded lightly. The words and Sexton's earlier peculiar behavior in the reception hall burrowed deeply through Martin's mind, competing with the urge to punish and inflict pain on the man who was the source of death and torment to everyone who was dear. It was Olga's presence, and her holding onto Martin's arm, that prevented him from taking a step of no return.

Sexton touched the breast pocket of his jacket and the door opened. Two plain-clothed security guards walked in, one of them the man who was knocked unconscious by a combination of a stun gun and a well aimed blow of the fist. "Put the weapon down," Sexton said to Martin. "And surrender what ever else you might have on you, courtesy of the Kawartha Facility."

"Call off your goons." Martin aimed the pistol. "I'm not ready to die. Not before you."

"You truly astonish me, Martin. What ever would make you think that?"

"A dark night on Lake Ruther."

"Wait, wait, wait! You're blaming me for the murder of your friends? Preposterous! Has Douglas really gone that far?" With the last words Sexton shot a questioning look to the woman.

"You're not denying it, then?" Martin asked gravely.

"My dear fellow, you're way off!" Sexton appeared genuinely offended.

"You're despicable." Borneman took a step toward Sexton, the two guards at the ready. "Do you realize that the only thing that prevents me from squashing you like a bug are my folks? You—" Martin made yet another step forward, the guards two steps behind. He was at the last straw.

"Wait!" Olga approached, and pulled his arm. "I think— I am beginning to understand."

"What are you talking about?" Martin shot over his shoulder.

"We've made it this far. Let him talk." She pleaded.

"Thank you, Miss Duchesne." Sexton bowed his a notch. He said to Martin, "I want to make it absolutely clear that neither I personally, nor any group you might be associating me with, had anything to do with the kidnapping of your parents. You have succumbed to a terrible lie, made worse by the tragic and unnecessary loss of lives. But you can't be blamed for not foreseeing the tragedy. It was beyond your control, the killings were planned and executed with cold blood and a terrible objective in mind. Admittedly, though, the plan almost succeeded. *Almost.*"

"I've heard this already. You're not telling anything new," Martin said through his teeth.

"Oh? Where have you heard it from? Ah, but of course — Douglas! Hmmm. Perhaps then, it will come to you as news when I tell you that Douglas is not quite the man you might have been led to believe he was."

"Surprise me," Martin said, while Olga's fingers tightened on his bicep.

Lawrence Sexton drew from the cigar, exhaled a blue cloud, and said, "Douglas Burke is a deep cover American intelligence operative."

35

Lawrence Sexton III savored the effect of his words. He exhaled a puff of blue smoke, and continued, "Douglas Burke has been with American intelligence since early 1970s. After a stint in Vietnam, he was assigned to the clandestine section responsible for the penetration of the Anglosphere countries. His British parentage, and an uncanny accent, assured him a post in the United Kingdom—"

"Spying on the closest allies?" Martin cut in with suspicion. He glanced to Olga, but received no support. The woman seemed engrossed in Sexton's every word. "Mr. Sexton, blowing smoke in my eyes does not make me blind to your obvious attempt to deceive. The question is: Why would a man like you need to result to such tactics?"

"A man like me?"

"Why would a man in your position — a friend to presidents and royalty, wealthy, and mighty — feel the need to feed us such a preposterous story? And the only logical answer is that we've gotten too close to the truth. Is that not so?"

"You are absolutely right on the latter point. You had gotten close to the truth the day you were recruited by the CIA."

"Preposterous lies of a cornered villain!"

"Oh, no, Martin! It's an example of a masterful intelligence plan. Your own background is what makes this carousel turn so effectively. A man who controls assassins is in the center of a conspiracy to assassinate the president. This alone is enough to ensure that no efforts are spared in stopping such a man. The entire security apparatus is occupied trying to locate the would-be assassin — every news channel broadcasts his image, every newspaper prints his service mugshot, and every police officer is told to be on the look out for the lone gunman. Meanwhile the real threat is able to grow unhindered."

Martin analyzed Sexton's words, and found no fault in the reasoning. His own suspicions of being framed gave him no counterargument. He looked at Olga, but seeing as she appeared as though under the spell of the old man, he exploded in anger.

"Give me my parents back!"

"Don't let anger blind you, Martin. Not now, not when you're this close." Sexton said slowly, and deliberately."

Martin's index finger tightened on the trigger.

"I want my mother and father back, and unhurt."

Sexton saw the proximity of a breaking point. He shook his head and said, "You were within arms' reach from them. At the Kawartha Facility."

The surprise was complete. Olga stood wide-eyed, gazing at Sexton. Martin was speechless, his face suddenly pale. He turned to the woman looking for confirmation, or denial.

"I assure you, Martin, I had nothing to do with it," she said, her deep eyes set on his. She turned to Sexton, and said, "Douglas may not be the most likeable man, but that is going too far, unless you can prove it."

Sexton disregarded her, his words directed at Martin. "Your eyes see that what your mind wants to see. You wanted to believe that your parents were flown to Europe, so you accepted Douglas' deception at face value, whatever proof he might have furnished to in support. From a strictly professional point of view, you cannot be blamed. Douglas is a pro—"

It was too much. Borneman approached the small table, and said, towering over the old man, "You son of a bitch!"

The security agents aimed their pistols.

Olga grasped Martin's arm.

"Wait, Martin! Wait."

To Sexton she said, "Your psychological mumbo-jumbo is misdirected. You're talking to a wreck of a person. Do not toy with us anymore, Mr. Sexton. Say what you have to say, or be damned!"

"You're right, Miss Duchesne. Ask."

"I want proof of Martin's parents being at the Kawartha Facility."

"Permit just one more question: What *proof* convinced you that they were in Paris?"

"A call was made. Martin spoke with his mother. She had enough time to convey that she was on a plane, flying over water—"

"And, naturally, Douglas convinced you that your parents were on the plane I flew on. Only, how could I have kidnapped your parents, and placed them on an aircraft carrying the official US delegation?"

"What?"

"You see, even Douglas makes mistakes. I suppose he assumed that I flew my own jet? Not so. My presence on the same aircraft carrying members of the US administration, along with a good number of business leaders, is a matter of public record. Many of the passengers will vouch for my being on that plane."

Olga was at a loss.

Sexton went on, "Now, allow me to tell you what really happened. You see, Judge Ezra Ferguson, to whom Martin turned for help, had been on our watch list since Arthur Latki began his research into the Basel Group. The judge's phone line was monitored. A call was intercepted, and traced to a private jet heading across the northern border, over water, to be sure, but the water being Lake Ontario." Sexton reached into his jacket pocket and produced his smartphone. He tapped on the screen, and to Martin's chagrin his own voice and that of Lydia Borneman poured out of the speaker. It was the conversation the kidnapper had allowed Martin to have with his mother.

Borneman was speechless, deflated.

Olga asked, "What about your name on Arthur's list? Your, and those of the other founders of the Basel Group."

"What of it?"

"You don't deny it, then? That you're a member of the Group? That you meet in secret? That you plot a New World Order—"

"Now, hold on a second. I have no intention of denying that I and a host of like-minded people meet occasionally, and discuss world affairs. But a New World Order? That is simply preposterous."

"Really? Why the secrecy, then?"

Sexton shrugged.

"Some of my friends are very shy when it comes to public attention. You cannot blame them. Given their position in society they appreciate the privacy. And the fact that our meetings are secret is simply to do with the desire to meet outside of the committing environment of an official occasion."

"You have to do a better job to convince us why we should trust you, and not Douglas."

"Alright. Let's talk about Douglas. Let's talk about the man who killed Martin's friends, and who kidnapped his parents."

36

Sexton released a puff, and said, his eyes on Martin, "The man whom you placed all your trust with, is actually responsible for all the misery that struck you. You had been used from the very start, beginning with your recruitment with the CIA. You and your friends were recruited to serve a purpose. Sure, some of you had the sort of skills that were exploited and benefited the spy agency, but these were nurtured in order to be used against you when the time came. The time has come."

Martin remained motionless, only his facial expression betraying the tremendous strain his mind was under.

Sexton continued, "Your journey started when a student by the name Chris Earle published that infamous paper on the CIA's activities aimed against the population of the United States. It caused a major shake up within the intelligence community, resulting in massive layoffs and reorganization. Among those who were forced to resign was

Douglas Burke, who, at the time, was back in America, and working for a group akin to the American Liberty League—"

Olga sighed.

Sexton paused, and shot a her quizzical gaze.

"We know your provenance, Mr. Sexton. We know your father was a founding member of the League."

"It isn't a secret."

"But you'd rather it was, is that not so?"

"On the contrary. I am proud of what my father did."

"Really? The financial support of the Nazi regime is something to be proud of? The plot to overthrown president Roosevelt in order to replace him with a fascist dictator is something to be proud of?"

"Are you finished?"

The look in her eyes showed that it was enough to paint a picture of a man and his view of the world.

"Had you done more thorough research, Miss Duchesne, you would known the true reason for my being proud of my father, who was the one who blew the whistle on the plot against the president. That single act of patriotic courage saved America."

She was speechless. Her eyes sought support in Martin's. She found him deflated, a man who lost all hope. It was that image that roused her. If there was anything to be had of this meeting it was to save Martin's parents.

"Is this why we are here? Are you responsible for the leaks about the plot against the current president?"

Sexton's expression was the confirmation.

"Is this why Douglas sent us here, to Paris, then? To stop you?"

"To an extent Douglas was acting on clues left for him. You are here because we needed to talk. But Douglas is not a fool. He allowed you to come here, knowing well that we'd have this conversation, and that it would have exposed him."

"Why would he do it, then?"

"I don't pretend to understand all of Douglas' scheming. Together, however, we may form a better picture. Ultimately, though, that is why you are here. With your insight into Douglas's operation we may be able to construct a plausible scenario of his scheming. We may be able to stop him from overthrowing the government."

"Ha! But you see — that is what Douglas accuses you of. You, and your Basel Group cronies. Douglas makes some good arguments, for instance — that of you having already chosen the president's replacement. Many people believe that is the way world leaders come to power — after receiving endorsement from the Basel Group."

"A fascinating conspiracy theory."

"Is it? What about those politicians who are summoned to your conferences, and soon after they become presidents, prime ministers, and the like?"

"Summoning?"

"Do you deny that you have met, or are about to meet the opposition's candidate for presidency?"

"Miss Duchesne, the opposition candidate is a very strong contender, with good chances of succeeding in filling the president's shoes. It is only common sense to get to know him on a neutral ground, before one has to enter into dealings with him as president, and according to protocol only."

"Why are your meetings shrouded in complete secrecy?"

"I promise to fill you in on some of the behind-the-scenes of our meetings. But if you don't mind, we have a more pressing issue at hand. And time is of the essence."

She considered his words.

"Alright. Let's put it aside for now. Tell me something about Douglas. What are his supposed goals?"

As was often the case where elevated social position was inbred, one assumed, often unconsciously, a condescending attitude toward the less fortunate. Sexton's orbit was so high above the common peoples that in dealings with them his generous use of platitude often caught him off guard, as it did in the case of this young obstinate woman. He was angry with himself for having to, inadvertently, put on a face for which he was neither inclined nor suited. He was not the kind of man to trifle. This was a man who dealt with equals reservedly, and with every one else from the position of the one whose word ought to be taken with reverence. The fact that this woman kept insisting on his proving himself and his word was deeply irritating, and amusing at the same time. He found it strange that there were people in this world who were not intimidated by the might that commanded nothing but submission.

Sexton pushed further back in his chair, and after puffing with an aristocratic gesture, he said, "You and I, Miss Duchesne, must meet some day, and have a chat of our own. I admire your ferocity. It's not something that I often get to see."

She raised her brows in a gesture of impatience.

"That's exactly what I mean," Sexton said. "But alright, let us come to the point. The truth about Douglas is that he is involved in a covert operation aimed at ensuring political unity across the American political scene. Call it the bonding element. His task is to eliminate all dissent, including that, which is burrowing through the administration. This should not really come as a surprise. Such unity, or, as we should accurately name it — dictatorship — is often considered the only guarantor of stability, and in a case of an empire, stability is crucial."

"Goddamn politics!" Martin said, at last, awaken from the stupor. "Is this why my friends died — to strengthen the empire?"

"I suppose, in a way, yes. You may put it that way."

"How did their deaths contribute to this master plan?"

"Their deaths were inevitable, however premature. You were acting parts in a play that was written with a different finale in mind. Arthur Latki's probing into the Basel Group was the trigger that cause the curtain to fall early. Inadvertently, Arthur had discovered Douglas' plan. Only, he made a fatal mistake. Arthur thought that he had found the Basel Group — an organization allegedly responsible for shuffling some of the highest offices around the world. It was not so. The Basel Group that Arthur uncovered, though was not aware of, was entirely Douglas' creation."

"Was it? How do you explain this?" Martin leaned over the card table. He picked up the pen and the pad that were used to keep bridge scores, and scribbled something down.

Olga peered over his shoulder. She nodded her head, approvingly.

Sexton read the words.

Buonarotti + Archibaldi + Sexton + Eenijde + Lutzenstein = BASEL.

Sexton's reaction was not what Martin had expected. The old man burst out laughing. He laughed so hard that he leaned all the way back, holding onto his belly. At last he stopped, tears in his eyes.

"I like a man who enjoys riddles. That's very good, you know. Only, you're forgetting that our group was formed by thirty-nine members. What you wrote here is akin to numerology. You see only what you want to see."

"Is it?"

"Martin, the name assigned to our Group by overzealous journalists was, perhaps rightly, derived from the place of the original meeting — Basel, a city in Switzerland. Here, let me show you something." Sexton flipped the pages and scribbled something down. He handed the small pad back to Martin.

"I don't believe it!" Borneman cried out.

Olga peered over his shoulder and gasped out. The page contained five names.

Borneman + Autry + Sadosky + Earle + Latki = BASEL.

"I'm afraid it's true," Sexton said coldly. "Your friend, Arthur, had stumbled upon a group of elderly businessmen, and former heads of state, who like to meet together, out of the prying eyes. The Basel Group your friend uncovered is much more sinister. Its name is derived from the first letters of your last names, an acrostic. Naturally, because of the name similarities we thought it prudent to look into your origin and purpose. We'd determined that the project was created and nurtured from the start by Douglas. It was his Trojan Horse, ready to be launched when the conditions called for it. He conceived of it and oversaw it every step of the way."

"You can't be serious!" Martin was overwhelmed.

Saxton was relentless. "Your friends, much as yourself, had no idea of Burke's existence, or of your true roles in his schemes."

"You can't be serious." Martin repeated, his voice weak.

"You can doubt your intellect, Martin. Some of the best minds doubted theirs, which often led to significant leaps for humanity's progress. But, to doubt the facts, to doubt your own eyes?"

Martin pushed back. He suddenly felt devoid of all energy and passion he so needed. He was in shock. The news Sexton presented him with was staggering. Jesus! All those years in the service he was but a dupe. Something broke in him, all reservations about Sexton vanished. It had to be this way. One, or the other. He had to believe somebody. He picked Sexton, not because the man's arguments were stronger, but because they were here and now. He opened up. He described the strange feeling when meeting Douglas for the first time, that feeling of recognizing the other person, never having met him before. Could it be that he had somehow matched the pompous, stern voice of the kidnapper, with Douglas?

Olga placed her hand on Martin's shoulder, her expression that of deepest compassion.

She asked Sexton, "What is the source of your revelations?"

"Connections." Sexton replied without a flinch.

"As in — your Basel Group connections?"

"Miss Duchesne, why is it so difficult for you to accept that our meetings have no malicious intent?"

"When men of your means and influence meet in complete secrecy it pays to assume the worst, particularly when backed by certain events that follow such meetings."

"The rumors of our electing presidents, prime ministers, and so on? I read the gossip column now and then, I know what's abuzz, and I assure you that all of it is sheer nonsense."

"Says you. What about the journalists and investigators who had disappeared, or had their family members killed when probing into your group?"

"That's a serious allegation. Would you care to amplify?"

"Douglas Burke." She said simply.

"What of him?" Sexton shrugged, bewildered.

"His wife and daughter dying in separate accidents—"

"Douglas? Married? With children?" Sexton appeared amused. "My dear woman, Douglas is as gay as the Jack of Hearts, and he has been since the day the CIA had found out and recruited him. As far as I know he has never been married, not even as part of his cover legend."

37

Lawrence Sexton III savored the effect of his words. The helplessness on his interlocutors' faces was absolute. He was considering his next statement when a muted sound drew everyone's attention.

Sexton gazed to his bodyguards. One of them nodded.

"Better answer that, Miss Duchesne, before your friend does something irreversible, or draws attention to himself."

It was Olga's mobile phone. It was vibrating. She answered it.

"André? ... Everything's fine. ... Couldn't. ... No, never mind that. ... We'll be out, soon." She ended the call.

The intermission acted as cold water on a hot head. Martin was able to gather his thoughts.

"Help me understand these several points," he said, and bent a finger as he went on. "The purpose of the special task force operating out of the Kawartha Facility. The reason Douglas let me out of his sight, and allowed this trip to Paris, knowing that meeting you would expose him. And above all — my parents. What is to become of them now?"

"You must be anxious to help your parents, and I won't impose on you anything, not before they are free and safe. Then you will expose Douglas, and bring out the truth about his operation and the covert section he runs out of the Kawartha Facility."

"Out of the Kawartha Facility?" Olga could not conceal her skepticism. "How is that possible?"

"Outsourcing is not limited to the business world, Miss Duchesne, and in this case it is mandatory. What Douglas is doing is McCarthyism on a scale not imagined by any of the dystopian writers. Our society, though deeply divided, is better educated and better informed than it was in the 1940s, and 1950s. To run an operation of this magnitude requires a covert approach. Using the Canadian facilities, so close, yet out of the prying eyes of the US population, provides just the right venue for unobstructed work."

"How could he do it? How could no one have discovered it? How could Canada allow it?"

"Oh, that's intelligence work at its best. The Facility was built largely from funds supplied by allied intelligence services, in this case mostly Pentagon's and the CIA's, with a large degree of free reign afforded to the main sponsors. To ensure the safety of his project, Douglas named it the Basel Group, knowing that any investigation would lead elsewhere. It's worked thus far, with the media's attention fixated on that group of old men and women, who are plotting a New World Order. Ingenious, is it not? It ensured that the hunt for Douglas' pet project would be unlikely to succeed. It fooled your friend, Arthur. It fooled everyone else who stumbled upon the name of the Basel Group. Meanwhile, Douglas continues to plot, unhindered."

Martin exchanged glances with Olga.

Unable to counter Sexton's revelations, she said, "Alright. Everything said here seems possible, even probable. Yet none of it matters unless you can prove your claims."

Sexton was ready. "Of course, I would not expect you to believe me blindly, and I am prepared to offer the proof you require. The funds for Douglas' operation are funneled through various financial institutions, some of which Martin's friend had an intimate relationship with—"

"Derek?" Martin cut in.

Sexton nodded. "Derek Autry helped launder the money that sponsors the project that led to your friends' deaths."

"The black vault! But how—"

"The funds were funneled though various financial institutions, among them certain affiliates of the Bank of France, whose president is a friend of mine. Money talks, as they say, and if you want to see what it has to say about Douglas and his project, you will meet me tomorrow, at the bank, ten sharp. You will be able to retrace the financial machinations that your friend, Derek, was involved in for the past ten years, and which were squirreled away for the purposes of an operation currently being carried out. An operation to topple the president of the United States, by forces from within."

Olga and Martin looked into each other's eyes. No words were necessary to convey that they had no choice but to agree to Sexton's offer.

He understood. "My men assure me that you are safe in the DST apartment. Nonetheless one cannot be certain of Douglas' scheming, and I would like to offer you protection—"

"No!" Olga objected. "We mustn't do anything that would alert Douglas, and if anything you say is true, then we must assume that our every move is being watched."

"Miss Duchesne—"

"Mr. Sexton! We are experienced field operatives. We'll take care of ourselves, and we'll be at the bank to see the proof you have in support of your claims."

Sexton agreed after short hesitation. "Right. I wish you would reconsider, though. The resolution to Douglas' plot is near, and it means that any day, and any hour, we may bear witness to new developments. To answer one of your earlier questions, Martin, the fact that you are painted as a ruthless killer, and an assassin bent on murdering the president, puts your being in Paris in a troubling light. One does not have to be an intelligence analyst to surmise that your visit here has a purpose. What that purpose is remains to be seen, but one thing is certain — you are vulnerable."

Martin reaffirmed Olga's words. "We can take care of ourselves."

Meanwhile...

"Is it true?" William Mittler asked as soon as he shut the door behind him.

"As the director of the FBI you should be among the first to know." Paul Bosworth replied.

"I was, but I still find it hard to believe. Why would the president demand your resignation?"

"Come now, Bill. We both know that the president is only a figurehead. They've gotten to him, and pressed him to get me out of the way."

The two men were sitting in an unmarked black sedan parked in the parking lot of a home improvement warehouse. It was late, the store nearing closing time, last minute shoppers rushing to the doors and not paying attention to two cars that were parked at a far end of the lot, one empty, the other occupied by two men, invisible from the distance of the falling dusk.

Mittler commented, "What is even more alarming is that he seems unaware of everything that's happening, or is about to happen."

"What could he do? His closest allies are conspiring against him. It's hopeless."

"There must be something we could do to stop it."

The former director of the Central Intelligence Agency replied, "There may be. But it will involve decisive action. No ifs, or buts."

Mittler swallowed the bite of the sandwich he picked up at a drive-through on the way. He was hungry after an all day in emergency meetings with his closest advisors. "I'm listening."

"They knew I would not join them. It was easy to foresee something like the dismissal. I've made contact with people I trust. They have contacts and resources which are being put to work. When the time comes we shall need your support."

"You have it."

"I know. But you must not show it just yet."

"What?"

"Make it appear as though you're sympathetic to the plot. It's not like you have a choice, anyway."

"How's that?"

"They are prepared to remove you."

The director of the FBI swallowed hard. "They wouldn't dare!"

"Bill, they are this close to a coup d'etat, and you're in their way."

"Jesus. You're right."

"Pretend to go along with them, or at least not to interfere. It won't be for long. We've picked up Borneman's trail — a sudden requisition for a safe house in Paris, but originating in Canada. Arrangements are being made to pick up the residents."

The director of the FBI exhaled a long whistle.

"Perhaps not all is lost, then. But do you have the resources to pick him up?"

"The chief of the immigration department is an old friend. I am certain that Borneman will be apprehended and will lead us to clues that will save this country."

38

"Impossible! A liar!"

André was beyond himself. In so characteristically French expression of outpouring frustration he was shouting and slamming his fists on the steering wheel. Having to wait in the car, uncertain, without a signal, was the build-up of fuel, and the disappointment of seeing his companions return without having achieved anything was the spark to set it off.

"Bordel de merde!" The Frenchman shouted out to vent his frustration. He turned to Martin, and said with reproach, "How could you've walked out of there with nothing?"

"Sexton's word is just as good as Burke's — neither can be verified, or disproved."

"There is a difference!" André protested. "Me and Olga. We've worked with Douglas for a year!"

What made it more difficult, nearly painful, was the certain closeness, a bond that was established between the new partners during the trip across the ocean. Martin found that the three not only worked well together, but also understood one another on a personal level. The meeting with Sexton placed a big question mark over that bond. Martin could not help but wonder whether his partners were victims of Douglas' scheming, or played an active role in everything that had happened since that night on Lake Ruther, and possibly beyond. It was most distressing to lose faith and trust in his new allies, and it showed on Martin's face.

Olga understood his predicament when she said, "My major in university was forensic accounting. I don't think I've gone too rusty, and am quite confident that Sexton's claims can be retraced through the promised paperwork. He must know my background, and the fact that he offered the access to the accounts is no coincidence. Unfortunately, it also means that he's likely telling the truth—"

"Or the books are expertly faked."

Olga shook her head. "If that were the case I doubt he'd choose the bank as the meeting place."

Martin nodded, agreeing with the observation.

"Oh, putain!" André would not have it. "Are you two so infatuated with one another, that you cannot see that Sexton is using us?"

Martin thought that Olga's face blushed before she replied.

"Have you ever noticed anything personal in Douglas's office? If my family was murdered, and I spent years trying to find the guilty, I'd have something to remind me why I was doing it, and for whom. A photograph on my desk would be just the kind of thing that would motivate me, day after day, year after year."

André found no counterpoint to the woman's argument, but did not abandon his contradictory position, keeping his doubts known, and helping restore Martin's confidence in his partners' innocence. He argued for the duration of the ride to the apartment, finding every possible reason for Sexton wanting to send the three of them astray. It became evident, however, that a seed of mistrust was sown in his mind too, when he did not object when Olga used a spectrum analyzer to sweep the rooms for electronic surveillance equipment that might have been placed on Douglas' orders. She found none, and André triumphed. Arguing rekindled, and would have gone on, had Martin not put an end to it with his sober thought, one that could only have been made by a newcomer to the existence of the mysterious Basel Group.

"Everything I know about the Group I've learned in the last two days, and at least half of it is a lie. Is it so inconceivable that some of what the two of you think you know about what appears to be one of, if not the most secretive organization in the world, is false?"

The Frenchman argued for a while longer, but his points were weak. Seeing as the conversation did not progress, he said to Olga in a conciliatory tone, "Maybe you are right on some points. I too thought there was something queer about Douglas.

Olga welcomed the attempt to ease the tension. She winked to Martin, and said, "That makes you a better judge of character, since I suspected nothing. Unless, of course, you have a special nose for these things—"

The Frenchman did not seem notice the last statement, and went on, "I should've guessed earlier. The way Douglas demanded sushi for lunch, supposedly for me, on account that I'm French, I suppose. Or that coffee that was for me, as though any Frenchman would ever be found near instant decaf! And what about that pungent cologne with a tinge of lavender that he wore? Or the impeccably ironed pants and shirts—"

Olga cut into his reverie.

"André, this may come as a surprise to you, but rumor had it that you were… you know…"

André did not comprehend at first. Then, suddenly, his face turned crimson, and he jumped up.

"Me?!"

"Well, you mustn't be surprised, really."

"What?"

"How often do you see guys wear pink mohair sweaters?"

"Pink is the new black! It is very fashionable in France!"

Olga and Martin burst out laughing.

André did not find it funny. With his face expressing the deepest offense, he said, "Gay? Moi?"

His companions could not help it, and laughed gregariously.

"So, you did not believe it?" André found hope in the laughter.

Olga said, after regaining her composure, "Well, I admit, I was a hold out. After all — don't most Frenchmen wear pungent cologne, and dresses impeccably, in pink sweaters, creased tight pants, and ironed shirts?"

"And what about all the passes I made at you?" André did not see the humor in her words.

"Actually, these only seeded more doubt."

"What?"

"You were unsuccessful, and what true Frenchman could not seduce a woman?"

André looked at her with gaping eyes.

"Oh, merde! You nearly 'ad me worried."

He stood up and left the apartment, slamming the doors behind him. He returned about twenty minutes later, a bag of groceries from Ed L'Epicier under his arm. He proceeded to unload deli sandwiches with thick slices of ham in between the bread.

Martin approached and checked the clear containers.

"What, no crispy, buttery croissants?"

"Very funny." André took his sandwich and sunk heavily onto the couch. A moment later the TV screen came alive, highlights of an earlier game of rugby seemingly occupying his every sense.

Martin ate his sandwich, satisfied that his companions were unaware of their boss's duplicity — if any existed. Having witnessed, and participated in the honest, unstudied, and improvised exchange between the two, he even began to doubt his earlier reservations about Douglas. What, he thought, could Douglas have hoped to achieve by allowing Martin to slip away from under his control? If Douglas was the mastermind of an operation so intricate, with Martin and his friends playing an integral role, albeit unbeknownst to them, for over a decade, sending him to France was either a sign of carelessness, or part of the game. Which was it?

39

It was quarter past nine, and the streets were buzzing with crowds rushing about.

"We 'ave company," André announced. "One at the bus stop, and another on the corner, right under the 'otel sign."

"You're right," Olga agreed after a moment of intense, if innocuous observation. "Looks like only the two of them, and judging by the look of them they seem to be local boys."

"Looks can be deceiving." André added with peculiar satisfaction.

They observed the surveillance team for a time.

"We should split." Olga commanded.

Martin objected.

"I don't know the city well enough, to say nothing about the field experience of losing tail."

André clued him in. "It's perfectly simple. 'ave you never watched spy films? You walk straight up, take some turns, walk through a department store, make a left, then right, watch your back, and waive a taxi, change it, then change again, and voila."

"We split two ways, and rendezvous at the bank." Olga cut him short. "But first we ought to find out if there's more of them. You and Martin. Back here in five." With these words she crossed the street.

The men watched as she maneuvered between cars that were stopped on red traffic light.

"Whoa! Some woman, no?" André said and turned in the opposite direction.

"Yes," Martin replied, and followed.

"She's got a lot of— fire. Can you say that in English?"

"Fire. You bet."

"Me and she. Tonight, maybe."

"What?" Martin thought he misunderstood the heavily accented words spoken over the noise of the rush-hour traffic.

"You know." André turned around, and winked.

The look in the Frenchman's eyes explained what was bothering him still.

Martin smiled. "André, at the risk of sounding gay, I'll say you're the most macho Frenchman I've ever met."

They turned left around the nearest corner, and continued for half a block, before crossing the street, and stopping in front of a window to a hardware store. André concentrated on the image reflected in the glass. His face was frowning when he pulled on Martin's elbow, and the two returned to the doorway of their apartment building.

Olga was waiting for them.

"Three in total," she announced. "One is watching the car."

"Merde!"

"The good thing is they're rookies, and not much of a challenge," she went on. "A worthy foe would not've been this conspicuous."

"A worthy foe?" Martin repeated. He glanced to one of the surveillance agents, who did not show any signs of discomfort associated with being found out.

"Someone wishing us harm. These three goofs can't even conceal themselves properly."

"Perhaps it isn't their intention?" Martin suggested. "Why are they acting as though they want to intimidate, rather than harm?"

They looked at him as though he said something revolutionary.

Olga shrugged. She glanced at her wristwatch, and said, "Rendezvous at five-to-ten at the pre-agreed location."

The pursuers proved better skilled than anticipated, and it took nearly three quarters of an hour to lose the tail. Olga and Martin were late for the scheduled meeting with Lawrence Sexton, and their tempers were running high during the last leg of the trip, in a taxi stuck in heavy traffic.

"Monsieur?" The taxi driver said to Martin. "I can go no more." His chin pointed forward when he added, "Le cordonne policier—"

"What? Quoi?" Olga sat up straight.

The driver pointed his finger to the radio.

"Le directeur général du banque… Shot, and killed, only fifteen minutes ago…"

To back his claim, the driver nodded ahead.

They looked to the imposing high wall of the Bank of France towering over a crowd that circled vehicles with flashing lights. Whatever happened must have occurred very recently. The shaken bystanders were in the way of constantly arriving police cruisers and ambulances. Olga and Martin paid the driver, and pushed on through the crowd. Once they reached the front a scene of carnage opened in front of them. The front wheels of a Peugeot limousine were on the sidewalk, just short of the driveway to the gate in the huge wall. From the distance of some thirty paces they could see the devastation made to the car by a heavy caliber weapon. The bullets ripped through the metal, shredding it to pieces; windows were shattered, with shards of glass sprinkled everywhere, and glistening in the flashing lights like diamonds. Some bank employees stood around, dumbfounded, while the arriving uniformed police were trying to keep order among the spectators.

Someone left the crowd and approached the two foreigners. He slipped his arms under their elbows, and said in his heavily-accented English, "The director of the bank and Lawrence Sexton. Shot about twenty minutes ago. Witnesses say that a man and a woman 'ad stepped in front of the car, and fired. They approached the window, withdrew a briefcase, and simply walked away."

40

They were walking quickly toward the entrance to the Métropolitain. Deep creases between their eyebrows expressed what words did not. All three understood instinctively that someone had foreknowledge of their planned meeting with Lawrence Sexton and his banker friend. That someone, as incredible as it seemed, could only be the man who dispatched them to Paris. With Sexton assassinated, which was only a means to the appropriation of the files that could have exposed his operation, Douglas had moved closer to achieving his goals. The only obstacles that still stood in his way were now walking to the subway station, driven by only one desire — to change the equation in their favor.

They had approximately twenty minutes — which was how long it took to get back to the apartment — to come up with a plan. The plan was simple enough, their only possible move — to confirm that what had happened was, in fact,

Douglas's doing. Without that certainty they could not act further. They agreed on that crucial step driven by yet another, a human, factor. Neither held Douglas in high esteem as a person, but believing blindly in circumstantial evidence was not enough to condemn him professionally, after all they had worked with their boss never suspecting him of playing a duplicitous role. Douglas might have been a disliked colleague, but these feelings were irrelevant, given the long list of accomplishments attached to his name. He was an ass of a person, a sentiment shared by many who served under his command, but he was also a veteran officer who had survived major political shakeups and deserved the benefit of the doubt.

They spotted the surveillance team instantly — two men standing in an alcove of a small craft store, feigning interest in sewing machines, their eyes centered on the entrance to the apartment building reflecting in the store's windows. The third man was out of sight, likely keeping an eye on the car that André parked around the corner the previous night. Standing in the staircase to the Metro, their heads barely above the ground level, they understood that capturing the third man was their best option. They agreed to shove the man into the Renault, and drive off to some remote place to question him.

It was time to make the move, but before they ascended to the street level, Olga said, "These guys seem different from the morning shift."

Martin, who had a good memory for faces, agreed.

"That's probably it, then — a shift change." André concurred.

Olga shook her head. "That is not what I meant. There's something peculiar about them. They look different, out of place, foreign."

The men each focused their eyes on the windows reflecting the faces of the two-person surveillance team. They scanned their clothes, or rather — the way the clothing was worn. Underneath long raincoats— never mind the warm, sunny day — the men's shirts were not tucked into their pants — a giveaway of a North American provenance. The bulges under the arms were all too telling that harm was intended. Indeed — something had changed. They decided to carry on regardless.

They waited for a train to deliver a load of passengers, and, mingling with the crowd, they began to ascend the stairs, one after another. André was leading the way, followed by Martin, with Olga trailing behind. They had a reasonable chance of passing without raising attention of the surveillance team, whose attention was on the apartment building. Assuming that only a three-man team awaited them was their mistake. They would never find out whether someone was waiting for them near the car. It mattered little, because, unbeknownst to them, someone else kept an eye on the Metro exit. It became evident when both of the men of the two-person team suddenly raised their right hands to their ears, and spun around to face the staircase.

There was only one thing to do, and André did not hesitate — he turned on his heals and headed downstairs. Martin did not. He could not. He recognized the face of one the quickly approaching men, and his legs froze in place. This was the confirmation they required, yet the realization of it, now unfolding in front of his eyes, though not unexpected, was numbing. It meant that all hope was over. His parents would be dead.

"Martin!" André pulled on his sleeve.

They had to go, and fast. With the passengers gone, they were now exposed, easy targets for even the least experienced shooters, but Borneman could not move.

"Martin!" the Frenchman repeated.

Borneman did not react, his mind desperately probing options that could turn the inevitable.

André took two steps up, and slipped his arm under Martin's elbow, pulling sharply.

Too sharply, Martin thought. He felt the full body weight of his friend, and turned to him. André had fallen to the ground. Stupefied, Martin raised his head, and looked to the approaching team. Compact automatic weapons in their hands left no doubts as to what had happened, bullets ripping through concrete being the additional, undeniable confirmation. André had been shot, but he rose to his feet, and started downstairs. It was that scene, coupled with Olga's pleading eyes, that roused Martin. He followed his friends.

41

They got off at the next station — the only sensible move for anyone expecting pursuit. André was injured, but able to keep pace, his teeth clenched. Two blocks later they located a church surrounded with a gated garden. It could not have come at a more opportune moment since André's trousers began to show signs of injury around the lower left thigh. Olga attended to the wound, which proved non-life threatening, but requiring treatment.

"A clean entry and exit, but you need help," she pronounced. "Is there a discreet doctor you can use?"

He gave her a look of injured pride. "It's only a scrape—"

"We need to stop the bleeding. It requires stitches, and I'm not the seamstress you require."

The Frenchman looked at her before his eyes ventured off to the street.

"Yes, you are," he said.

She followed his gaze.

"Oh, no! No, no, no!"

"If not you, then Martin."

Borneman did not understand. He said so.

"We don't 'ave time. I'll be an impediment unless you patch me up." André nodded to the street, and explained, "That corner store has liquor. Pick something strong, clear. I'm thirsty, too. A bottle of water will do. The place next door, the boutique. They'll sell you needles and thread. Go."

Martin did not argue. He understood that in the field his experience was far surpassed by his two friends. He came back several minutes later with everything André had called for.

Olga examined the purchases.

"*Spirytus*?" She read the label on the bottle,

"I asked for the strongest. The seller said the Polish thing was what I needed."

"Indeed. 98% alcohol. If it doesn't burn another hole, it should help the existing one."

She poured the liquid on the wound.

André clenched his teeth but did not utter a sound. His face turned pale as the needle pinched the skin.

They were occupying a bench in a shaded area of the church garden. Dense leafy shrubs intertwined with a wrought iron fence providing significant privacy, with the only concern being the front gate through which passersby could see the trio, but the presence of a bottle at the feet of the bench was enough to explain the writhing.

Soon the area surrounding the wound became numb, and the pain bearable. Color returned to André's face.

"Tell me: How do you like field work so far, *deskman*?" André noticed Martin's pale face and could not help the biting remark, though it was delivered without malice.

Olga replied, instead, with relief expressed by a smile, "I wonder if I sewed up the correct gaping hole!"

They all smiled.

The woman continued, "Glad you're feeling better, but you still need a doctor."

"The kind of doctor I need most right now is in that bottle." André reached for the Spirytus.

"Not so fast!" Olga poured some of the liquor on her hands to rinse off the blood. She mixed the rest with water, and handed it to André.

He took a swig, and then examined the label.

"It tastes like something from a medicine chest," he said.

"It is."

"And they drink this in Poland?"

"Does it help?"she replied with a question.

"It does."

"Then no wonder that they do."

She took the bottle, drank from it, and passed it to Martin who followed in her example.

André extended his hand.

"Sorry," she said. "We need to stop the bleeding, and this won't help."

She and Martin took turns to empty the bottle, drinking in silence, each pondering the events of the day.

At last Martin asked, "Anyone else saw what I saw?"

The looks in their eyes told him that they did.

"It was the redhead from the Kawartha Facility. What's his name?"

"Jack— something." Olga replied somberly.

"Jack-what-the-fuck. It means that Sexton was telling the truth." Martin summarized.

"That's not the worst of it." Olga said.

"What could be worse?"

"The fact that we've been lied to, and we don't know why."

They each reached for the bottle, and caught themselves realizing that it was empty.

"Right." André said. "Drinking our sorrows away will not 'elp."

"But it appears to be all that's left to do," Olga said, while her eyes, inadvertently, ventured off to the corner store. "We can't turn for help to our agencies, not without knowing the full extent of Douglas' penetration."

André looked at her.

"It is unlikely that we should ever find out the full truth, but even a tiny fraction of it may 'elp."

They saw it in his eyes that the Frenchman came up with a plan. They awaited details with their eyes fixed on his lips.

"I will 'ave to 'ack."

"What?" Martin gasped out with disappointment.

"I will 'ack."

Borneman looked helplessly to the woman.

She shrugged.

"I'll start with the DST servers, and go from there." The Frenchman said with irritation, and stood up.

"A hack." Martin understood at last.

"You 'ave computers in America, don't you?" André said over his shoulder, and limped to the street.

They followed him. In a city as abundant with coffee shops it took only half a block to locate one that offered Internet access terminals. Olga and Martin kept watch outside, while the Frenchman did what he set out to do. He emerged some ten minutes later, a deep crease between his brows.

"Let's move," he said. Several blocks later, as they waited for a green light at a crosswalk, he explained, "There's good news, and there's bad news. The first surveillance team, this morning, was from the immigration. They received a tip about three illegals staying at an apartment that was reported for suspicious activity. Frankly, in that part of town, that should be any apartment, given the population of illegal immigrants. The strange thing is that the team was called off about quarter to ten, this morning."

Olga and Martin exchanged glances.

"Just when we thought we lost them." The woman said.

"We didn't. Their orders changed." André said, mercilessly.

"Was about the good news?" Martin asked.

"You pick which is good: Word is that Lawrence Sexton and the director of the Banque de France were killed by a man and a woman who matched your descriptions. They were aided by a driver bearing an uncanny resemblance to me."

"Shit." Olga said.

"How could this be good news?" Martin asked angrily.

"They— or we, are described as rogue agents serving an unnamed, but clearly a malevolent force."

The light changed. They crossed the street. They walked another block, in silence.

"I don't get it." Martin said. "Why would Douglas confirm our identities, instead of simply finishing us off? It's like he's handed us over on a platter."

"We did get away rather easily, didn't we?" Olga agreed. "Sorry, André, but in hindsight, it is rather remarkable that a team of supposed assassins would bangle the operation so badly, at a distance of some dozen steps."

"That is, perhaps, the good news." Martin thought out loud. "Douglas needed to extract the evidence held against him by Sexton. He sent us to Paris to draw it out. As you may recall," he said to Olga, "Sexton suggested that Douglas letting me out of his sight wasn't necessarily a thoughtless move. Well, we helped him extract what he was after, but apparently our part in Douglas' scheming isn't over. He's still got a role for us to play."

Olga grasped his elbow. "And that is the really good news! It means that your parents are safe."

He nodded. "For now."

"And that is Douglas' biggest mistake."

The Frenchman's words startled them. They gaped at him in stupefaction.

André explained. "Douglas should've understood that we'd see through his scheming."

"Perhaps he did! Perhaps we are meant to see through it!"

"I know I do! Jack wasn't 'ere to assassinate us. 'e was 'ere to send us a message. Feeding our details to the French is a part of it."

"The message being?"

"That we are to return."

"What for?"

"I'm sure Douglas thinks 'he 'as a plan, but it doesn't matter. What matters is that 'e underestimated us, and it will be the end of 'im!"

Olga and Martin exchanged glances.

The Frenchman went on, a grin of satisfaction on his face, "It gives us time to prepare a strike against this ass'ole!"

42

Hotwiring a Citroën sedan took Olga under a minute. Sitting behind the wheel, with André as the guide, she drove the vehicle along the busy périphérique without asking questions. It was not until she was directed to join the N12, heading for Brest, that she cast the injured friend questioning looks. The Frenchman's reasoning was simple: the priority lay in leaving France, and while expediency was preferable, it was even more important to achieve the goal safely. They understood that Douglas wanted them back in the Kawartha Facility — sending his sidekick, and feeding the French with their identities, was a message. It was the only way to persuade all three of them to return, since neither would trust Douglas having learned from Sexton the truth about his scheming. That he expected them back was as encouraging as it was disheartening — it meant that Douglas had additional plans for them. Unfortunately, it also suggested that they had no choice. André was determined to take the latter into his own hands.

"How do you propose to do that?" Olga asked.

"Douglas expects us to play into 'is screenplay, to do the expected."

"He wants us back in the Facility."

"Precisely. And we're going to be there, but on our own terms, maybe even with a little twist."

"A twist?"

"I'll stay behind, and create a diversion, something that will keep Douglas guessing. An element of surprise is our only chance."

They did not argue with the logic. All that was left was to agree on the details.

"Keeping Douglas' 'hounds occupied in France will buy you time."

"Did you say: Douglas' hands?" Martin asked.

"Douglas' dogs! That's what they are. They will follow my scent, or rather the scent of money. You will leave your bankcards. I will use them to convince the dogs that we are still in France."

"It might work." Martin said thoughtfully. "Not for long, but it may buy us time."

"I don't know if I like us splitting forces." Olga said.

"It's necessary. Plus — we'll be working together, if at a distance. It's the kind of long-distance relationship that will work."

They appreciated the humor — it lessened the tension and helped the spirits run high. André seized the opportunity to lat out his plan, convincing his friends that together they could outwit Douglas. As every intelligence officer, or indeed any cop in the world, André left certain aspects of his work out of the official reports that were filed during his work on various cases. Some things that were found out during an investigation, but were not pertinent to the case, were not mentioned but kept in a private folder for future use. Every cop in the world had his own sources of information that were kept out of the official channels. They invariably came in handy when restrictions imposed on security forces hindered performance. André too had his sources to fall back on. One of these sources was a fisherman named Kerloc, who could be found in a tavern in the small town of le Coriquet on the shores of the Chenal du Four.

Jacques Kerloc was a retired fisherman whose sons carried on the family business. Illegal fishing and smuggling of goods to and from the Channel Islands and beyond, by way of Ile D'Ouessant, was the main occupation of Kerloc and sons. But the business was able to remain operational only thanks to a rookie DST officer's scarcity of words when it came to filing reports some years earlier. Kerloc was a crook, but he was not connected to the case André had worked on at the time. Rather than pass him on to the cops, André kept the findings of the old seaman's activity to himself. This was the time to repay the favor.

Kerloc had fulfilled his promise. He had arranged transport for André's friends — a two-engine aircraft. It would take off before sunrise. He was glad to do it, he owed André more than that. He wondered who the couple were, but then again — he always wondered who were the people that he helped smuggle to a better life. André's friends were his friends. Kerloc smiled at the thought. His friend would have been helped by the local doctor by now, and no doubt was waiting at the tavern over a tall glass of absinthe. Kerloc licked his lips and smiled at the thought of returning to his second favorite occupation after smuggling.

Olga pressed deep into the seats of the small aircraft, watching the brightening sky. Her mind worked frantically. The parting with a friend under such circumstances, the unknown of the days to come, and the terrible suspicion of the true objectives of the colleagues with whom she worked for over a year, day after day, had a disheartening effect. She was struck with the full magnitude of the loneliness that loomed ahead. She had no one to turn to, no one to trust and fall on until more information was available on the scope of Douglas' schemes. They teach spies resourcefulness and survival skills, but those always have a clear direction: contact the nearest station, return home, or survive until help arrives. Without the station to turn to for help, without someone to trust, one is all alone. Loneliness of a spy is one of the most heartfelt.

She shook her head to part with the gloomy thoughts. Her eyes fell on the man across the aisle. As she glanced at her companion she realized that regardless of how bad one had it, there was always someone else who was worse off. She watched Martin rest his head against the window — a tired and torn man. His was not an enviable situation. Hers was a professional conundrum, but his was personal. Then, suddenly it struck her. There was no *him*, or *her*. It was *them*. They were not alone. They had each other.

The trip across the Atlantic was arduous for one seeking quick passage. The route via Faeroe Islands, Iceland, and Greenland, was dragging due to low flying altitude and aircraft used. A favorite among organized crime groups, it was a safe and established way. Planeloads of cash from the drug trade in the United States and Canada destined for laundering through banks in Luxembourg and Liechtenstein, before being transferred to South America, covered the route with regularity of scheduled airliners.

The length it took to cross the Big Water was not easy for one desperate for a resolution, but the shared misery and looming danger acted as a magnet. Before the landing on an ice strip on Baffin Island they had caught up on each other's biographies with the hunger of long-lost friends. They found that their conversation, purposely personal in nature, devoid of the professional haunts, was more than a way to pass the time. It worked as a binding element.

They had already covered topics from elementary school, family trips, and eccentric relatives, to books they read. It was time to become more personal. The onboard menu, while consisting of simple sandwiches shared by the pilot and his sidekick did not lack alcohol, which proved to be as friendship-binding as it is justifiably famous for. They were ready to talk about anything.

"Is there a Mr. Duchesne?" Martin asked during the last leg of the trip across the ocean.

"Too many overtime hours to find time for one. And, to keep him." Her voice was devoid of self-pity.

"And on the inside?"

"In CSIS?" She said it in a voice that meant — don't make me laugh.

"It's one of those professions where dipping your pen in company ink is outright recommended." Martin smiled.

"Really, though. Think of the single or unattached guys at the CIA." She paused, but it was clear that she did not want the subject to end. She needed to vent. She looked out the tiny window, and said, "The only ones worth anything are on the outside, but it doesn't last. There's only so long they can keep up with the charade. Sooner or later they begin to ask questions, turn jealous. Not really surprising, I suppose, what with the periods of absence that sometimes have no good cover story."

"Hear, hear. We're not that different from celebrities, who, for better or for worse, only date and marry within own circle, only we do it out of the limelight."

"Is that why you and—" She blushed.

"Jeannie?" He caught her eyes just before they shifted away. "I felt that we actually hit it off as normal people do. Only, it didn't last, either."

"Is it over?" This time she did not look away.

He thought about it before replying.

"I think so."

"Oh?" She caught the hesitation.

"I do feel for her, what with the ordeal she went through because of me. I mean — I don't even know if she's alright." He paused abruptly, realizing he was making excuses when he actually did feel guilty for having involved Jeannie.

"She has vast experience in the field, does she not?"

That she does, he thought. A little too much, given her specialty, so much so that it often left him jealous, wondering what she had been up to in her pursuit of targets — male representatives of foreign diplomatic and business missions.

Olga did not pursue. She knew what Jeannie's job involved. She understood that in such circumstances a breakup was unavoidable, if no less painful.

43

They switched aircraft on an ice strip in Iqaluit, whereby another one delivered them to a private aero club in the outskirts of Ottawa. Communication with André was not possible while in the air, but now required immediate attention. With the resources at Douglas' disposal it was crucial that any communication be conducted securely. To achieve any level of surprise, Douglas had to be convinced that all three of them were nowhere close the Kawartha Facility. It was perhaps the only way to save the lives of Lydia and Oliver, assuming they were still alive, which was not out of the realm of possibility — what was another day or two for a man who had the means and resources to pull off a scheme of such magnitude and carry it out for as long as Douglas did? Indeed, it was in Douglas' best interest to keep his collateral safe until such time when the obstacle that was Martin was no longer in his way.

André would ensure that their whereabouts would be traced to Paris, and they had no reason to doubt the scheme. It was reasonable to expect that the bank cards issued by the Facility would remain operational — withdrawing money was traceable, and Douglas would keep the cards active in order to keep abreast of the fugitives' whereabouts. Unfortunately, it also meant that no cash could be withdrawn in Brittany, now leaving the two with limited financial resources. The arrival on Canadian soil was the point in which the shrewdness of Douglas' position and the difficulty of her own became most apparent to Olga — Douglas' connection with the Canadian security apparatus, and particularly the unknown extent of it, meant that Olga could not turn to any of her sources.

In essence — they were broke.

"Have you stashed some emergency funds, somewhere?" Martin asked without much hope.

Olga shrugged. "I don't know how it works south of the border, but here you're more likely to owe the service than to scrounge anything out of it. The red tape is terrible. Besides, I never conceived that it would actually come in handy some day."

They had little money and no prospects of acquiring any more without raising alarm that would inevitably ring at the Kawartha Facility. Yet they desperately required a vehicle, and reliable communications equipment, to say nothing of the almighty cash.

Olga suggested, "Any ethical objections to stealing?"

The question took him off guard. Objections? Despite his training with the CIA, and his holding a job responsible for the lives of field operatives, it was perfectly obvious who in their two-person team held the upper hand, who was the leader in the field. This woman had proven, day after day, that no amount of theoretical training could outperform true field experience. He knew that she was not really struggling with ethical barriers — after all the rule of survival, as taught at the academy, was that there were no rules; one took any steps necessary to accomplish one's goals. She had proven already that no such barriers existed for her when she hotwired the car, or used the drug cartel's aircraft to sneak into Canada. So what has changed? He studied her face closely and suddenly he understood: It was not a cold-blooded and ready to use any means necessary intelligence operative talking; it was a woman determined to uphold a feminine image in his eyes.

He shrugged. "We have a job to do."

Jimmying a lock was an easy affair. They were in and out of a computer repair shop in minutes. They hotwired a car that they singled out in the parking lot of a small suburban mall, and abandoned it an hour later in a residential neighborhood. Downtown Ottawa was cluttered with office and government buildings. They crossed the Rideau Canal and passed the Château Laurier. The area was popular with students of the Carleton University. Trendy, if unassuming, restaurants and bars dominated several square blocks. They entered a bar where several groups of youthful patrons occupied all but three of the smallest tables. Two waitresses meandered between the tables taking breakfast orders, and giving Olga and Martin enough time to assess the loot. The knapsack they picked up in the computer shop contained whatever they could stash in it in haste — some cash, a credit card that did not expire for another year and might be valid, a notebook computer, as well as several other items. Martin powered on the computer. It was not the newest model, but they chose it purposely, for it was unlikely to contain tracking devices. He exhaled deeply upon finding two open wireless networks, one of them provided by the bar. Four postings under prearranged nicknames, all belonging to André, awaited in the previously agreed on Usenet groups. In all — two messages were broken up into two separate postings each, and each part was submitted to a different group, each containing half a message, in case of intercept, though chances of either message raising attention were remote considering the cipher being used. It was simple but effective. To a casual reader they were innocuous messages containing descriptions of restaurant menus, with prices. Numbers and letters. It was all a cipher was. Should either message be targeted by electronic surveillance, they would not stand up to the modern decrypting capabilities of the eavesdroppers, however, the messages would have to have raised attention, and the chances of it were next to nil, unless André was under surveillance. Martin remained positive in that respect. In any case he expected the affair to be over within days, knowing that even the ECHELON required time to filter intercepted data through its dictionaries, before the data was analyzed and properly distributed to interested parties. Time was what they were up against, to be sure, but time was what worked for them just as it did for the enemy. The winner would be the one who would make better use of it.

Martin wanted to ask a waitress for a pen and paper in order to decipher the messages André had posted.

Olga was wary of the time it took to locate the newsgroups and the messages of interest.

"Save them to the disk. We should move."

The nearby stores selling fresh produce from local farmers attracted shoppers from across town, and finding a car suitable for the next leg of the journey was a breeze. Removing the plates and switching them between two cars took less than ten minutes.

Olga explained, "Most drivers won't notice their plates were changed. Switching plates between different makes will give us extra time when the car is reported stolen. A day or two is all we need." She noticed Martin's gaze. "A miracle tool, though standard issue, so to speak."

Martin extended his hand. She handed him a very thin piece of extremely durable polymer — no thicker, or bigger, than a credit card. Made for intelligence operatives and crooks who required emergency tools for their trade, it easily passed through unwanted scrutiny, such as airport scanners; it fit in a wallet, and upon inspection resembled an ordinary credit card complete with appropriate logos, an account number, and cardholder's name. Only under close observation one noticed the perforations that concealed various curves, sharp edges, and holes shaped into hexagons and other forms. Each shape could be punched out, and what popped up was a tiny but useful tool. In all, the card contained a screwdriver, a saw, a can opener, and, as Martin had just found out — what amounted to a license plate remover.

They were on the road heading southwest of Ottawa before Martin deciphered the messages posted by André. He read them out loud. In the first one the Frenchman was not certain how long he could keep up with the charade, and he urged quick resolution. He ended the message with a warning that no other form of contact was to be initiated until the integrity of the safe house provided by André's friend in Paris could be confirmed. In his second message, André described the safe house and the help he received through the friend — a colonel in the Directorate of Military Intelligence. He urged extreme caution as the source of the information that followed could not be confirmed. Word was out that after the assassination of Lawrence Sexton, the Basel Group had entered into talks with the dismissed Director of the CIA, apparently on the latter's initiative. Together they released a warning and a call for Martin to beware of Clarity.

"What's Clarity?" Olga glanced at him from the driver's seat.

"Clarity is part of the few truly secure networks in the world, not subjected to the NSA's eavesdropping; this on the express wishes of the Secretary of Defense. The network is used between the top brass at the Pentagon and the White House, and Clarity is the emergency line."

The woman shot him a peculiar look.

He explained. "It is part of the new and increased role the Pentagon plays in the national security arena, whereas the

Defense Secretary gets a free hand in decisions necessary to protect the United States."

"So the Pentagon wants to talk to you, and wants to make sure that no one eavesdrops." She whistled, impressed. "What do you think?"

"I think we have nothing to loose by contacting Clarity, but we should remain vigilant. André is of the same opinion. He sends a number for a secure relay station provided by his buddy from the military intelligence."

Olga thought about it for a moment, and said, "I think you're right — you have nothing to loose and everything to gain. Just let's hope that the relay station is as secure as André thinks, or the element of surprise we are banking on will be lost."

"But only if Clarity proves hostile."

They considered the possible implications of contacting Clarity, and decided to use the cellular phone that was left in the car. Being on the move was safer than standing at a phone booth if the relay station proved not as secure as André believed it to be.

Martin dialed the number to the relay station, followed by the number to Clarity. The relay station automatically re-directed the call through a series of secure proxy switchboards that were scattered around the world. Tracing the call, while by no means impossible, would depend on the duration of the conversation, and the encryption used to hide the proxies.

A series of clicks and high-pitched sounds followed, and the phone was answered before it rang.

"Martin?" A worried woman's voice came on the line.

The sound was as clear as though the woman was sitting in the seat beside him.

Martin recognized the voice instantly. He replied in utter astonishment, "Jeannie?"

44

It was Jeannie, alive, and well.

"Martin! Thank God you are alright!"

"They told me you were captured!" His voice combined worry and disbelief.

She cut him short, and was speaking hurriedly, as though afraid the line may go dead, "I'll tell you all about it another time. Suffice it to say that the episode hadn't gone to waste. I found out things. Scary things. Things you ought to know. There's a man called Douglas Burke. He's done a lot of bad things. He's a traitor, Martin. He's fooled a lot a people, lots died because of him, and lots more will die if he isn't stopped. I cannot underestimate how dangerous this man is. So much so that his plotting has solidified interagency cooperation. The CIA, the Pentagon, even the Feds, we're all working together to bring this man down. We've tracked him to a site called the Kawartha Facility. It's a top-secret intel installation in Canada—"

"Jeannie, I—" Martin tried to interject but she did not hear him.

"Martin, there's more. This man, Douglas Burke, he's the man responsible for the kidnapping of your parents, and the killing of your friends—" She hung her voice abruptly.

Martin could not help but say it, despite gentle nudges from Olga, "I know."

"You know?"

"I know about Douglas Burke. I know about the Kawartha Facility, I'm heading there right now—" The nudge into his ribcage took his breath away.

Jeannie's voice was filled with alarm. "Martin, you mustn't!"

"Yes, I must! Douglas has got my parents!"

"I know. We've dispatched a team to the Facility. They know about the hostages, and are instructed to rescue them!"

Good old Jeannie! She did not waste her time, but neither will Martin.

He said forcefully, "I'm going in, Jeannie!"

"Douglas is extremely dangerous." Her objection lacked some of its earlier vehemence.

"So am I when I'm pissed, and I'll be damned if I sit on my ass while my parents are at the mercy of this psycho!"

She tried to reason with him. "This is a highest-priority national security case, Martin. It is being handled by a multi-agency task force—"

"They can all got to hell! The CIA, the Feds— Jeannie, the Feds had the cabin under surveillance, and they allowed my friends to be slaughtered! I won't let them mess it up with my parents!"

His words were met with a momentary silence. At last the woman spoke, "I understand, Martin. All right, then. You don't trust anyone but yourself. But do you trust me?"

He hesitated, but only because, at last, Olga's signals had reached him.

He replied mechanically, "Yes."

"I won't let anything happen to Oliver and Lydia. They will be alright, you hear me? But you must promise that you won't do anything on your own."

"Jeannie—"

"I'm sorry, Martin. I can't let you mess up this operation. What I'm offering you is that you wait for me, and we'll go in together." She paused for several seconds to let the words sink in. Then she added, in a different tone, "Lookit, Martin, things might not've worked out between us, but we were good friends, and friends help friends. I'm here for you, and for Lydia and Ollie. Let me."

The surprise of hearing Jeannie's voice wore off, and with it came rational thinking. He knew that Jeannie was right. He could not do it alone. He needed help.

"All right," he agreed.

All that was left to do was to schedule a meeting place. The motel Jeannie suggested was located some twenty kilometers from the Facility, on the outskirts of Bancroft, only hour away for Martin, but five hours to the rendezvous.

"I don't like it, not one bit." Olga voiced her opinion when the call was ended. She was angry that he gave away their location so easily, but she suppressed the urge to reproach — it could not possibly make any difference now.

They did not speak for the remainder of the drive. Martin sensed Olga's reproach, even if she did not dress it in words. She did not have to say anything on the subject — he was angry enough with himself. He could not help giving away their location and intentions, even if these were given to a friend and an ally — one does not reveal such sensitive details over the airwaves, particularly where his own communications equipment is not secure. The incident made him realize that he was losing grip of his mind; the pressure caused by the treachery, and magnified by the proximity of his parents, affected his judgment. He understood it, if belatedly, and glanced to his companion, his eyes filled with appreciation for her level-headedness. Soon his mind was occupied with her presence, recalling the moments they spent together, and imagining those still to come.

45

The Woodman's Inn was not the sort of motel one would spend holidays in, not even a weekend, unless one had no choice. The Kawarthas did not lack lodgings that drew visitors regardless of the season, which left some who appreciated the remoteness and the privacy of the Woodman's, however uncomfortable and unwelcoming it may have been. Olga and Martin belonged to the latter group, who found the establishment ideal for the sort of meeting that would commence in a mere four hours. With only two cars in the parking lot, and one of them belonging to the receptionist — as Martin casually verified — the place offered the much-needed privacy to plot the next move.

Having taken adjoining rooms, they convened at Martin's. Refreshed, they set out to study the crude plans of the Kawartha Facility, as drawn by Olga on a scrap of paper. Their aim was to establish the most likely location of Olivier and Lydia's detention. It was not an easy feat. The Facility comprised kilometers of underground corridors, conference rooms, offices, and strategic command centers, all guarded and accessible by way of electronic and biometric identification passes. It was the use of the passes that helped narrow down the criteria. The areas Douglas could hold the elderly couple were limited to those to which his task group was restricted. And restricted it was, for whatever its importance, Douglas' operation was but a small wheel in a huge tribe of the intelligence community that was housed in, and operated out of the Facility — apart from the CSIS, Olga's employer, there were also quarters assigned to the CIA, the MI6, and numerous other services of the Anglosphere countries. Olga decided to concentrate on the most secure, and thus restricted areas Douglas' section was assigned — the communications center. It was a logical choice, and the most likely, as being the only one to which neither she, not André, had access to. She highlighted the layout of corridors that led to it, as well as explained the nature of offices that surrounded it. The time Martin spent at the Facility helped him visualize the location, which, in turn, led to building confidence that a successful resolution was possible.

The clock on the wall was ticking. The realization of the passing time, and of the nearing resolution, was unnerving. In several hours the fate of his parents would be decided, and Martin could no longer think about the upcoming operation. He needed a reprieve, anything to offer his mind a break from the endless plotting. He watched the woman, and he admired her ability to contain herself, to concentrate on the task at hand, and to remain positive. He realized how close they became in those past several days. She was not only a supportive colleague, but also a compassionate soul, whose presence he so appreciated in these times of uncertainty. There was no doubt in his mind that had this been anyone else he might not have been able to hold on to his senses during the trip across the Atlantic. Ever since he found out about Douglas' treachery he lost his wind. It was

Olga's positive energy that fueled his. The inability to act would have driven him insane if not for the woman's presence. It was in the small confines of the aircraft, during the long flight, that he first felt the closeness that could not be mistaken for anything but affection, and a mutual affection at that. It was evident now, in no uncertain gestures, or words, that his fledgling feelings were returned. It was as though a spark flew between them. Sitting shoulder to shoulder over the drawn plans, their fingers touching as they followed the lines of the corridors, they both realized their feelings. Feelings that could not be ignored.

Suddenly, Olga rose to her feet, her face blushing. Their rooms were joined by a set of two doors, the arrangement working as a suite, or as separate rental units. She disappeared behind the doors, and Martin thought he heard the lock turned. He was considering his next move, when a knock on the main door drew his attention.

He glanced to the wall clock, and decided to disregard the visitor.

The knock was repeated, louder, more forcefully.

Martin rose to his feet and approached the door.

"What is it?"

A woman's voice called his name.

It could not be! Bewildered, he glanced to the clock again. Three hours to the scheduled meeting.

"Jeannie?"

With the chain in the latch, he opened the doors a notch.

Jeannie Domagala stood outside, a smile on her lips.

He took a step back to unlatch the thin chain, when the door flew back at him, breaking the lock, and knocking Martin to the ground.

Two bulky men rushed inside, and pinned him to the ground. With the corner of his eyes Martin saw a semiautomatic in one of the bully's hands, while the other scanned the room, checked the bathroom, and tried the door handle to the adjoining room — it was locked.

Jeannie entered the room.

46

They observed one another for a minute or so, speechless. What Martin saw in the woman's eyes was enough to dispel any doubts about the forced entry.

At last Jeannie said, trace of genuine sadness in her voice, "I hope you can appreciate how difficult the situation is for me."

Martin staggered to his feet, the barrel of a pistol aimed at his abdomen. One of the thugs motioned him to sit down, and Martin complied, taking a corner of the bed.

With his eyes on the woman's, he asked in a grave voice, "Did you kill my friends?"

"Of course — not!" Jeannie was offended. "What do you take me for?"

"For someone whom I thought I knew, and loved—"

"Oh, spare me the sentimentality! You died for me that night on the lake."

"But I'm still alive."

"Douglas enjoys the challenge of risky games."

It was the dispassionate way in which she said it that roused him from the state of incredulity induced by the surprise of finding out her treachery. He assessed his chances. The room was small, but, regardless of its size, he doubted if he could reach the pistol held in a firm grip, and aimed at his head. He did not allow the hopelessness of his situation to dissuade him — he was left with a single option, and he had to try. He had to.

He spoke only to divert the attention away from his feet — moving them ever so slightly. "Douglas will be exposed. There are bank records in France—"

She made a gesture with her hand, as though waving off a pesky fly.

"With no hope there is no pain of disappointment," she said. "I suggest you forget about it. There are no loose ends. The Bank of France — that sounds mighty fancy, and one would not want such questionable associations. The director of the Bank purged all records from the system, so as not to slander the institution. The only hard evidence was kept inside his private residence — in itself an impenetrable fortress, hence your travel to Paris, to help draw the evidence out."

Martin placed his right foot forward, ever so slightly ahead of his left one, and braced himself on the edge of the bed frame. In order to mask the move he acted surprised, and said, "There are always loose ends, no matter how carefully crafted an operation."

She looked at him closer, and for a moment he thought she noticed what went on in his mind.

"It's not too late. You have a role to play. It was written for you and your friends, but you can carry on."

"What makes you think I will participate?"

"You will."

"Alone, where the original script called for five?"

"You and your two new friends will do just fine. Oh, don't look at me with these puppy eyes. Of course we'd not let the Frenchman and the Canuck out of our sight. See, I know the woman's here. One of my men is waiting for her, next door."

It took extraordinary effort to conceal the rage her words evoked, and even greater to act as though he could not care less. The only sign that his blood was boiling, urging him to lunge for Jeannie's throat, was in his eyes — he could not bear looking at her. Turning to one of the thugs, and recognizing the face as that of the driver who picked him up from Judge Ferguson's, Martin said through his clenched teeth, "How's your head?"

The thug's only reply was a caressing movement of his thumb sliding gently over the handle of the pistol.

"The only question is — how painful you want it to be?" Jeannie went on. "You can try and put on resistance, in which case we shall have to use appropriate measures to elicit your cooperation, or you can accept your fate, and you won't feel a thing."

"Really, Jeannie? What about the pain in my heart?"

He thought for a brief moment that something stirred in her, but it might have been one of these circumstances — not uncommon among field agents — where they experience what can only be described as a premonition, a warning that arrives from the depths of the unknown.

Jeannie's eyes drifted to the phone, a split second before it began to ring.

"Answer it," she said.

Martin did not move.

The woman approached the bedside table and brought the telephone over. She picked up the receiver and kept it between her ear and Martin's, with the palm of her hand covering the microphone.

The words that poured out of the speaker rendered him speechless.

"Hi, sweetie! What's taking you so long? Been waiting down here forever. Come down already, the beer is getting flat."

245

Jeannie replaced the receiver. She glanced to the two thugs, and said, "She's in the bar. Both of you, go, and bring her over, quietly."

She stood back, and drew out a pistol from her holster. The thugs left, and Jeannie approached the door to the adjoining room. She knocked, while keeping an eye on Martin, the barrel of her pistol never swaying away from his torso.

"What did you do to my parents?" Martin asked, while simultaneously flexing his muscles.

"They're safe, and will remain so, as long as you do what you're told."

She listened at the door, and repeated the knock.

"Are they at the facility?"

"Is there a safer place?"

She knocked again, and listened at the door. The lack of response was not what she expected.

Martin could sense Jeannie's alertness and frustration rising. It was now or never. He was about to lunge at her, when he heard it. Something in the adjoining room was moved, as though a chair was dragged on the floor, followed by the sound of the lock being turned.

Jeannie relaxed, and half-turned to the door.

"What the hell took you so long?" she said, and reached for the door handle.

At that moment the door flung open, hitting Jeannie on her shoulder and her face, the force of impact throwing her across the small space that separated her from the bed. She landed in Martin's arms. Blood tricked from her nose and the upper lip, but she did not lose the grasp of the pistol.

47

Olga rushed in to the room, her arms extended in some form of hand-to-hand combat style. She froze in place at the sight of the most peculiar scene — that of two bodies, intertwined, and swirling around in complete silence.

It was Martin's fault. The sight of Jeannie's bloodied face delayed his reaction, but the moment was seized by the woman, anger and hate making her strong, giving her the energy of a puma. She clung onto his neck, choking him, viciously trying to strangle her former lover. He could not bring himself to fight back, the force of her attack throwing him into a spin. With the woman clinging to his neck he kept turning in place.

Olga stood aside, watching helplessly the swirling mass of arms and legs. Realizing that it would be up to her to end the silent wrestle she approached, and attempted to separate the two, in the process receiving a powerful blow from Jeannie's swaying boots. The impact threw her to the small space between the bed and the wall of the bathroom cubicle.

The door to the room swung open, and one of the thugs walked in. He was stunned by the sight, but it lasted only a moment.

"What the fuck!" he roared, and reached to his holster.

With the pistol in his outstretched arm, the man wavered. He could not risk firing, lest he injure Jeannie. He observed the scene in helplessness, his anxiety rising with every turn of the bodies, as the woman clung the pistol in her outstretched arm, held straight by Martin's strong grip of her wrist. With each turn of the bodies, and the pistol aiming at him, the thug had to duck. At last, unable to withstand the pressure, he raised his arm and aimed for the mass of two bodies. He waited for just the right moment. When it came he squeezed the trigger, while, simultaneously, his arm was kicked up by a leg that appeared from behind the cubicle wall.

The sound of the shot was still ringing in the confines of the room when Olga's heel landed in the killer's throat in a figure skater's pirouette.

At the same time Jeannie's grip loosened, and she slid off Martin's back, her body slumping onto the carpet.

Martin's head was spinning, and he would have, perhaps, fallen, had Olga's arms not slid under his arm pits. She allowed him to slump onto the bed, where Martin watched in awe as the thug frantically grasped for air, his hands embracing the crushed windpipe. Diverting his eyes from the scene of the painful death, Martin's gaze rested on the body spread out on the carpet. He focused on the dark blot on Jeannie's forehead. His lover lay dead at his feet, and Martin found himself strangely relieved.

"Help me!"

The voice reached him as though from the clouds. He looked up, and saw Olga struggling with the thug, dragging his body away. It took him a while to realize what she was trying to do. He rose up, and together they dragged the thug along the hallway, propping his body against the door, thus blocking it. Martin watched as Olga went back, quickly picking up whatever belongings she could find among the terrible mess scattered about the room. Before leaving, she frisked the two bodies, taking particular care in removing ID cards that hung around their necks. She pulled on Martin's elbow, and they rushed to the adjoining room, where a body of another man was stretched on the floor, laying in the small space between the bed and the bathroom cubicle. Martin did not show surprise, breezing through the room in a dazed state.

The downstairs lobby was brightly lit. They crossed it in several brisk steps, and realized their mistake a moment too late. In order to reach the doors they had to pass by the entrance to the bar. With the lights subdued there, anyone passing through the lobby was as visible as a bright moon passing on a dark sky.

A bullet shattered the door frame, confirming that they were, indeed, noticed.

Another bullet shattered the passenger side windshield as soon as they sunk into the car seats.

They ducked. The parking lot was lit indirectly from floodlights above the entrance to the motel, turning the fugitives into blind targets on a shooting range. They had no choice but to try for it. Olga started the engine, and hit the reverse gear. With both their heads below the dashboard, she changed gears, and pressed on the gas, turning the wheel. They heard the bullets grazing the metal of the getaway vehicle, and thought they heard the cursing voice of their pursuer. Soon they were surrounded by dark forests and starless sky.

"We go in now!" Olga shouted through the noise of the wind coming through the shattered window.

With one hand on the wheel, with the other she felt for the bag she threw on the gearbox. She found the mobile phone she picked up from Jeannie's pocket, and keyed in a number. Martin asked no questions, listening to the credentials she gave to the Ontario Provincial Police officer who answered the call. She did not mince words describing a bomb threat at a secret government facility located in the Kawartha Highlands.

48

Ten minutes later they turned off the highway, and drove along an unmarked gravel road that curved its way between huge granite rock. The ID cards seized from Jeannie and the thug had opened the automatic gate that led into the compound that housed the Facility. The guard who manned the post was there only for dealing with visitors, and possible irregularities; he merely glanced at the vehicle occupants. It was the security check inside the building that worried Martin. Here security personnel manned detectors that all employees and visitors went through. But the detectors scanned the bodies for objects not allowed inside, as well as those banned from being taken out. The ID cards, believed to be foolproof, were the ticket in. It was the universal human folly of believing in digital technology that allowed Martina and Olga to enter one of the most secure locations in the country unhindered. They passed through the security based on the supposed fail-proof digital fingerprints of the

IDs, but the ease with which they entered the Facility had alarmed Martin.

"I don't like it," he said. "The shooter must've alerted his cronies by now."

"I think it spells good news," Olga tried to sound reassuring. "It means that whatever is happening, has not corrupted the entire system."

They took an elevator to the fifth level below ground. The corridor, cut in granite rock, was narrow, and reminiscent of sterile science labs, with the architects having done their utmost to conceal the rock behind the walls so as not to cause claustrophobic phobias among employees. It was eerily quiet down here, save for the hum of the air vents. Olga led the way past empty offices — deep recesses cut in the rock — meeting no one on the way, which was not unusual given the hour. It was not until they reached the area that served as a kitchen that they ran into a woman and two men, who stood around the coffee percolator, arguing. Olga and Martin's arrival startled the team. The woman's hand froze midway delivering the coffee mug to her mouth, while one of the men smiled uncomfortably, and the other one muttered a curse, and started for the door, past the newcomers.

Olga stood in the doorway, blocking the way.

"What's the matter, Paul? Seen a ghost, or something?"

The man did not reply. He was the communications officer. His normally pale face was paper-white.

"Where are they?" Olga pried.

The three stood uncomfortably, neither volunteering to answer.

"Where are the Bornemans?" Olga repeated forcefully.

Two of the officers exchanged looks, and shrugged. They appeared genuinely puzzled.

The communications officer turned his head, avoiding eye contact.

"Paul?" Olga approached him.

He said nothing.

The woman did. She said, "What are you doing here? How did you even get in? Your passes were revoked!"

"By whom?" Olga asked.

The woman shrugged, and said, "You're supposed to be arrested."

"Care to tell my what for?"

They looked nonplussed.

"We've just been wondering about it ourselves," said the third man. "Perhaps you could tell us what's going on?"

"Really, Dan? You have no idea?" Olga said sarcastically.

The expression on his face was that of genuine puzzlement. It angered Olga.

"Enough of this nonsense. Where are they?"

"What the hell are you talking about?" the woman asked.

"I'm talking about this man's parents, Kathy." Olga pointed to Martin. "The Bornemans whom Douglas kidnapped and is using as collateral. That is what I'm talking about." She turned to Paul, and added, "They're in the comm. center, are they?"

The communications officer shook his head, but did not raise his eyes.

"There's no one here, Olga!" Kathy cried.

"Look for yourself," added the man called Dan. "Everybody's gone; only the three of us are left, and our orders are to start packing."

Olga was at a loss.

"They're dupes, just like you," Martin said.

She looked at him. She recognized burrowing resignation in his eyes.

"I can feel it in my gut that we are close," she said with conviction. She turned to the three officers, and warned, "If I were you, I'd start looking for good lawyers. You'll need them."

They were too stunned to ask: Why?

"You— We've all been participating in an operation to overthrow the government of the United States."

They looked as though they were punched below the belt.

"I thought something funny went on in here," the communications officer said. "I swear, I had no idea that it was this bad, though!"

"What are you talking about?" Kathy and Dan asked in unison.

"It's Douglas! He's been doing… things."

"What things?"

"Things he shouldn't have."

"Goddamn it! Can you be more specific?"

"Like rerouting traffic behind my back."

Kathy looked at him as though she was beginning to understand.

"I thought the comm. center was off limits to anyone, including Douglas?" she said.

"It was."

"He couldn't possibly use the comm. center, his pass would not let him." Dan said quietly.

"He did not. He used the comm. through a remote site."

They were perplexed.

"Hacked?" Kathy asked.

"No. It was a built in backdoor entry."

"What does it mean?"

"It means that all those security measures that preclude unintended use of the comm. center were built with the bypass in mind. Douglas was using our comm. center from a remote site, in order to mask his true location."

Kathy and Dan looked at Paul, then at Olga. Their faces confirmed their innocence to the scheming.

"Did you not think of alerting someone?"

"I did. I was told that everything was fine. But it smelled, so I've kept logs, you know, to protect myself when shit finally hit the fan."

"Can you tell where Douglas was connecting from?" Olga asked.

"Sure can." All eyes on his face, Paul explained, "Level seven."

The revelation stunned everyone, save for Martin.

"I don't get it," he said, helplessly.

"Bad news, but it explains a lot," Olga clued him in. She pointed her index finger to the floor, and said, "Two levels below. Sort of a diplomatic section, untouchable, off limits to Canadians, even though it's on their soil, or underneath it as it were. It's used by the Pentagon."

"Pentagon? Here?" Martin asked doubtfully.

"Actually, it's much worse. It's entirely run by the Pentagon's S3."

49

Minutes later they were on their way to level 7. Kathy and Dan insisted on coming along, and hesitated only a moment, upon seeing Olga emerge from her office with a Glock.

"I suggest you arm yourselves, too." Olga said.

The idea that Douglas could be involved with the Strategic Support Section, or S3, was incredible, but to suggest the need for a weapon was absurd, for regardless of the agency affiliation they were all on the same side.

It was not quite so obvious whose side the S3 was on, according to Olga. She gave Martin a quick rundown as they rushed toward the elevators.

"Rumors about level seven have been around almost as long as the Facility itself. When its existence had leaked out it caused uproar among the opposition parties, with the government continuously refusing to confirm, or deny, the reports. When the rumors of level 7 first emerged, the general perception among the staff occupying the other sections was that if there indeed was level 7, then why not 8, 9, or even 29? To this day the Canadian public doesn't know the answer."

"What is the answer?"

"According to those in the know — level 7 is very hush-hush, and off-limits. It houses the S3, which conducts reconnaissance in Canada, as well as in other allied countries. It fills the niche that was left void because of limits imposed on the CIA's activities, which, as rogue as they were, were still bound by some rules of conduct and responsibilities. The S3 is not bound by such conditions. Responsible directly, and only, to the defense secretary, the unit comprises highly trained officers that are pulled from various organizations. Among its staff are intelligence officers, linguists, interrogators, technical specialists, spin doctors, propagandists, and special forces, among others—"

"Special forces?"

"It is, in fact, the main reason of concern for countries that house these units, usually unofficially, hiding the fact from the legislative branch of the government, as in the case of your rendition sites. Often employing mercenaries, with the ability to strike at any given time, in any spot on Earth, and on sole orders of the secretary, not surprisingly the unit became a diplomatic sore point in US relations with its allies."

They had stopped in front of the elevator banks. Olga pressed the key.

"Why is the S3 in Canada in the first place?" Martin asked.

"In the first place? Because it is so rogue, and operates so far out of the scope of the US judicial system, whether civilian or military, that it would have to be shut down by your law enforcement agencies."

"For doing what?"

"Perception management. Overthrowing governments. You name it."

"And the Facility serves as what? Headquarters of the S3? Why here? Why in Canada?"

"It's like being home. One can work on domestic US issues, away from the prying eyes of watchdogs and the likes."

"Here we go." Kathy announced.

The elevator doors slid open and they filed in.

Dan pointed to the keypad, and asked, "How do we get there?"

Martin looked at the keypad. The lowest key was 6.

It was the last, or the lowest, of the staffed floors of the Kawartha Facility. What was below was officially described as the remainder of the old mineral mine, access points to which were blocked in order to seal off the Facility from unauthorized penetration — a necessity given the unknown extent of the mining shafts, many of which were naturally occurring. Each of the levels that housed offices and labs, stretched out for many kilometers, but no floor was identical, as the architects of the Facility had utilized the naturally occurring corridors — cracks, really — in the huge granite rock. As it was based on naturally formed tunnels, as well as man made shafts, with no level resembling the next, finding the location of the Bornemans' likely detention was not an easy task. Olga hoped that Jeannie's pass would lead them to it. She was not mistaken. As soon as they descended to level 6, the card's display changed, showing a layout that included entry points that were otherwise unmarked. One such entry was a huge reinforced wall that slid open as the sensors detected the pass. A narrow and brightly lit shaft, not unlike all the others in the Facility, led them to another wall that slid-open when the sensors detected the pass cards. Here the corridor descended, and split two ways, small plaques and arrows on the walls pointing toward different sections. Olga led the way to the right, where the corridor was much wider, and lined with doors on either side. Some doors were made entirely of steel, others had glass windows. The first common-use room they passed was a lounge, with armchairs, pinball machines, card tables, and newspapers. A television set was switched on, and tuned to a news network. Not a soul was present. They passed dozens of empty offices and living quarters until they reached a canteen with fresh groceries and a bar. It resembled a self-contained unit, which explained, perhaps, why no one has ever seen any of the S3 employees in the general cafeterias. Voices pouring through the open doors indicated that level 7 was not abandoned, after all. Indeed, as they walked by they saw that the canteen was also a movie theater equipped with a huge screen. Some half a dozen men were focused on a game broadcast, not paying attention to the hallway behind their backs. Loud sounds were pouring from surround speakers and concealing the intruders' footsteps.

Unnoticed, they passed the canteen, then a bank of vending machines, and entered a short corridor with a set of steel doors in the middle, and another door at the end of it. A panel above the first door had two small lights — a green and a red. The red light began flashing as they neared. The door had no handles, and prying at it yielded no results.

"What now?" Martin wondered out loud.

His question was drowned by the sound of a shot that was followed by another, and another. Olga had fired three rounds to a spot in the door where she expected the lock.

Martin understood. He pried, but the door would not give in.

"Up there!" Dan pointed to the upper frame. "I bet it's exactly the same as ours."

He was correct.

Olga fired three more rounds, exposing a bolt.

Martin and Dan rammed into the door together, and this time it gave way. Behind it was the communications center — the most secure of all offices in any intelligence agency where an environment secure from modern eavesdropping techniques was required. The room was dark, the only sources of light being computer monitors. Banks of computers and electronic equipment lined the walls. They provided enough illumination to expose three figures standing in the farthest corner. Two of them were the Bornemans, and the third was the communications officer with headphones over his neck, and an automatic pistol in his hand.

50

"I won't hesitate to use this." The communications officer warned, his pistol aimed at the newly arrived. His face was partly obscured by the overall darkness, but his voice betrayed extreme anxiety.

"Let them go," Olga said calmly, with a commanding voice.

"I have my orders!"

"Let them go if there's any decency left in you."

"You've forced your entry into the property of the United States. You have less than two minutes to leave the premises, before this place blows up." His voice was shaky, indicating his deteriorating self-control.

"Our comm. center is wired to self-destruct if security is broken." Dan announced dispassionately, merely stating the obvious.

With Kathy and Dan behind her back, and Martin at her side, but as though not present — his eyes fixed on his parents' — the resolution was left to Olga. Her mind was working frantically. Shooting the officious officer was the foremost option, but by no means offering a certain outcome — the dark and confined location could result in injuring the Bornemans.

Olga's unenviable quandary was answered by dramatic circumstances: A string of violent obscenities were followed by shots fired in rapid succession. Ducking, she span around, to witnessed a scene of carnage. The man who gave them chase at the motel was standing in the doorway, cursing, while simultaneously squeezing the trigger of his automatic. Kathy, being closest to the door, and in the line of fire, was thrown forward by the impact of the bullets, her body hitting Martin, both falling onto the ground. The turn of events had exposed the communications officer, who, being already at his wit's end, had returned fire. Lacking field experience, he failed to properly assess the situation, and emptied his magazine into the one who was, undoubtedly, his ally. He continued to squeeze the trigger long after the assailant's body hit the floor.

Olga was the first to come to her feet. Martin followed, and rushed toward his parents. Dan stood up slowly, his left hand clasping his right forearm, his face in pain. Two bodies remained on the ground, lifeless, oblivious to the drama unfolding in the small confines of the room.

Olga assessed the situation in a single sweep of her gaze. With her eyes on Martin in the embrace of his parents, she cried, "We've got to go!" Seeing as her words had no effect, she approached and tugged on Borneman's shoulder. At last, the gesture roused him to action, and Martin led his parents out of the comm. room.

Olga followed, passing Dan who stood over Kathy, his eyes darting between her dead body, and the communications officer. Olga tugged gently on his arm, but this time the gesture had a different effect. Awakened from a paralyzing shock, Dan lashed out, in two steps reaching the officer, his good fist landing in the man's jaw, and continuing the mutilation without caring that he was hitting the wrong person. In Dan's sorrow, the communications officer, still holding the gun in his drooped hand, was the epitome of evil that killed Kathy. The two of them fell to the ground, where the attack continued. Olga tried to separate the two men, but in the process she received a powerful elbow blow into her abdomen. Picking herself off the ground she saw the futility of her attempt — she could not possibly stop the man who was avenging the death of the woman he loved, an affection that was known by his colleagues.

She was ascending the narrow corridor to level 6, following in the Bornemans' footsteps, when she heard a series of contained explosions. Dimmed lights encased in protective crates began to flash, as the four continued to climb to the surface. Soon they were joined by others, some in a state of panic, and still others who contained their fear behind a mask of stoic calm.

The main floor was in upheaval. Plain-clothed officers of the Kawartha Facility were mixed with uniformed security personnel who failed to gain control of the panicking crowd. It was no use. An explosion was heard through the elevators shafts, and, to some extent, through the staircases. As secure as the Facility may have been, working deep under ground brought out the deepest fears of being buried under tens of thousands of tons granite rock. Compounding these fears was the never satisfactorily explained presence of the Pentagon's rogue unit in the deep shafts of the country's premier intelligence center. In the havoc that ensued no one was checking passes and ID. The four fugitives — who otherwise would have plenty to explain — were now able to flee into the crisp air of a September night in the Kawartha Highlands.

51

They drove for about an hour, passing police and emergency vehicles that headed in the opposite direction. At last Olga pulled off the highway, and found a quiet spot on the bank of the Otter Creek, where, with the soothing sound of flowing water in the background, they spent much of the night catching up on the events of the last days. With the affection satisfied, they spent the remaining hours before dawn in pursuit of the most plausible ways to scatter the clouds that hovered over the days to come. Keeping absolute secrecy in the confines of the S3 quarters was not possible, and keen observers that the Bornemans were, they drew conclusions from the smallest details, such as the growing tension among the staff, even snippets of conversations that no one bothered to hide from them, with the majority of officers not even aware of the role the elderly played. It was thus that the Bornemans were able to deduce that a major operation was about to take place, but what this operation entailed they could not tell. One clue involved the talk about an undetermined weapon.

"Any mention about its potency?" Martin asked.

They could not tell any more than the staff being convinced of its effectiveness.

It was not enough to draw conclusive answers.

Martin asked his parents to recall any words, or terms, that were used in conjunction, or in a conversations involving the mention of the weapon.

The elderly thought for a minute, before they began to speak, each word stirring memory in the other person.

"Effective range. … DNA. … The national guard. … Deployment. … Containment. … Genetic modification. … *Pohtoos*—"

"Potash?" Olga cut in.

They both shook their heads.

"No. It sounded more like *pohtoos*."

"POTUS, perhaps?" Martin suggested.

Olga looked at him, suddenly understanding. She said, her voice incredulous at the realization, "POTUS! The President of the United States!"

"They're going to do it!" Martin said in a like manner.

"To do what?" Lydia asked.

"They are going to kill the president, and overthrow the government."

The mother and the father looked at him doubtfully.

"They seemed the least likely to fit the bill."

"How's that?" Martin asked. "Does an assassin look the part?"

"It's not that," Oliver tried to explain. "It's more to do with what they represent — they were soldiers, Martin. Why would the military want to assassinate the president who keeps the wars going, finding new territories to conquer and occupy, and laying foundations for ever-growing military presence in all aspects of public life? It just doesn't make sense."

Martin shrugged, while stating the obvious. "That is the key — if we find the sense behind the plan, then we'll find who benefits from it."

"But where do we start?"

"The Kawartha Facility seems the obvious place."

"We can't go back," Olga said. "There'd be little point in it, now that the S3's presence there has been confirmed, and the OPP, and the RCMP, are on the scene. With that kind of a spotlight they'd have fled by now."

"Then we follow them."

"How? We don't even know who they are."

"Mom? Dad?" Martin would not give up.

The Bornemans exchanged looks.

"Everything about them spelled military," Oliver started. "From the way they carried themselves, to the way they interacted, though, instead of weapons, they used computers. When they walked us to the washrooms, we could make out what was on their computer screens — schematics, and graphs. They worked on those around the clock."

"What were these schematics of?"

The parents exchanged glances.

"Couldn't tell. Except, perhaps, that one time, when the door to one of the rooms that was usually closed, was opened, briefly, just as I was passing. Inside looked as though a science lab, not that different from ours, at Georgetown. The first thing that caught my eye was a huge digital TV screen, with a man in a white frock giving a presentation to an audience of some higher-ups, judging by the reverence displayed by the presenter. On the screen was a DNA sequence."

Martin said after a period of baffled silence, "Military scientists, and DNA. What the hell could they be up to?"

"Jeannie, and her thugs, were unlike any scientists I ever met." Olga was thinking aloud.

"Jeannie?" Lydia asked in alarm. "Wasn't your… lady friend, called Jeannie?"

"You mean — you haven't seen Jeannie among the staff?" He replied with a question.

It was too much for Lydia. "Lucky for her she did not show her wretched face, or she'd've heard from me!"

Oliver embraced his wife, attempting to calm her, but Lydia would not have it. She went on, venting what she suppressed for years. "You should never have allowed yourself to be recruited by the CIA, not after all our family had been through! Bunch of liars and hoodlums! And that woman— how could she! Oh, Olie!" She turned to her husband.

Oliver said to Martin, "The day you quit your association with the CIA we celebrated. We thought it would be over. When will it end?"

"Mom— Dad—" Martin was at a lack for words. He looked to Olga for encouragement.

She said with merciless agility, "There's only one way to confront the enemy who wants to fight. We'll give them a fight."

52

The first glow of rose-colored sunrise garlanded over the horizon when they pulled in to a farm near Bobcaygeon. The owner was an Ojibway man whom Olga had befriended some years ago, when natives joined forces in waves of protests that swept through the province. Joe Crow and his family were placed under surveillance by the country's security services. Olga and other officers who were part of the intelligence team investigating the Ojibway, and who quickly realized the absurdity and illegality of their orders, simply passed the time by learning the locals' customs instead of spying on them. Joe Crow was very much involved in the peaceful protests, but the orders to report on all his, and others' relations, and whereabouts, were what many officers despised after an unarmed protester was shot dead. It was perhaps thanks to this approach that Joe was able to stay on his farm rather than sit in jail while maple syrup season — his main means of income during those last months of winter — passed him by.

Joe Crow owed Olga a favor, and giving shelter to two fugitives was a bargain compared to what he would have suffered had she not been lenient in her reports. Joe's children, now teenagers, adored her for the colorful tales of foreign lands she so interestingly painted during the closing winter months that she spent under cover of a substitute teacher in the local elementary school. Olga was a welcome guest on Joe's farm, and her friends were friends of the family.

Joe proved helpful in another matter. A cousin of his lived in Quebec, a short hike from the border, and would be able to guide them across to the United States. They could abandon the stolen vehicle, and drive Joe's pick up to the cousin.

The Bornemans were not content to be left out of Martin's pursuit, but they accepted the need to give their son a free hand. Their being captured was a tremendous hardship, as well as a restraint, on Martin's actions. He could not permit personal affairs to affect his judgment again. They parted not without sorrow, the mother's eyes glistened with tears.

It was not until they reached the suburbs of the capital city that they could use wireless networks to connect to the Internet, and download a message from André. It contained an encrypted URL address to two other groups where two messages awaited. Each contained a part of a telephone number, and a demand for an immediate contact. Once again the call was to be relayed through the secure switchboard of the military attaché of the French embassy in Ottawa.

"I suggest we treat it with caution. Don't want another Clarity surprise," Olga said. Make it quick and dump the mobile out the window. These things can be located to the exact spot."

Littering was not necessary — the mobile phone that they picked up the day before had already been disconnected, and the one they appropriated from Jeannie was surrendered at the security checkpoint at the Facility. They drove on till they found a bank of payphones in the west end outskirts of Ottawa, outside a busy discount mall, where weekend crowds rushed by with excitement that only bargain-hunting bestows. It was a good place to make a call and disappear.

Olga made the call.

"Everything we feared is about to materialize!" She said five minutes later, after Martin pulled Joe's truck out onto the street. "André was contacted by a Basel Group member." She glanced at the notes she made on a scrap of paper. "A Frenchman named Pierre de la Tour, who insisted that Douglas is about to launch a coup d'etat."

Martin turned his head and gaped at the woman.

"Eyes on the road! Eyes on the road!" She cried out.

He hit the brakes. The truck might have been old, but Joe kept it well maintained. The fender bender with the car in front of them was missed by a touch. Still, Martin was more excited by the news than the near miss.

"Can André verify the source?"

"He's working on it, but says it's as good as verified, because the intelligence circles are abuzz about an imminent coup in Washington. The conspiracy is wide-spread. André says that the armed forces stand behind it, and there is even a hint as to who has been chosen to replace the president. Can you guess?"

"We went to France to attend the same meeting were the Basel Group summoned its favorite. Apparently the Basel Group lost out to Douglas and his camp."

"Care to take a wild guess who that might be?"

He glanced at her, perplexed. He thought about it for a minute, and gave up.

She said the name.

He looked at her, again. "I don't believe it."

"Think about it. Being the military's pick, it would have to be someone popular with the military, as well as with the public so as to achieve some level of acceptance of the coup. He doesn't like the president, and his policies, and is tired of playing the second fiddle."

"I thought they were friends, though."

"Apparently his friendship with the president is not as strong as the bond that developed with Douglas. De la Tour claims that the connection goes way back to the days when Douglas and his candidate served in Vietnam. As POWs they spent months locked up in the same cell."

To Olga's surprise Martin smiled, as one does at seeing the end to a long, and arduous road.

He said, "Don't you just love it when the pieces of the puzzle begin to fit into place?"

"We're still missing many of the pieces. The question is: How do we find them?"

"We're going to pay a visit to the Vice President."

53

Joe Crow's cousin lived in a small cottage on Châteauguay River. He was well known in the area for the wooden native carvings, which he sold at the Huntingdon country fairs. The artistry was not enough to pay the bills, and George Tortoise picked apples on local orchards, or poached in the woods on both sides of the border. More importantly — he knew the ancient trails that were used to carry contraband across the border, only nowadays, instead of furs, George smuggled tobacco and alcohol. It was a nice supplement to his measly income.

Even though George insisted that he could drive them across the border by means of a dirt road that he used regularly, Olga did not want to take that risk — too much was at stake. They decided to cross on foot. They left after sunset the same day. George parked his pick up behind the Garden's Delights store, just off the highway, and they walked the two kilometers to the border. The path meandered through the woods, forking in several places. Martin admired the native man's ability to find the right path without the use of a GPS device. He tried, just for fun, to memorize the number of left and right turns, but had to give up. If truth be told — he thought they walked in circles. As it later turned out they did — George wanted to make sure the pass was safe.

Two hours later they reached the home of George's friend, Henry Ruisseau, where they spent the rest of the night. In the morning Henry drove them to Malone where they got on the bus.

Later that day two messages from André presented a gloomy prospect for their investigation.

Through De la Tour, André appropriated a document that proved that his earlier revelations were true. Douglas Burke had done a short tour of duty in Vietnam, where he was the commanding officer of the battalion in which the vice president had served during the final stages of the war. Only Douglas Burke was then called Douglas Brooke. The scanned Pentagon documents were posted on a secure server located in the Netherlands and owned by the Basel Group. Those included photographs and service records of Douglas and the vice president.

The documents looked authentic enough, and although with caution, Olga and Martin decided to treat them as such.

The second message demanded an immediate contact via the secure telephone relay at the French embassy.

They used a payphone located at the shopping mall, not two blocks from the motel, their heads close together to make use of the headphone.

"Our asset at the Eglin Air Force Base in Florida 'as alerted us to a break-in, which occurred last night," André began. "I wouldn't think much of it 'ad Martin not mentioned the conversation with 'is parents the day before. Eglin is a major munitions storage, and a weapons research center."

"Oh, God!" Olga understood.

"I'm afraid it's true," André confirmed her fears. "We don't know what was stolen, but from the report from our asset, we must conclude that it is something major. Our source tells us that the researchers from the base 'ave gone berserk, although the military officials are downplaying the incident."

"Oh, I think we cannot have any doubts as to what happened down there," Olga said. "Canadian Intelligence has been aware of research into new types of weaponry being conducted at that base, and we are as interested in finding out more about it as the French are, and indeed the rest of the world."

"What types of weapons are we talking about?" Martin pried.

"Of the more interesting, albeit futuristic, they are researching antimatter weaponry," said the Frenchman.

"You enjoy popular fiction, do you André?" Martin winked and realized belatedly that André could not see his ironic gesture.

"The common thought is that these are still a long way off," André agreed. "The primary issue being the containment. But my friend suggests that it's part of a disinformation campaign, and that, in fact, antimatter weapons are closer to completion than we are led to believe. Still, I think that we're dealing with something else, just as experimental, but infinitely easier to 'andle."

"Such as?"

"Our source says that a delivery was made recently to the Eglin Base from the biolabs in the Dugway Proving Ground."

"A biological weapon?" Olga asked.

"That is the big question," was André's reply.

They thought about the implications. Too many questions mounted, none could be voiced. Time was running out.

"We can't stay in this booth much longer," Olga said.

The Frenchman was an experienced officer and came to the point, wrapping up the conversation, "Our source says the operation at Eglin was done extremely smoothly, almost as though aided from the inside, which supports the case that the military is in on it. Of course the entire incident might only be a coincidence, but a pretty darn timely coincidence, if you ask me."

Before hanging up, they agreed that another form of contact must be worked out, preferably over the Internet. Then Olga and Martin wandered the streets for over an hour before arriving at the motel. They did not talk much on the way, their concentration on making certain that they were not being followed.

They checked in to the motel separately, having chosen one that did not insist on credit cards, and stayed on different floors. The wallets taken from Jeannie and her sidekick contained credit cards and bank cards, none of which they dared use for fear of being traced. The three hundred and sixty dollars in cash, also found in the wallets, was not a lot of money, and they realized with dismay that they would soon have to get a hold of more funds.

On the way the stopped by the nearby shopping mall, and came out with two bottles of red wine, and some basic provisions.

About an hour later, and with the first bottle emptied, Olga returned to the topic they left off when they hung up with André.

"The base is a major weapon development site. I don't believe in coincidences, and am inclined to agree with André that the supposed break in is connected to our trouble."

"The plotters need a weapon to carry out the coup? What kind of a weapon would they need?"

"Other than the tanks, and missiles, and the entire military arsenal?"

"Perhaps it's not enough? Perhaps the plotters fear stiff opposition, and need something more powerful."

"This antimatter stuff?"

"Antimatter, or positron weapons, are the most powerful energy source known to us, much more powerful than thermonuclear weapons, where one gram equals the destructive power of tens of thousands of tons of TNT; they are of great hope for the military as they leave no nuclear fallout, and as such the military actually stands a chance of using them in battle without destroying the planet."

"But isn't antimatter weaponry a thing of fiction?"

"I'd call rather it a wish list. Given their potency someone out there is after them for sure."

"Just how powerful are we talking?" Martin asked, and topped up her glass.

"In layman's terms?" She thought about it as she turned the glass in her hand. "If you had very deep pockets, and could produce steady containment to fit this wine glass, and were to detonate this anywhere in D.C., this country would be left without government. Luckily for us and some 7 billion others, we're talking about incredible sums of money, where a commercial production would run into billions of dollars per gram. I doubt the Pentagon has room in their budget for such expenditures at this time. This isn't the Cold War."

They sipped their wine for a few minutes, before Olga picked up the subject.

"Since the base is a well-known research center, it is possible that it was not the potency, but the weapon's novelty that attracted Douglas."

The wine was doing its thing. Gone was the tension of the past days. They discussed deadly scenarios without that tinge of urgency that would be there otherwise.

"Perhaps you're right," Martin nodded. "Perhaps it's not a weapon itself that was the subject of the heist, but a research to the development and production of it? But, assuming that it was a weapon, and we ought to take it into consideration in light of the plans for the coup, what could Douglas do with it? What kind of weapon could he use? How would it be transported? If we could answer any of these questions we might get an idea of what his plans are."

"Eglin is an Air Force base, which may suggest that whatever we're dealing with is air-delivered." Olga suggested.

They were sitting on the bed, the second bottle of the inexpensive wine nearing the bottom.

Olga tapped her finger on the glass requesting a top up. While Martin was pouring the wine, she said, "Why would Douglas need a whole new weapon, when he's got the military backing him?"

"And he's had one at his fingertips all along: the Tox-Chip, with which he could kill off whoever is implanted with it?"

"Perhaps the way the death is delivered is of importance? Perhaps he wants to apply the shock of gore? Death through the Tox-Chip is undetectable, as the toxin is entirely absorbed by the body, whereas, say — a bomb — may deliver a more psychological impact."

Not able to come to a conclusion they drank in silence for some time, each pondering multiple scenarios, but finding no satisfactory answers. After days of poor sleep, and excessive stress, they were both exhausted. The alcohol was calming and relaxing, but on the downside their minds were slowly dissipating into nothingness. The conversation waned. To rekindle it they talked about their intelligence work, slipping further back, to college years, and childhood.

Talking about college brought back memories of Martin's friends, and the murder at the cabin.

Olga touched his arm and spoke gentle words that only made him more vulnerable.

She leaned over and embraced him.

54

The electoral office was located in a leased space, in a spacious, ground-level venue, three blocks from the J. Edgar Hoover building. Several unmarked SUVs were parked at the curb, with Secret Service agents spread out strategically outside, indicating the presence of a distinguished guest. It was shortly past 6 in the morning, and Vice President Rick Manley was not impressed.

"How dare you!" He uttered through his clenched teeth.

"Did you not serve under Douglas Brooke?" Martin persisted, unmoved.

They were sitting at the table in the farthest corner of a large room. The polling team had showed up in full to shake the hand of their candidate. They moved the posters and pamphlets around in an effort to look busy, all the while glancing at the angry figure. The vice president was unlike the person they knew from television. Gone was the image of a composed and quiet, nearly submissive senior citizen, his entire bearing epitomizing an angry beast.

"Who put you up to this?" Vice President Manley asked composedly, in stark contrast to his facial expression, making his words the more ominous.

"As I already told you on the phone—"

"Your conscience!" Manley cut in, barely able to contain himself. "I remember, but I'd like to know why you're bringing this up now?"

"Why am I bringing up the fact that you served under Douglas Brooke, and spent months with him in a POW camp? Why am I bringing it up now?" Martin said mockingly, his words intended to be the answer.

"Don't trifle with me, son!" Manley warned. "I've served my country to the best of my ability, and as honorably as permitted at time of war. That part of my life is well known to the American people; it is part of my campaign. Standing in the front lines, ready to give life for this great country is not something the opposition's candidate can boast of."

"Does it really matter which old man can get a longer-lasting erection? Why don't the two of you settle this like men, outside, in the back alley, instead of mudding the entire nation with your filthy backstabbing?"

"It's clear you know little about politics."

"Enough to know that only social degenerates vie for political office."

"That's a matter of opinion that you are free to express because you live in this greatest of all places."

"I thought I did, until—"

"Yes, yes! At last you come to the point. That is what you said on the phone — that someone on my staff is involved in… irregular electoral activities."

"A coup d'état is not a mere electoral irregularity, though it probably has become such in your politico doublespeak."

"Enough of this! You said you have proof of my staff's involvement. Speak now, or I'll have you arrested." Manley nodded to the Secret Service agents who stood at the ready not five paces away. "What is your proof of this preposterous allegation?"

Martin pushed back in the chair.

"I am it." He said.

"Explain." Manley did not show surprise.

Martin described the events of the past days, starting with the murder of his friends.

"Which part of your teary story suggest that I am, somehow, involved?" Nothing in the politician's voice, or on his face, indicated that he had foreknowledge of the events.

"Your previous association with Douglas, starting with the military service."

"You are talking about ancient time, long before you were even born."

"Of course, it's only secondary to your injured pride."

"My what?" Manley looked at him, puzzled. Then he burst out laughing. He laughed a long time, before replying, "I'm a politician, or a social degenerate, as you just suggested. Do you think I could be driven by such human emotion as pride?"

"Your injured pride has little to do with being a human being, and everything to do with being sidestepped in your bid for the presidency. You've been plotting with Douglas to overthrow the government because the Basel Group chose not to put your candidacy forward. Frankly, I don't give a damn who gets to occupy the Oval Office. I want Douglas. Give him to me."

Manley froze during Martin's emotional outburst. Changes on his face indicated growing anger mixed with incredulity.

"Now you listen to me. I don't know where you got all this nonsense from, but if I find out that you're Douglas' plant, I will have your balls fed to my dogs."

He stood up, turned to one of the Secret Service agents, and said so Martin could hear, "Shoot him if he so much as lifts a finger."

"With pleasure, Sir." The agent grinned, as his hand rested on the butt of his pistol.

Vice President Manley drew out his smartphone; he fiddled with the keys, and pointed it at Martin. He took a snapshot, and walked away dialing a number.

He returned not five minutes later, his face changed.

"So you're *that* Borneman." He said.

"Come now, Mr. Vice President. You knew who I was from the start, which is why you agreed to see me in the first place. Either that, or it's your guilty conscience."

Manley waved off the agent, and continued in an appeasing voice, "I'm a politician. I have no conscience. I thought you'd know that being the son of your parents, and running The Hill Gazer. I have nothing but deep respect for their work. You are their son, but that is not why I agreed to meet you. It's because you said things about events which you should not be privy to, and because you are a part of them. A huge security machinery has been put on alert because of you. I don't know how you became involved in this, but I will find out. Meanwhile, you can start by telling me how you learned about Douglas, and be as attentive to detail as you can. The future of this country depends on it."

55

"You've been duped and you should know this much by now." Vice President Manley summarized when Martin's narrative ended. "I gather from your employment with the CIA that you're not so innocent yourself, and so it should not shock you when I tell that the unit I served in, under Douglas' command, was an intelligence operation disguised as an army battalion. It was short-lived, disbanded if you will. Douglas was pulled back to more important tasks. Officially Brooke died in action and Burke was born… and then disappeared. He resurfaced in another part of the globe, and with a different set of objectives." Manley hesitated for a moment. Then he said , "Douglas was what you might call an assassin, but not just your typical contract killer; he was more of a policy guardian. He took care of the most prominent cases — political, and military leaders, chiefs of intelligence agencies, the cream of the cream of those whom our country considered obstacles to freedom and democracy.

You can verify this by following Burke's postings versus death announcements, or sudden resignations from government posts. His last assignment was to the United Kingdom, and in a somewhat evolved capacity. He did not have the mandate to kill, but rather to help steer that country's policy in the right direction. As a highly placed mole, his position came to reap rewards when Europe was uniting. Douglas was there to ensure that the key people in the British administration knew what was important to the United States. His presence, as well as access to key, if dirty, information, assured good cooperation."

This sounded all too familiar to Martin. He said, sarcasm permeating his every word, "Let me guess — Douglas made sure that no matter whom the voters cast their votes for, the candidates would be people sympathetic to our policies. Isn't this how it works in the United States?"

Manley did not appear to be put down by the cynicism. "The White House does not govern unilaterally. The people are still represented by their elected officials, and their voices cannot be disregarded by the president." He added in a voice that signified the end of the subject, "I am aware of your work with The Hill Gazer. I understand where you stand, but this is not the time to debate our political differences."

"Mr. Vice President! Everything that's happened has to do with the politics."

"We'll have a heart to heart about it someday, I promise, but now we must save this country. America cannot afford to be weakened from within, not now, not when outside forces threaten to overtake us economically, when banana republics are turning red again, and when the Middle East regimes want to detonate their WMDs on our soil—"

Martin watched the statesman speak with the zeal that was in stark contrast to the man known from television — a mere stooge who posed for photo ops. He was now a man with clear vision, a man who would not stop from carrying any means necessary to forward his way.

Martin asked, "Is this not why you have teamed up with Douglas? Are you not scheming to conduct a coup, to replace the administration, and institute tyranny or, as the doublespeak goes — to consolidate power, in order to strengthen the country?"

"Nonsense!" Manley shivered in anger. "Preposterous lies!"

The vehemence in the vice president's voice confused Martin momentarily. He recovered, and pressed, "Are you not conspiring together? Were you not involved with the commission that appointed Douglas to the new role, that gave him the new identity?"

Manley considered his reply for a few seconds.

"Douglas was assigned a job vital to the interests of the United States."

"Assuring political unity across the nation. I've heard that before. But are those the interests of the people of the United States, or of the elites?"

Manley was losing patience. "Look, son, I can't give you Douglas. This man knows enough to bury this country politically. I can't risk letting you mess this up."

"The man has taken possession of a deadly weapon, probably a WMD, and you worry about the political fallout?"

"How did you figure out it was Douglas' doing?" Manley asked in a tone of voice that spelled out respect for Martin's investigative ability.

Martin kept a stone face. It was true, then. Douglas did break in to the Eglin Base. He pressed, "Every spy holds a powerful trump card — it's called information. But information, combined with weapons, and no oversight, means power. And power, as you know, corrupts. Douglas' ability to wield power is dangerous and must be stopped."

Manley dismissed the idea with a wave of his wrist. He said with confidence, "A single man cannot alter the course of history."

"Perhaps not, but one man's idea certainly can when it finds enough followers. Douglas is not working alone, he must have powerful backers to have gone this far. Together they will change history. He must be stopped. They must be stopped."

Manley shrugged, and said, "I am assured that Douglas will be caught within a matter of days." He glanced at his wristwatch. "I think that you've been through enough already. Step aside and let me deal with this."

"Your jumping to each others' throats does not interest me, but Douglas killed my friends and kidnapped my parents. This is personal. I want the son-of-a-bitch."

"Son, this is too serious for a slip up. My advice to you is to leave it. You must drop it, or I'll have you locked up until this is over."

"No, you won't." Martin reached in to his lapel, and presented a miniature microphone. "Amazing what you can get at a civilian hobby store these days, eh? This conversation is being transmitted, and recorded. Lock me up, and my associate— associates, will go public." Martin stumbled and to cover his embarrassment added in a raised voice, "I want Douglas!"

"Amazing! You're actually blackmailing the vice president." Manley studied Borneman's face, and seeing as the young man was not bluffing, he said. "Alright. But, I need time. Let's apprehend Douglas together and figure out whom he is working with. It might take time, and I hope to God that time is on our side. Let me know where you're staying, and we'll contact you when the time comes."

Martin shook his head in disappointment.

"I might have been a chair warmer at the CIA, but over the last few days I had a share of field work. I'm not going to sit idly by. And I was never fool enough to fall for such a blatant brush off, anyway."

"Amazing." Manley said without a trace of sarcasm that his expression suggested.

Martin matched the tone when he said, "Just standing up where my country failed."

Vice President Manley pushed back in the folding aluminum chair and studied Martin's face for several long seconds, weighing his decision.

"I understand that your dissatisfaction with the government goes back to your employment with the CIA. You must tell me about it some day. I promise to hear you. The CIA is in dire need of major overhaul and voices such as yours are invaluable. For now, however, we must not argue. A skillful killer with a deadly weapon is on the loose."

Martin made several attempts to learn about Douglas' whereabouts, but the politician would not have it. Further arguing was of no use. The vice president turned to one of the Secret Service agents to organize a safe house for Martin and his associates. Martin observed the natural authority with which Rick Manley delegated his staff, and declined these offers. He was not about to trust the man, regardless of how convincing he had sounded, or what office he held. As far as Martin was concerned — the only person he could trust was himself. And Olga, a voice added in his head.

He walked out of the quarters more confused than when he had entered them. He was inclined to believe that Manley was not involved in the coup. The vice president's replies were consistent, his performance perfunctory; on the other hand his insight to Douglas' role was incredible, confirming that he possessed the information that Martin was after. And thus Martin was inclined to believe that Manley had nothing to do with Douglas' scheming. He did not advance in his investigation, true, but he gained a potential ally. If the vice president was not plotting with Douglas, then it meant that huge law enforcement machinery could be at his disposal. Perhaps Douglas could be stopped, after all. Still, Martin's gut was telling him that equally powerful machinery was aiding Douglas. It had to, for to achieve this level of treachery one had to have strong backing in places of influence. Very high places, indeed.

The thought was so disturbing that he unconsciously looked over his shoulder, almost certain of being watched.

He increased his pace and continued thus through several blocks before meeting with Olga at an agreed location.

Meanwhile, the operator of the video surveillance equipment took off his headphones, and dialed a number on his mobile phone. He held his breath as Borneman walked by the van with tinted glass. He knew that the passerby could not see in, but it always made him uncomfortable when they stopped to see their own reflection, to fix their hair, or just pry and see what could be hiding inside.

"Got him on camera, very clearly." The man spoke to the handset.

"Good. Now get out of there and report to base."

He hung up and quickly folded and secured the equipment. He stepped over the cables and sunk into the driver's seat, started the motor, and joined the traffic.

The head of the Secret Service detail in charge of the vice president's safety team folded his mobile phone and watched the van move out of the parking spot. He gave silent orders to his officers. The four plain-clothed men who were under his command had spread out. The office was staffed with six personnel who had volunteered to do the early shift. They had come to pick up the flyers and buttons early just for the chance to shake the hand of the vice president.

Rick Manley despised having to be outgoing, something every politician had to be if he were to succeed in office. Once secured in his position, as any politician, he seldom mingled with his subjects, but this was crucial time for his political career. He had to fall from the pedestal of greatness, and shake the hands of those whose efforts would help assure his return to office for second term. He was shaken by the conversation with Borneman, yet he could not afford to turn back on these poor folk who volunteered their time so that he and the president could be reelected. He put on his best smile and gracefully waived the nearest one to approach. Where were they, though, he thought. Why were they standing against the wall? Why were the Secret Service agents pointing guns at these people? He called out to the chief of his security detail, but instead of an answer he was faced with a barrel of a gun.

56

Washington. D.C. was not an easy place to do spying in these days when even such typically touristy activities as videotaping popular landmarks were met with suspicion. With informants on the payrolls of all security agencies snooping on their neighbors and visitors alike, it took considerable effort to find a place that did not insist on a credit card — that quintessential tool for surveillance. Their stay was arranged by André, and although not as comfortable as a hotel, the run down two story house offered that which privacy-seekers required — no unwanted scrutiny, and no additional guests. It was a private house leased by a front company belonging to French intelligence, and purposely kept in a state of controlled disarray in order to blend in with surrounding properties. They moved in after dusk, the day before, carrying with them some purchases made in the local mall, including, among other items, an Internet video camera for the dated laptop, and provisions that included nice wine. They did not have to deny themselves anything this time, assured by the Frenchman that a considerable amount of cash would be at their disposal, left in the house for the oft-passing field agents.

Once settled, Olga used a communications suite to connect with André.

The Frenchman listened to their account of the meeting with the vice president.

"The fact that you walked out of that meeting is a good sign — it means that not everyone is participating in Douglas' scheming. That said — I wouldn't trust a politician, not implicitly." André said.

"Nor would I," Martin agreed. "Which is why we must step up our efforts."

"Do I detect in your voice that you've come up with a plan?"

"I wouldn't go as far as calling it a plan."

Olga looked at him, a question mark in her eyes.

Martin explained, "We have to face the facts — Douglas is beyond our reach, and with the kind of support for his plot, he is out of Manley's reach, too. Given what we already know, and what we suspect, the resolution to Douglas' operation is near, which leaves us with only one option to confront him before he strikes."

Olga understood immediately.

"I don't like it!" she said.

André required several seconds to process the meaning of the Martin's words.

He said at last, "Neither do I, but Martin is right. We've no choice." Then he added, "Our sources confirmed that a biological weapon was lifted from the air base. We don't know what it was, but the video surveillance that our agent received, leaves no doubt that whatever took place was not a break in, but was orchestrated with full participation of the military."

Martin nodded. "It only highlights the need to hurry. The fact that a phony story was leaked, is a clear sign that they are about to make their move."

"But we've six weeks to the elections." Olga attempted to stall the inevitable.

"I don't think we should treat this deadline seriously, seeing as the success of Douglas' operation depends, to large extent, on deception."

She could not argue with the logic, but Martin could detect worry in her eyes.

"I'd like to set something straight," he said. "From the beginning, from the day I, and my friends, were recruited, I was slated to play the role that comes to its final performance. You, on the other had, got involved in it quite by chance—"

"Oh, no, no, no, mon amie!" The Frenchman cut in. "You won't brush me off this easily. I'm with you to the end."

"We both are," Olga seconded. "At this point it isn't only about you, though I wouldn't leave you to face it alone, even if it were."

"Alright, then we've got to do it. In order to get close to Douglas, we have to make him come after us."

"Actually," André corrected with a blink of an eye, "we only need you as the bait."

They smiled, welcoming a diversion from the stark reality.

"Are you coping?" André asked with concern. "I can tell by the looks of you that you've become… intimate. Yes?"

They did not reply, the question taking them by surprise.

"Bah!" André continued with a smile. "It's too bad for me. I would like to ask you, Martin, to take care of Olga, only I think she might do a better job of caring for you. No?"

They laughed.

Suddenly, the smile vanished from the Frenchman's face. With his head turned away from the screen, he muttered, "Merde."

"What is it?" With smiles still on their lips, they concentrated on the dark area of the screen that drew their friend's attention.

André did not reply immediately, listening intently. At last he relaxed, and looked directly into the camera. "It's nothing. Just some kids—" He stopped abruptly, and jolted up. The video shook, as the table where André was sitting at, suddenly fell to the ground. They heard noises resembling a scuffle, and the video feed ended.

"André? … André? … What's happening? … André?"

The Frenchman did not reply. The connection was lost.

Olga was first to regain her composure.

"We've got to get out, now!" She stood up, and headed for the doors.

Martin began to gather their belongings.

"Leave it!" she commanded over her shoulder, and reached for the door handle.

It was too late. The door flew out of its hinges. Several men poured in, wielding weapons, and shouting orders that fused into an incomprehensible clamor.

57

The room was bare and drab. The hours he spent in it, contemplating the peeling paint, and moldy patches under the ceiling, had began to blend in his mind. When he did not nap on the inflatable cot, he trotted between the doors and the wall with a window that was boarded up with thick plywood. He kept track of time by the meals he was served, and the number of times he had to relieve himself into the galvanized bucket that they left for him in the corner. Every hour resembled the previous one, until something changed on what, by his count, was the third day. He was sitting at the small wooden table, having just finished the microwaved TV dinner, when the guard — a stocky man with the neck of a bull — came back for the tray, and left the door open on his way out. Martin's entire being concentrated on the world behind the doors — a huge hall, like that of a processing plant of sorts, but furnished with banks of computers, electronic equipment of indeterminate purpose, and tactical presentation screens. This was a familiar sight, not unlike those Martin used in his days with the CIA, when working on particularly resource-intensive operations.

The view told him what to expect, and Martin was ready.

It was the strong reflexes of the two agents who accompanied Douglas that prevented Martin from inflicting the hated man with any lasting pain. He leaped out from the chair before Douglas made two steps through the door. He practically flew over the table, and managed to land one blow of his fist into Douglas' jaw, before the guards overpowered him.

Two minutes later Martin was seated in the chair, the table pinning him to the wall, rendering him immobile.

Douglas massaged his jaw, and said without a trace of the British accent, "I suppose I deserved it."

"Send your dogs away, and I'll show you what else you deserve," Martin hissed out.

"I'm sure you would, alas, neither of us should risk being injured before our roles are played out."

"Nothing you can do to force me to play in your sick scheme. Not anymore," Martin said with the expression of utmost hate.

"Ah, but the most interesting parting is only coming up. It's the grand finale, with you as the main attraction."

"The only finale I see is you dying a painful death."

"You might still get your wish," Douglas said without trace of irony. "In fact, the forty-odd years in this business has taught me that it is the most likely outcome for both of us. After all — we're only pawns."

"You may as well kill me right now, then, because you will not get my cooperation. You cannot coerce me. They are out of your reach—"

"The native's little farm in Ontario?" Douglas's brows arched upwards. "Is this all that you base your confidence on? What is it? Your face is pale, as though you're surprised. You shouldn't be. Did you honestly think that you could stop an operation of this magnitude?"

Martin tried to push the table away, ready to leap out again, but two sets of strong arms made sure that he would not. He breathed heavily, hatred in his eyes.

"I promised they wouldn't be harmed, as long you played the role that was written for you."

"You son-of-a-bitch!"

"My promise stands."

"Kill me, or I'll kill you!"

"You'll get your wish. I can't promise that I'll do it myself, though, I assure you, nothing would give more delight than watch you die. I'm a professional, however, and in my view business always goes before pleasure. The operation is in progress, and it must go on according to the script."

"I told you — I won't play. You won't make me."

"But you are playing, and you are performing as expected." Seeing the perplexed expression on his victim's face, Douglas took out a folded newspaper from his side pocket, and threw it onto the table. He explained, "The vice president is your latest hit. You've assassinated him during a visit to his electoral headquarters. The closed-circuit camera shots leave no doubt about it."

Martin scanned the front page. Several images, stills from video cameras, showed him entering, and leaving the place where he met with the vice president. The headline left no doubt that the vice president had been assassinated. Martin clenched his jaws. Douglas had him cornered. He wanted to shout, but suppressed the urge. To react now would be tantamount to admitting defeat. He lost, he no longer deluded himself, but honor and dignity was all that he had left, and he would be damned if he let Douglas take it away from him.

Douglas said, "Aren't you interested in the details? I thought a master planner like you would appreciate the beauty of the most elaborate intel op in recent decades. I'll grant you that wish, and answer your questions about it.

After all you'd only tickle my pride, since the op's been my prized achievement from start to finish."

"It's full of holes." Martin spat out.

"Really?" Douglas' face showed unfeigned concern. "Such as?"

"Your killing my friends, for starts."

Douglas watched him for a long time before replying.

"I would've thought that you had it figured out by now. I really did. But now I see why the vehemence in pursuing me, instead of disappearing from my radar after you got your parents out of the Kawartha Facility."

"What?"

"Martin, Martin… I did not kill your friends. Far from it. The five of you were an integral part of the plan. All of you were supposed to be here today. It's true that I made do with you alone, but it was a stroke of luck."

"A stroke of luck?"

"Someone wanted the five of you to die that night. But you survived, and I took advantage of it to carry on with the operation."

"You did not kill my friends?"

"I told you — they were an integral part of an operation that was a decade in the making. Why would I kill them off?"

"Who, then?"

"The Basel Group, of course."

58

It was too much for Martin. He sat speechless, his eyes on Douglas'. Was the spy telling the truth? What possible benefit would the deception mean? He had Martin in his claws, literally, pinned and immobilized between the table and the wall, and surrounded by armed thugs, unable to flee, or disturb his plans. Unable? What if a chance still existed that the plans could be altered, or otherwise spoiled? Would Douglas not try to deceive in order to ensure cooperation, especially now that the resolution was near?

"Why would the Basel Group kill my friends?" he asked.

Douglas looked at him with feigned disappointment.

"I would've thought that you'd have it figured out after talking with Sexton. I even considered picking you up, and transporting back in a sack, but Jack, my officer, convinced me that you'd come back on your own. Frankly, I am disappointed. I thought you were better—"

"Ha, ha!" Martin burst out. It was a nervous laughter, one intended to hide his despair.

"I'm a scoundrel, I admit." Douglas said. "But I have no reason to lie to you anymore. The Basel Group killed your friends when they learned of your purpose, albeit unknown to you."

"That you wanted us to assassinate the Group's candidate for president." Martin understood at last.

Douglas smiled appreciatively.

"Then Arthur was right: the Group wanted— still wants the seat for its own pawn." He thought about it some more, and added, "Which means that so do you. You, and the Basel Group, have your own puppets. It means that you are going ahead with the coup."

"Can you guess whose strings are being pulled by whom?"

Martin sighed, and said deprecatingly, "Does it matter? Two candidates vie for the office, and both are plants, serving not the people, but special interest groups. The question is: Whom do you represent?"

"Very good!" Douglas clasped his hands, but did not answer the question.

"My question stands." Martin said, his mind racing.

Douglas, the self-proclaimed scoundrel that he was, said with a devious spark in his eye, "Tell you what. I'll let you sit on it—"

"Ha!"

"Did I say something funny?"

"Funny? You've just divulged that your scheme is not as full-proof as you'd like it to be. Admit it — you're afraid I can still spoil your decade-old plan. I'm right, I can see it in your eyes."

Douglas shrugged.

"You know it as well as anyone, that no operation is considered successful until it is completed. There's always—"

"That element of surprise." Martin finished Douglas' sentence.

"Precisely."

"Then you can't really be sure that I haven't made plans."

"I can't be sure. But I can take it into consideration, and prepare for various eventualities."

"Did you consider *all* eventualities?"

"Again, no one could do that, but at least I know that I have nothing to fear from you."

"Aren't you taking serious risk, considering how much is riding on your scheme?"

"Not at all. You see, the woman— she already talked. I know what you know."

Martin froze.

"You mustn't be surprised," Douglas continued mercilessly. "Given how much is riding on this op, one cannot play a gentleman, not that spying is that honorable to begin with."

Martin clenched his teeth in helpless anger.

Douglas noticed.

"She wasn't harmed, not physically, anyway. She had to be persuaded to talk, though — you know how it is. I know how passionately she feels about you. I'm telling you this as, a sort of a friend, as we're all kin in this business, regardless of the side we serve. Yes, she does feel for you, Martin, and quite a lot."

Martin said nothing, aware that Douglas' words, whether true or not, were meant to kill hope.

"Wouldn't you like to know what will happen to her?" Douglas went on.

Martin raised his face. He did not reply, and he did his best not to show how much he wanted to ask that very question, but what words would not tell, his face showed instead.

"I thought you might want to know. I'll tell you. I love a good love story, the more tragic the better. I've rewritten the play so that both of you will star in it till the end."

Martin remained silent. He was curious. He wanted to know, but he did not want to give this man the satisfaction — it could only seal his defeat.

Douglas shrugged.

"Suit yourself, then. But to show you that I'm not entirely heartless, and certainly not afraid, I'll allow you to try and figure it out." He turned to one of the thugs, and said, "Bring him a screen." Then to Martin, "One thing I always missed about America, when I was posted elsewhere, was that everything is televised here. Not everything is shown, of course, but a TV crew is always where there's action." He stood up, and started for the doors.

"Burke!" Martin stopped him. "Where's the weapon?"

For a moment Douglas looked as though he might answer, but in the end he only smiled.

Then he said, "One clue, just for the fun of it. When it is all over, it'll all be linked to you."

It was not enough.

"I know you did not have to break-in to steal it. It was an inside job, which means that the military is involved in the coup. What do you need a special weapon for?"

Douglas sneered. "Think, Martin. Think!"

59

Martin realized why Douglas' plan would work the moment the guard brought in and powered on the small digital television set. The answer was right here, or rather behind the doors the guard had left open. The men Martin saw at the far end of the large hall, seated at an elongated table, and talking to Douglas, looked familiar. He concentrated his eyes, and gasped. He recognized several prominent members of the administration and the security apparatus, and several others whose faces Martin knew, but could not assign names to. They stood shoulder to shoulder with the figure whose bearing epitomized a man in charge — the Secretary of Defense. They were all in it together. Douglas Burke was working with men who represented the nation's most powerful security agencies, and the military. All this suggested that it was not an operation orchestrated by a rogue deep cover agent. It was a full home-grown coup d'état. He clenched his jaws, biting his tongue until the pain became unbearable. It occurred to him that he had missed the only chance to stop, or to otherwise stymie the plot, when he did not realize that both — the Basel Group, and Douglas, were in a race to instill their own candidates in the office. By playing one against the other he could have averted the coup altogether. It was too late now. Or was it?

Some of Martin's questions were partly explained by one of the agent-thugs, who brought in water and food. Now that Douglas had set things in motion, the guard was more talkative than in the previous days.

"When this is all over, there will be a lot of questions. The one thing we don't want to hear is: Where were the security services when the coup was being planned and carried out?"

"I fail to see the reasoning." Martin said in a voice soliciting further explanation.

"Well, we caught the assassin, didn't we? Too late, of course, but we did."

"An assassin! Who? Me?" Martin played along.

The thug shrugged.

"You can't be serious. I won't admit to anything of the sort."

"Who says you'll ever get the opportunity to talk to anyone?"

"You gonna kill me? What is this, an Oswald remake?"

"Nah, better! And bigger."

On another occasion Martin tried to appeal to the thug.

"How can you do this? You're Homeland Security! You're supposed to protect this country!"

"That is exactly what we're doing." The thug sounded as though he believed it.

"By killing the president?"

The thug appeared insulted. "You know, Douglas warned us not to talk to you. He said you used to be some sort of an egghead in these things—"

"You're way off, pal. I never planned to kill off my own government administration! I never worked against my own country!"

"You just don't get it. What we're doing is for the country."

"How's that?" Martin sounded puzzled. His mind was working frantically. Could he take this guy? He was a thug, taller and better built, and — God knows — he was in better physical shape than Martin. Even if Martin knocked him down, which would be an accomplishment in itself, how could he ever hope to get through a room full of them? The thug had a pistol, but so did the rest of them. If Martin overpowered him and took his gun he could shoot several more, but not all of them. He would never get away. They knew he could not. They were certain he would not, or else his legs and arms would have been tied. Furthermore — they appeared oblivious to his presence, perhaps they knew that even if he managed to free himself, somehow, he could not stop the inevitable. That was what the thug had in mind. It confirmed the worst.

"You look and sound like you were in the military. Did they not teach you to train your weapon against the enemies of the constitution? How can you watch them plot such a treacherous act?"

"Treacherous? We are trying to stop the traitors!"

"By overthrowing the government?"

"By ridding this great nation of those who are trying to undermine our democratic principles, our way of governance."

"You are doing exactly what you just spelled out."

"Sometimes one has to act seemingly against the law in order to preserve the greater good."

"You are traitors."

"I was taught at school that only history can make such pronouncements, and even then it is all up for interpretation," the thug replied, a grin lingering in the corners of his lips. He started for the doors.

"Wait!" Martin stood up. The agent looked genuinely annoyed and unlikely to carry on the subject. "Tell me at least what happened to the woman I was with?"

"The Canuck?" He shrugged. "She's being prepped for her role. Eat your food, it's the last you get." He left the room and locked the door.

Martin tuned in the television set, and flipped the channels until he found one that he was looking for. The preparations for the funeral celebration were being broadcast. The cemetery was cordoned off, the podium for the speaker being set up, along with hundreds of fold up chairs. Security was tight. Uniformed and plain-clothed police, the secret service, and military units were patrolling the area. To kill the president in these conditions could only succeed through an inside job. Martin's professional experience left no doubt in his mind that it required the cooperation of a good number of people, in key positions, and that a scapegoat would be required. Of course he understood that he was the scapegoat and that he would not be permitted to outlive the operation, but even so — to plant him as the assassin required an unprecedented level of logistical support. It confirmed that was an all out sanctioned operation. But, why was he the only one not seeing how all the security agencies could get together and agree to kill their president? How was cooperation possible in evil deeds, while mutual effort for the country's defense was not?

Several hours passed, and Martin was no closer to finding the answer, when the thug-agent returned, couple of sidekicks behind him.

"It's time for the show."

Two agents ushered him, at gunpoint, into a navy-blue van with government plates. The agents offered no explanations, nor answered any of his questions. They pushed him inside, and sat on either side, leaving the door open. He saw people coming out of the factory, carrying cases and boxes, and packing everything into the other cars.

Then he saw her. Two men walked Olga, steadying her as she dragged her feet. She was dressed in a smart suit, not unlike the female agent he had seen on the way to the parking lot. She was not beaten, or at least there were no visible signs of it, but she was evidently medicated. She did not hear Martin's shouting, and soon no one else did as the doors to the van closed shut.

60

Martin's mind worked frantically during the long ride in the sealed van. He expected to be framed for the assassination of the president, but could not fathom how to get out of the predicament. He hoped to get better ideas once he visualized the exact location the plotters chose for the deadly act. If worst came to worst, he reasoned, he would scar himself, turning his body into a message board, for the investigators who would dissect every aspect of the heinous act. He was considering these, and other options, when the van came to a stop, and the doors slid-open. He recognized the cemetery where the preparations for the state funeral were being broadcast from. He was ushered to a large mausoleum, and, to his surprise, was locked inside, all alone. The plotters must feel supremely confident, he thought, and immediately began to scout the place for anything that could be turned into his advantage. It was a large structure, built with fantasy, and detail, worthy of baroque architects. Two intricately carved sarcophagi stood on the marble floor, side by side, bathing in colorful lights that were cast through stained-glass windows. Marble vases stood at the head of each sarcophagus, in between them a tall candleholder shaped as an olive tree. His eyes wondered up the bronze tree, and his heart froze. All the way up, underneath a round cupola, was a crude platform, constructed using several planks of lumber, and supported by steel scaffolding.

Reaching the platform was difficult. He managed to pull himself up on the steel tubes, and sat on the platform gasping for air. The cupola was encircled by stained glass, with one panel removed, and offering a view of the cemetery. He peered outside and saw hundreds of people who were sitting on fold up chairs, watching a podium where someone was delivering a speech, the distant, but incomprehensible words reaching Martin's ears. It was far, but not impossible for a sharp shooter, he estimated. He realized that whatever was planned, had to happen momentarily, hence the plotters' confidence in dropping Martin off, and leaving him alone, as though nothing could alter the course of events. Determined to prove them wrong, he shifted his gaze, expecting to find the actual killer, knowing that the shots would come from his proximity in accordance with the expected ballistic report. He saw nothing, the small broken pane not providing adequate angle of vision. He took a swing to break more glass, when his arm froze mid way through the gesture.

It was Olga.

She was walking along the path between the tombstones, toward the podium. The security agents, who were scattered nearby, showed no concern, which, in itself was not out of the ordinary, given that she was dressed as any female agent. The unusual, which should have alerted the Secret Service, was the automatic pistol in the woman's hand, swinging with every movement of her arm, as she continued forward. Every step was brining her closer to the podium, yet no one seemed concerned.

Something should have happened by now, but did not.

Martin called out to her, but Olga did not hear him.

She continued on, walking as though in trance, drawn to the podium.

Martin's eyes glided above her, and he saw the stage was now taken by a familiar figure. The familiar posture of the senator who was running against the president in the upcoming election, had approached the microphone. It meant that the next speaker would be the president, which left Martin with little time. He had to do something, and do it now. With the swing of his elbow he broke a panel of glass, and then another. He called out Olga's name, but she did not react, perhaps unable to hear him.

Someone else did. A Secret Service agent who was posted several feet in front of the mausoleum had turned around, and looked up. He raised his wrist to his mouth, and spoke to it hurriedly, but whatever he sad, was drowned in a dry, but powerful blast.

A shot was fired nearby.

Martin's eyes gazed above the tombstones, to the podium.

The senator, and the apparent candidate of the Basel Group, has been assassinated, his body frozen momentarily, and then suddenly slumping backwards, to the floor.

This was not the time to ponder the surprising turn of events. He had to act, now or never. He pushed back to take a kick at the window, and his shoulder hit something hard. A bell hanging under the ceiling of the cupola began to toll, its deafening sound sending flashes of pain through Martin's head, its piercing noise resonating under the skull. His hands embraced his head, his body writhing in pain, and setting a chain of events in motion. The scaffolding rocked, once, twice, and began to collapse just as the gate to the mausoleum opened and two men rushed inside. One of them carried a sniper's rifle in his gloved hands, whereas the other had a pistol, ready to shoot the supposed assassin. Both had enough time to utter short cries before the scaffolding, with the full weight of the person sitting on the platform, crashed onto them. One man died instantly, his head split open by a steel tube, while the other was rendered immobilized by the weight that pinned him to the cold marble floor.

Martin rushed outside, ducking as bullets whizzed by. He rolled and crawled behind monuments, his moves propelled by the desire to make it as difficult as possible for the plotters to turn him into the murderer. He knew that his prints were all over the scaffolding, and would be placed on the murder weapon, but the longer he survived, the more people witnessed the incident, the more questions would be raised, the more difficult would be the answers.

The agents began to advance on him, and he knew his time was up. He took the last breath, and was ready to skirt away when something caught his eye. He thought he was hallucinating, perhaps as a result of the tremendous emotional pressure. He blinked, and looked closer, but the image did not disappear. It was not possible! Not possible!

Martin stood up to call out the name when he was hit with the first bullet. Then another. And another. The world spun in front of his eyes, and he slumped onto the grass. He watched the events unfold, but was unable to move. At first he saw legs, lots of legs, as they approached, and hovered above him. He heard voices, but they began to wane, gradually dissolving into a hum, before complete silence surrounded him. Soon the legs began to dissipate, only to be replaced by other — clad in different footwear. He did not feel it, but the sensation did not escape him that he was being picked up, and carried away. Unknown figures flashed by his eyes, most wielding guns, running, shouting, their faces displaying shock and fear.

He was dropped to the ground, but felt nothing, the realization apparent only in the sudden change in the vantage point. As he lay on the ground — a gravel path — his eyes followed the havoc that swept the stately mourners who attended the funeral, and were now scattering in all directions. Some Secret Service agents, with handguns and radios in the hands, stood bewildered, unable to control the situation, unable to comprehend the unfolding events, watching as their colleagues were firing, and being fired at by a growing number of uniformed police officers.

Something landed on the ground, next to Martin's head. It was a body of a police officer, his legs kicking convulsively. It took extraordinary will power to turn his head away from the dying man, but the view that opened up was even more terrifying.

Not more than twenty paces away stood Olga. She was motionless, seemingly removed from the events, as though unaware of everything that was taking place around her. Someone ran passed by, bumping in her, and the impact turning her around. The person who had run into her had come into a sudden stop, his eyes on Martin's, his intent evident in the hate that sent fiery sparks out of the man's eyes. It was Douglas, a pistol in his hand, as he was headed for Martin, ready to finish off where his men had failed. Apparently he recognized the woman he had bumped into, and in a cruel desire to cause premortal pain, he turned around to face her.

Martin watched helplessly as Douglas raised the pistol, and pointed the barrel into Olga's chest.

A weapon went off, but it was not Douglas'. A man with large FBI letters on his jacket had materialized behind Douglas, and fired. Douglas spun around in place, and fired at the agent. Both fell to the ground. Douglas was injured, but not dead. He staggered up to his feet, aimed again at the woman, and fired.

Martin watched in horror as Olga fell to the ground. He watched as the hated man turned toward him and began to approach. It was the scene that had just unfolded before him, that added the strength necessary to act. Martin's arm reached out to the fallen body of the police officer, his fingers probing until he found what he hoped would be there. With the butt of the pistol in his hand, he raised his arm, aimed, and squeezed the trigger. The mark of the bullet hole in Douglas' forehead was the last image he saw.

61

Loud agitated voices woke him up. Opening his eyelids was a struggle, and trying to focus his eyes sent a series of pain shocks through his temples. When he overcame the pain, he found himself in a corridor with moving walls, and blurry figures that passed by with lightening speed. The motion ended eventually, the confinement of the walls disappeared. He felt himself being lifted up, toward strong bright lights that seemed to penetrate under his skull. He closed his eyes and the pain ended.

He came to again. He could hear voices nearby, but did not move, afraid of the pain, of what he would see. Two males voices were speaking excitedly. At first he could not understand the words. In time he picked them out, one by one. Soon he could make out whole sentences.

"Should've left the motherfucker to die—"

"Ergh. He's just the trigger. Someone had to hire him and the others—"

"They'll smoke them out, one by one. They'll trace the chain of command—"

"Ergh. Maybe not. It ain't no regular shmoe who can come and shoot in that kind of a crowd—"

"Maybe, but—"

The voices faded away.

The shouting woke him up again. He did not have the energy or the will to move his head or to open his eyes. He could tell they stood somewhere close by the clarity of their voices.

"I don't know about that, agent!"

"But we've got to talk to him!"

"He's lost a lot of blood! This man has been unconscious since! He's on a ventilator, he can hardly breathe on his own, little else talk—"

"Jesus! He's got to talk! He's got to talk—"

"He might as well be talking to Jesus right now, agent!"

The voices faded away, again.

The bed was shaking, side to side, forwards, and backwards. He opened his eyes. He was in a small enclosed place. The hum of the engine and traffic noises gave away the location. He was being transported in an ambulance. Where to? He wanted to ask. He could not. The rocking of the vehicle was so comforting. He closed his eyes.

When he opened them again, he found himself in a large bright room with huge windows covered with light draperies. An IV stand towered over his bed, and he could hear the beeps of medical equipment nearby.

"He's up," a female voice said.

A nurse and a plain-clothed male appeared on either side of the bed, and observed him closely. The male proceeded to perform a series of checks on the patient.

"The worst is over," he pronounced.

"It's the first time he stayed awake the whole time," the nurse said.

The man leaned over the patient.

"Can you hear me?"

Martin's lips moved but no sound followed. He cleared his throat. It came with difficulty.

"My name is Dr Michael Hlinka." The doctor leaned closer. "Can you tell me yours?"

He muttered something out.

"Good." The doctor smiled and walked away several steps, nurse following. They talked for several minutes. Martin could not make out their words. His mind drifted away, and he slipped into nothingness.

He woke up now and again. He could tell the passing of time by the changing light outside the windows. He was confined to the hospital bed, too weak to move, too disheartened to fight for his life, and too indifferent to notice the others fighting for him. His companion during those days was the nurse. She was the first thing he saw when his eyes opened, and the last when they closed. Occasionally she would lean over and turn him to his side or sit him up and massage his back. The doctor would come back several times a day. Each day he would try to engage his patient with small talk, without success.

Days turned into weeks.

Martin was able to eat solid foods and walk to the adjoining washroom by himself. He was able to talk, but scarcely said a word. He made observations about his surroundings, but never asked any questions. He was afraid of the irrevocability of answers to questions that mounted in his head. He felt stronger with each passing day and now that he could, he often approached the windows and marveled over the evidence of changing seasons in the outside garden. He saw gardeners sweeping the fallen leaves and tending to shrubs, but never noticed any other patients. He understood that he was not cared for at a hospital. The room he was in was a luxurious bedroom on the second or third floor of a grand estate, as he concluded from the view of the outside world and the richness of the furnishings inside. It told him something. Someone had removed him from the hospital and nursed him to health in a private residence with the help of a hired medical team. This was someone with resources, both financial and human. Who was it? The answer came eventually, as he knew it would.

62

Martin had never seen this man before. He was inconspicuous, of meek physical build, yet somehow managing to project a great aura of respectability and power. He walked in through the door with the confidence of the man of the house, and approached the bed, a stack of newspapers and magazines under his arm. He sat in the chair where the nurse used to spend most of her days, and focused his eyes on Martin. Both observed one another for a minute or two without uttering a word.

"The doctor assures me that you will be good as new in a few weeks," the stranger began. He spoke clearly and slowly, accentuating every word, as one does to the injured or elderly. "You have made a remarkable recovery, although for a while we were not at all certain that you would pull through. It's like you've been away, or asleep, and returned, or woken up to a new reality. Here." He placed the newspapers and magazines at the foot of the bed. "Brought these to keep you up to date. Read. I'll see you when you're ready to talk. Tonight, or tomorrow. Take your time." He awaited some reaction and when none came he stood up, and started for the door.

"Who are you?"

The question stopped the man half way through the door. He turned around and gave his name.

"Your name doesn't mean a thing. Who are you, and why am I here, which, I presume, is your house?"

"To answer your first question — I'm a patriot." The reply was delivered quietly, as in mourning. "As for your second question — We couldn't let you die. You're the last surviving link to the farce that took place in front of the eyes of the world."

"Who's *we*?"

"A group of likeminded people who refused to stand idly by when such blatant disregard for the law was taking place, laying to waste centuries of democratic achievements, and making mockery of our country."

"Would this group have anything to do with a certain city in Switzerland?"

A reply was not necessary. Martin knew the answer.

"It's the common goal that binds us together, not geographical assignation."

The spark in the man's eye signified that Martin hit the spot.

"What goal is that?"

"To ensure that this country is governed by law, and in accordance with democratic principles."

"Is this why you tried to plant your own president, a fraud?"

"Plant a fraud? We gave the people of this great country a choice where there was none."

Martin did not reply immediately. He studied the face of his host. The slim lips, and the sharp nose, signified a man who was used to getting everything his way, but the probing eyes were sincere.

"I understand now, more than I did when all this began. I had time to think it over," Martin spoke with zeal, feeling the anger rise in him — anger that was simmering for weeks inside the weak body. "You tried to plant a puppet president. Don't deny it."

The man replied with sadness in his voice that was matched by the expression in his eyes, "I won't soap your eyes, you're too smart to see through such blatant deception, anyway. Yes, it is true, we had plans for change. As did the majority of voters. But, our decision to support the opposition candidate was born in response to those who were determined to keep the president in office regardless of the outcome of the elections. What do you think you and your friends were meant to achieve? You were nurtured from the very start to play your part in this scheme. You were the BASEL group — an elite band of assassins and intelligence operatives. Your group was formed all those years ago for just the occasion — to kill the candidate that your puppet masters did not support. It makes no difference whether you knew about the scheming or not, whether you actually squeezed the trigger, or were used as scapegoats. You served the purpose you were intended for."

"I thought you said you wouldn't soap my eyes with lies," Martin said without raising his voice. Lies. He was lied to all this time. Everybody lied to him, and he expected nothing else from this man. "Douglas told me what you did."

"Douglas told you!" The man purred through his bottom lip. "I would've expected you to know by know that Douglas is the last person you should trust." Something in the patient's eyes told him not to expect an argument on the subject. "And just what did Douglas tell you?"

"Douglas deserved to die. I am glad I killed him, but as much a bastard that he was he told the truth — You killed my friends."

The man pushed back in his chair, and raised his head, as though studying the high ceiling. At last he looked down,

318

into the patient's eyes, and said, "You deserve the truth. We did kill your friends."

Martin exhaled deeply, but said nothing.

"We killed your friends because we believed that it was the only way to stop the madness. We believed that it would stop Douglas' operation, after all you were the patsies that he needed to pull off his scheme. Alas, you survived, and Douglas seized upon it, he rescued his operation. Whereas his original plan called for an entire cell of skilled assassins, he settled for one, added couple more on the way, and carried on. You, the woman, and the Frenchman, sufficed."

It pained to hear the killer boast about killing of one's friends. Yet the straight out admission did not propel Martin to avenge the deaths. Hearing these words now, possibly the only words of truth, had the opposite effect. A sense of closure took over him.

The man realized what was going through Martin's head. He added, "You must understand that we had no choice. Douglas' plan was about to be set in motion, and we had to act fast. What we did was conducted in the interest of the country."

"Expendables — that's what you are". Martin quoted the words of his instructor from the Farm.

"Come again?"

"Is it over?" Martin asked.

"Certainly not. That's why you are here."

"What does that mean?"

"It means that for as long as you're alive the game is not over."

63

"Now you listen to me," Martin spoke through his teeth. "It's over. Get it? Douglas is dead. Arthur, Bobby, Derek, Chris, Olga, André— They're all dead!" He motioned his hand as though waving off a pesky fly. "You can forget about it. I'm through. You— You can go ahead and kill each other. Just leave me out of it."

The man replied with a resigned expression, "Wish it were this simple, but you are still in the center of it all. Perhaps now more than ever."

"I wanted Douglas to pay for what he did to my friends. I put a bullet in his head. Now, as it turns out, I killed the wrong person!"

Cold shivers shot through the man's spine. He checked himself and said, "There are no bullets enough to stop what Douglas set in motion. Do you have any idea what is happening out there? Well, of course you don't! How could you? You have been unconscious for most of it. Let me tell you, though — you can reverse it."

"Of course. No less." Martin said with as much sarcasm as he could muster. "Only, whatever else you have in store for me— You can count me out."

The answer had visibly let the man down.

"What do you want then?" He asked resignedly.

"I want to be left alone."

"Yes. You said so, and I can understand it—"

"Can you?"

"Sure. You lost your friends, and got entangled in a mess that almost took your parents' lives. You are asking yourself — was it worth it? So what if they made a mockery of this great nation? As long as they leave you alone! Well, let me tell you something: It's not going to happen. They will hunt you down for as long as it takes. And if they can't find you, they'll go after those that matter to you. They'll find them sooner or later, Martin. What do you think will happen then?"

"No one is going to find them," Martin replied in a voice that did not match the conviction that his words suggested, Douglas' insinuating that he knew the whereabouts of Oliver and Lydia still vivid in his memory.

"Do you honestly think it's so hard to re-trace your route from the Kawartha Facility, through a certain native's home, to Washington?—"

"Goddamn you!" Martin sat up.

"Relax! You parents are safe. We anticipated this. We got to them first, and moved them to a safer place."

"Where?"

"A Native reservation on Manitoulin Island. They're safe there. Even so, should we receive so much as a hint of danger we'll move them again, and again, as long as it will be necessary. But the question is: How long are you prepared to subject them to this life, on the run?"

Martin fell silent. He knew the man was right. It would continue haunting him for the rest of his days. Still, could he be blamed for wanting to put all this past him? The driving force behind his pursuit — vengeance and desire to punish — it all died with Douglas, and watching Olga's death brought about inertia. How much more can a man endure?

Martin's host grew impatient. He was not getting through to Borneman. He tried to understand him. Martin had lost his closest friends, he watched his parents die in a sick display of psychological cruelty, and then brought back to life only to be threatened with losing it again. He was a man who lost the woman he was falling for, and then watched her being shot by the man who had caused all his sorrows. A man who had gone through such psychological strain could not be expected to stand up and fight once more when he had nothing to fight for. All this was understandable, and expected from any man, but Borneman was not any man, the job he did for the CIA was not assigned to average men. So why was he taking it so emotionally when his psychological profile had cleared him earlier for the tribulations that would inevitably come with the job? Was it the compound of all the things that happened since the night on Lake Ruther? Was it something that came later? Was it perhaps the woman, Olga? It suddenly became clear. Martin did not know what really happened.

"What about the woman?" the man asked in a last attempt to rouse a broken man to action.

Martin was too exhausted to protest. He only murmured, "Lay off."

"She's alive, you know. Her condition was serious — she was in a coma for two weeks — but she pulled through. They believe she died that day, which is just as well. She's safe, with your parents, and recuperating."

Martin sat dumbfounded. He felt tears building in his eyes. They were tears of helplessness.

"Both of you survived thanks to the sharp mind of the director of the CIA," the man continued. "Bosworth suspected something wasn't right with the way you and your friends were recruited, and handled, all those years. He set up a special unit to investigate what happened, and discovered that his deputy was involved in non-sanctioned operations, including your extraordinary recruitment and rise through the ranks of the CIA."

Martin pressed his knuckles to his eyes to cover his emotions. He thought the ordeal was over, but he was wrong. There remained too many unknowns to rest.

"Who was running the deputy?" he asked.

"He was under Douglas Burke's thumb for many years, though he wasn't exactly an unwilling cooperator. He was much interested in out-sitting his boss and jumped at the first opportunity even if it meant participation in the coup d'etat."

"And the director only clued in at the eleventh hour?"

"Directors of the CIA are only figureheads. The top spy is the deputy for operations. When you disappeared after that night on the Lake, which brought a chain of events, Bosworth tried to find you. He received intelligence about your going to Europe, and his men in Switzerland apprehended three people of matching descriptions, alas they proved to be decoys sent by Douglas. Then, the director got wind of your presence in Paris. His friend, the director of the FBI, alerted the French immigration, and they were about to apprehend you when Douglas' reach proved deeper and the immigration agents were called off. Bosworth would have caught up with you eventually, had he not been dismissed. Still, he would not let go. He contacted us."

"Us?"

"Us, you know — what you thought of as the Basel Group. We joined forces with the director and his loyal supporters. It wasn't easy to work together. We each thought of the other as the enemy set on destroying this country, but eventually we grew to understand that there was a common enemy who posed a big threat. To get to the heart of it, we had to find you first. Your chip was deactivated, so finding you was not easy. That's when we realized that your friend, Olga, might have one, after all she was a field officer in a very secretive agency. This had to go through the very top and very carefully, as we knew enough of the reaches of the conspiracy. Some members of our group are personal friends of the prime minister of Canada, and we were able to—"

Martin interjected, "Come on, did you not mean to say — our member, the prime minister of Canada?"

"Through the office of the prime minister," the man did not correct, "we obtained the frequencies and the ID of Ms Duchesne's chip. We tracked you both through Ontario and Quebec, to Washington, until you were taken out by Douglas and the signal disappeared. Now, you're not going to like what I'm about to say, but you should know it was necessary—"

"Finish it." Martin's eyes were set on his host's.

"Olga's chip is different from the one you were implanted with. Basically it transmits data. It has a recording capability, albeit small, so every now and then it has to dump data to receiving stations. It records sounds within a small range, enough to pick up casual conversations, and sends it out when storage reaches its limits. When you isolate the inevitable gastrointestinal noise the result is quite clear." The man paused and waited patiently for Martin to voice his anger.

"You knew we could've used help," Martin said quietly. He was astounded, but too tired to object more vehemently. His head was spinning. The conversation proved more strenuous than he could handle after weeks in the company of his own innermost thoughts.

"We couldn't do much about it. The data was monitored by Douglas. He knew everything you'd been through. To interrupt it in any way would have alerted Douglas. We couldn't afford it, we had to have enough evidence against him, but more importantly — we had to find out more details about his plot. Unfortunately you disappeared after the vice president's assassination. We knew you were taken to a location somewhere in the outskirts of Washington, but we lost the signal. We did not get the signal back, until you were on the way to the funeral where you were to be framed for the next hit. Bosworth suspected something to that effect, thanks to the analysis of your progress, the conversations, and your visit with Manley. We pieced it together and sent an army — literally — an army of cops to the funeral. Douglas did not expect it. The chaos that ensued saved your lives. Unfortunately it didn't really stop Douglas' plan. It was too late."

"They got the president, too." Martin concluded.

"The president? No, of course not!" The man shrugged.

"How do you mean? What the hell was it all about, then?"

"Martin, everything that happened was to ensure that the president remains in office, especially in light of his waning chances at winning the elections."

64

The man spread his arms in a gesture of helplessness.

"I'm sorry. In the heat of the discussion I forgot that you were out of it for weeks. I should have let you read the papers first. I had them prepared for you chronologically. It's a step by step of the death of democracy." He nodded to the stack.

Martin stared at the newspapers piled at the foot of the bed in disbelief.

"Douglas — although at the time I did not know it was him — told me on the phone that he wanted me to kill the president!"

"He would. Remember that at the time you thought you were speaking with the Basel Group. You thought we wanted our own candidate in the office, and the president stood in our way—"

"Was it not true?" Martin barked.

"Yes," the man replied unapologetically. "We did what every citizen, and every corporation in this country, does: we supported the candidate of our choice. But we did not have to kill the opponent — the president. Our candidate, the senator, would have won the popular vote. Exit polls did not lie. Douglas knew it, and killed the senator."

"And the vice president?"

"The vice president knew about Douglas, and the plot, and was against it. He would not have allowed it to be swept under the rug. Douglas killed him."

Martin chewed on the revelations he learned. Then he shook his head.

"I can't believe the president would play along, only to stay in office four more years."

"There's more to it than a mere term in office. Presidents of this country are only nominal figureheads, with true power hidden in the shadows. The conspirators orchestrated a coup under a false flag operation — the Basel Group being the scapegoats — and *uncovered* a conspiracy that allowed them to arrest and disappear their opponents, which in turn allowed the president to call for extraordinary measures, and to suspend the constitution."

Martin studied his host's face. He saw no signs of deception in the blue eyes.

"Jesus."

He reached for the newspapers, brought them closer, and fumbled through the pages. They were organized in an ascending order, by date. Among the titles he recognized dailies from across the country, as well as some from overseas. He scanned the headlines with growing shock, and had to put them down several times in order to suppress overwhelming anger and anxiety.

"Why not give me the run down?" He suggested after a while of frantically fingering through the pages.

The man was prepared for the request. He spoke monotonously, the way someone reciting a well known and documented event in history would.

"The first few days the media speculated on the identities of the killers of the vice president. When the identities of conspirators, including you as the ringleader, were released, they were met with bigger shock than the killings themselves. This launched a campaign of purges. Thousands were arrested, even more were discharged. The CIA and the Bureau were hit the hardest."

"Did everyone simply take their word for it?"

"You can hardly argue with the Homeland Security and the Pentagon when they cry in unison that the president has granted them full range of security and policing powers, as would be expected in such extraordinary circumstances. Naturally evidence had to be presented. Everything — from killing your accomplices on the lake, to escaping police custody, and so forth, including your conspiring with the foreign intelligence operatives, was announced and presented at a highly publicized conference. The video showing you leave the party headquarters minutes before the electoral office blew up, and the discovery of a French military spy who had stolen a new super weapon from the Air Force base, was about as much as this nation could take. The Frenchman was found in a van outside the cemetery, accompanied by a Middle Eastern intelligence officer from a country America is at war with. They were thought to be ready to launch a genetic bomb that could wipe out the entire population of DC. Again — the swiftness of action on the part of Homeland Security and the military had averted a tragedy — the Frenchman was shot dead, but the Muslim got away with the potent weapon. The announcement that the bomb was only one of several that went missing was all that the Congress needed to pass a resolution granting the president the extraordinary powers that included extending his mandate for as long as was necessary to restore peace and security in the country. The United States was in a state of emergency. The conspirators received what they were after."

"What the hell is a genetic bomb?" Martin asked.

"A dream weapon. Not a bomb in a traditional sense, as there's no big explosion involved. It provides a devilishly innovative way of wiping out the enemy according to their genetic profiles. Such a weapon would target only Caucasians, or only Muslims, or only Blacks, or the blue-eyed, or a particular sex, leaving everyone else alive and well. Its finer version could target specific geographical areas. It could be fine-tuned all the way down to the individual DNA, killing only a predetermined person, with or without his or her relatives. Its effects can be instantaneous or delayed. Programmed and released anywhere in the DC area it could kill the president, or the entire staff of the White House. Imagine what such a threat could achieve politically."

Martin recalled his parents describing a lab-like environment at the Kawartha Facility where Douglas' people worked on DNA sequences. He asked, "How does it correlate with what happened?"

"You mean: what if the weapon could target only a certain voting group?" The man winked, but Martin was not in a joking mood, and he continued. "We can only guess. Perhaps the weapon needed to be tested and what better opportunity than to do it under, what you might call in the intelligence world — a false flag operation, whereupon you blame it on someone else and at the same time further your own agenda."

Martin took a deep breath. He hated to admit to himself that the man's version of events was beginning to add up to a very plausible, if incredible scenario. He would have, perhaps, dismissed everything as a sack of lies had he not been a part of the events.

"What did the implicated foreign states say about their alleged involvement?"

"The connection with foreign agencies being irrefutable, diplomatic relations were suspended with the countries involved. Through the president's mouth the conspirators vowed swift retaliatory action and declared that several defense initiatives were being given immediate priority. To show the world that America was serious, the military was put on DEFCON. The United States was preparing for war. But it was just soap in our eyes. The true reasons behind it all were to institute martial law, to place soldiers on our streets, and to put an end to any and all dissent. No right to assembly, no student-protesters on streets, no labor actions, no Occupy Movements… To say a word against the state is to be arrested and detained indefinitely."

"And me? You said they are looking for me. Why have they not found me?"

The man smiled, but his eyes remained sober. "They are looking for you, but we are not without resources. The security directives warn that anyone found aiding the terrorist will be considered an enemy combatant and dealt with according to the provisions imposed at time of war. They are looking for you and are convinced they will smoke you out."

"Will they?"

"I suppose it all depends how long it goes on, how long they can keep up the charade. If history teaches us anything, it's that no tyranny lasts forever, and sooner, or later, they will have to ease their grip on the nation."

"What is to be done?"

"I'll be painfully honest with you — at present not a whole lot, but the sheer fact that we have you proves that this country still possesses forces strong enough to stand up to them."

"Stand up? How?"

"They stand on shaky ground. The president is not as willing a participant as they would like him to be. There are people who know what really happened, what really precipitated the events, but they have no compelling proof to present it to the nation. We can present that proof, and the conspirators know about it. We need a human face. You have a story to tell, and as long as you are alive they won't dare go all the way."

"Which is?"

"You name it. Few hints: a president-puppet for life, one party system, police state—"

Martin thought about it for a minute or so before replying. "Seems to me that things aren't as hopeless as you paint them if the possibility of reversing the course of history still exists."

"You're right, we're quite a long way from becoming a place like North Korea, and, frankly, I doubt they want it to go that far. Still, we're talking about America where strong and centralized leadership exists for the purpose of suppressing liberties, a country whose outside policy is based solely on economic expansion on the barrels of weapons, and citizens of this country are overburdened with supporting such a state."

"You've described America as we know it. What's new?" Martin shrugged.

The man replied with zeal that could only be attributed to someone who cared passionately about the subject, "America as you knew it is on its last breath — an unsustainable giant. Intelligence think tanks give us a decade on the outside before we become completely dependent on foreign capital, labor and production. Unfortunately, the remedy the conspirators see is in rapid conquer of the vital sectors of world's natural resources and infrastructures, by all means necessary." The man paused, but seeing as Martin remained dubious, he continued, "Let me put it this way: this country is insolvent. Furthermore — America is plummeting from her pedestal of a superpower. Unfortunately, the way the conspirators are trying to remedy this process, is only making things worse. Instead of slowly descending, we are crashing down for a big splash, and the first victims are the citizens of this once great nation."

"Again, what is to be done?" Martin shivered. It has suddenly become chilly inside. He had noticed that the man was cold too. The climate control, it seemed, has malfunctioned.

"We're in a state of emergency. There is no room here for such niceties as hearings, lawyers, and other things of the bygone era. This has to be done one step at a time, and in accordance with their tactics. We let them know we have you, that we know what happened, and we'll take it from there, step by step."

"You're not calling for the people to rise?" Martin asked sarcastically, suddenly tired of the conversation.

"The people?" The man was taken aback by the suggestion. "Revolutions start when the people have nothing to put in their mouths. People will give up their civil liberties in exchange for food, for basic luxuries of life, for entertainment. Supplying the people of America with those needs, and who would want to get off their comfy couch and fight, when a good game's on TV, and a bucket of chicken drums on the table?"

"How am I ever to change this, then?"

"As I said — the average American won't care, but your coming out with the truth is a step forward. The world will react. The Canadians and French will see to it, after all a great injustice has been done to them. The change will come from the outside. America will be forced to listen. No country, great or small, can exist in isolation. Ours in particular. We depend on the world now more than ever. Here, let me show you something—" The man paused. Something drew his attention. He listened intently for a while, and relaxed. "Those darn leaf blowers, they make so much noise." He stood up, to pick up a remote, and switched on the entertainment center. He located the appropriate video file on the hard disk of the video recorder, and pressed the play button. A newscast filled the large plasma screen mounted on the wall across the room, and sound poured out from speakers that Martin could not locate.

The grim-faced president, appearing a decade older, started off by saying that the unthinkable had happened. The enemy had struck with boldness and cruelty. The Air Force has confirmed that a small but incredibly potent biological agent was stolen from its laboratories. The agent was developed for defensive purposes. Now it has been turned into a weapon, and has been deployed on American soil, killing much of the population of the township of Apsley. Located only two hours from the nation's capital, it was the very place, as was recently revealed, where several assassins conspired to bring down the American government. Apprehended by the Homeland Security agents, the treacherous terrorist cell was believed to be neutralized, but it was supported by international groups aided by foreign governments and traitors within the United States. The superpower's security apparatus failed because the identities of the perpetrators did not fit the profile. No one could have foreseen that the world's greatest democracy, the freedom-spreading Messiah in the quest to bestow its values on the world, would fall under attack from its own and from its allies. A potent weapon of mass destruction was in the hands of skilled specialists who aimed to bring the United States to its knees. The crisis had reached the highest proportions. Acting on FEMA's executive orders, and backed by Congress, the president had suspended the Constitution. The elections were called off indefinitely, and a state of emergency was declared. Special conditions were to be strictly observed, and would be enforced with all powers given to the head of state in such circumstances. The National Guard patrolled the cities and villages alongside specially empowered military units. Communications restrictions were instituted, with international telephone, radio, and internet traffic, subjected to censure and monitoring. The Department of Homeland Security has been busy detaining thousands of dissidents and enemies of the state, with hundreds of thousands more being sought. Authorities implore the public to contact local Homeland Security offices with tips on suspicious and politically incorrect behavior among neighbors and strangers alike...

The recording went on in a similar vein, but Martin and his host were no longer listening. Something strange was happening in the house.

"It was probably backfiring in the parking lot—" the man said, but bit his tongue.

This time they both heard what sounded like a pat of a gun. And it was very close.

The man stood up, his face pale. "I better see what this is about."

He flipped open his mobile phone and started for the door when it flung open. A man walked in, a semi-automatic in his hand.

"You!" The man of the house roared. "How did you—" He did not finish. One shot in the forehead silenced him forever.

Martin did not watch the body slump onto the floor. His eyes were fixed on the newcomer. They did not play tricks on him that day at the cemetery, after all. The man he had seen walking away along the green path, between the gravestones, was now standing in front of him.

"Under different circumstances I'd say I couldn't be happier to see you alive," Martin started calmly.

"As would I, Marty. Believe me, as would I."

"Do me a favor, Bobby. Shoot me now or my heart will burst open."

65

"Don't you want to know why?" Bobby Sadosky asked after a minute of silence.

"I'm tired, Bobby. Tired and… disappointed. Just finish it off before someone stops you. I don't think I'd like to see my best friend die again." Martin's eyes were set on his friend's. He realized why Bobby did not shoot him yet. Every killer hits a time when he needs to reconcile.

"I've never known you to be this sentimental," Bobby Sadosky said, while distant gun fire could be heard from various parts of the residence.

"Blame it on the drugs." Martin tried to joke. He added after a while of studying his friend's face, "I guess you don't know your friends until you know them."

They sat quietly, each with their eyes set on the other.

"Jesus. How could you, Bobby?" Martin broke the silence.

Bobby replied, quietly, "They said it was for the good of the country."

"Is there any country worth killing your friends for?"

Bobby looked at him closely. "Tox-Chip, it was supposed to be painless. You wouldn't have known what hit you, had it worked. It pains me, Marty, it really pains me to know that you know. Me, I could live with it. I've done worse things."

"Worse than killing your best friends?"

"Believe me."

"For the good of the country—" Martin said with sarcasm.

"Yes, Marty, for the good of the country. Isn't that why we all joined the CIA?"

"Is that why you sold out to the Basel Group?"

"You may think it silly, but I had no idea where the orders came from. I was duped. They said you wanted to kill the president. Derek, and his black vault, seemed to support the case. So I did it. For the good of the country. You would've done the same if it was the only thing to do. "

"Would I? Would I have blown off the faces of my friends?"

Sadosky did not turn his eyes. "It's nasty, but it's a job someone had to do."

"They were your friends, Bobby."

"You know as well as I do that there are no friends in this business. What mattered was the country. The CIA thought they could stop the Basel Group, so they fixed this op—"

"Can you ever fix it so that you can live with it? You killed Arthur, Chris, Derek. They were your friends, Bobby. They would give their lives to save yours. You know they would, so don't tell me that you were duped."

"But it is a part of it." Bobby nodded to the corpse. "He's dead because he hired me on false premises. He said he represented the CIA. He said you wanted to kill the president."

"And you simply did it."

"I've been recruited because I'm good at something, Marty. Years ago someone came up to me and said, for the first time in my life: 'Son, you have a talent. Why not turn it into good use?' I've been doing it ever since—"

"For the good of the country." Martin said mockingly.

"It's politics, Marty. Politics is shit. That's why people like me exist — to keep the country stable."

"Do I still pose a threat to the country's stability?"

"Now more than ever. Douglas was an asshole, who deserved to die, and if you hadn't done it, I would. But he was right in one respect — he came to me and told me everything about they way we were recruited, and the dirty purpose we were to serve — and then he said that the dirt must be wiped clean, for a clean start. For the good of the country."

Martin said nothing.

"Don't you want to know why I agreed to it in the first place?" Bobby asked pleadingly.

"I think I've learned most of it now." Martin sensed that Sadosky came to the moment when he needed to reconcile.

"But don't you want to know why I really did what I did?"

"Not any more, Bobby." Oh, how he wanted to hear it. He forced himself not to give his friend the satisfaction.

"I think I owe this much to you."

Martin heaved a sigh. "You don't."

Bobby ignored it. He said, "It was Jeannie, actually."

He got Martin's attention.

"I loved that bitch. At first— We ran into each other overseas. She said it was over between you two. So, we hit it off. It was good. Real. Then I learned about her. You know— I said she's got to stop, now that we're together, and all. But she wouldn't. She kept going out with guys. Part of the job, she said." He paused for a moment, then said, "Marty, I understand things after the fact. She was in on it from the start, she worked with Douglas. She did what she did best. You and I, and the others— We were all recruited.

337

Douglas had plans for us. But then you and Art— You left, and Douglas' plan went to hell. So Jeannie— she spun her web around me to bring the two of you back, or to silence you forever. You and Art had done a lot of bad for the CIA. I had hoped you could be turned around, but then this man came, and I got confused—"

"Bobby, it doesn't matter. If it wasn't you, it would've been someone else."

"No, Marty. No! We should've talked."

"Bobby—"

"Marty! We should've talked. You and me. Long time ago. You know— about Jeannie. It would've cleared things between us, and I would've been able to think more clearly. You have no idea how I dreaded the meeting, and facing you. Then this thing happened, and I was glad you walked out of there alive. It meant we had another go at it—"

"What about the others? What about Chris? Derek? Nothing? You don't feel anything? What about Arthur? Still nothing?" Martin was angry and he hated himself for showing it. He did not want to give his friend the satisfaction of seeing him emotionally broken.

"Art shouldn't have meddled with the ICC!"

"Jeesus, Bobby! You actually believe in this crap? We were all dupes from the start, just as every other agent. We're only expendable tools."

"I know I'm dead. I know they'll whack me, and sooner rather than later. The things I've seen and done— People like me are bound to end up this way. I just wish things were different between us, between you and me."

"Yeah, me too, Bobby. Just promise me one thing, though."

"Yeah. What's that?" Sadosky did not look into his friend's eyes.

"Let them be. They're out of the way. They're old. They don't know anything. Can't possibly harm you, or those you represent."

"Not me. But they can do great harm to the cause. They were at the Facility. They watched. They heard things they shouldn't have."

"Bobby! They had no idea what was going on," Martin said wearily.

"Promise?" Bobby studied his friend's face. "Alright."

They sat quietly for several minutes. Neither said another word. At last Bobby Sadosky raised the pistol in his outstretched arm, and gazed at Martin. Their eyes locked. Both glistened with tears.

THE END

From the Author

THE BLACK VAULT was inspired by true events:

Following the Great Depression of 1929, America found herself at a precipice. Only a series of drastic socio-economic changes could ensure stability and return to prosperity.

Franklin D Roosevelt spearheaded the necessary Change, yet within a few short years wealthy industrialists and politicians plotted to overthrow the President. They formed the American Liberty League (ALL), a group dedicated to protecting the members' wealth and privileges through whatever means necessary, including a coup.

The ALL members were afraid of the President's nationalization and Social Security plans, which they considered dangerous to their interests. They plotted to replace FDR with a puppet dictator who would serve their interests. 500,000 soldiers stood by, awaiting orders to storm Washington.

The United States was about to become a fascist dictatorship when one man saw right from wrong, and his moral reservations averted the coup.

The conspiracy was stopped, yet no one associated with the coup was ever held accountable.

Were the plans of the wealthy aristocracy shelved for ever? The old truism comes to life in THE BLACK VAULT: History repeats itself...

About the Author

As a former top-secret government courier, Jack King was privy to all the ins and outs of covert maneuvering on a global scale. He has turned his work experience into a series of novels that resonate with authenticity. The corridors of power, with their backstabbing, greed, and corruption, are the focus points of Jack's books:

Agents of Change: With its antiquated political and banking systems, rogue military-industrial complexes and flawed educational systems, the world of today is a relic of the imperfect past, and Agents of Change are ready to right what is wrong.

WikiJustice: There exists a place where no one stands above the law, where individuals and corporations are held liable in ways, which fit their crimes... WikiJustice.

The Black Vault: Secret funds, obtained by illicit means, used for the purpose of conducting black operations.

In the 1930s a group of wealthy industrialists plotted to overthrow President Franklin D. Roosevelt and replace him with a puppet dictator. The coup failed because of moral reservations of a single man.

Can one man stop a conspiracy to overthrow the current-day President?

The Fifth Internationale: Now that the Iron Curtain had come crushing down, and Soviet satellite countries switched allegiance to the United States, their communist spies are no longer needed. Hundreds of thousands are discharged, but not retired - they form The Fifth Internationale, building a global conspiracy that will allow ⌐ manipulate world governments to their own end.

⌐int your browser to **SpyWriter.com** to connect